## Fairest of Them All
"Medeiros pens the ultimate romantic fantasy."
—*Publishers Weekly*

✦

## Thief of Hearts
"Emotional, funny, sensual, and spellbinding, this is a marvelous read!" —*Romantic Times*

✦

## A Whisper of Roses
"Ms. Medeiros casts a spell with her poignant writing. . . . An outstanding reading adventure from cover to cover. Great!" —*Rendezvous*

✦

## Once an Angel
"An enthralling love story that grabs hold of your heart."
—*Romantic Times*

✦

## Heather and Velvet
"Fast-paced, exciting . . . a terrific tale . . . thrilling romance."

—Amanda Quick, *New York Times* bestselling author

# The
# Bride
## and the
# Beast

## TERESA MEDEIROS

Bantam Books
*New York  Toronto  London  Sydney  Auckland*

This edition contains the complete text
of the original hardcover edition.
NOT ONE WORD HAS BEEN OMITTED.

## The Bride and the Beast

A Bantam Book

PUBLISHING HISTORY
Bantam hardcover edition published June 2000
Bantam mass market edition / April 2001

Library of Congress Catalog Card Number: 00-023707.

ISBN 0-553-58183-X

*Published simultaneously in the United States and Canada*

Bantam Books are published by Bantam Books, a division of Random
House, Inc. Its trademark, consisting of the words "Bantam Books"
and the portrayal of a rooster, is Registered in U.S. Patent and
Trademark Office and in other countries. Marca Registrada. Bantam
Books, 1540 Broadway, New York, New York 10036.

PRINTED IN THE UNITED STATES OF AMERICA

OPM   10  9  8  7  6  5  4  3  2  1

*To the memory of Debbie Dunn,*
*who not only loved romance but lived*
*one of the sweetest ones I'll ever see.*
*And to her steadfast hero, Phil.*
*You keep those angels organized,*
*honey, until we get there.*

*To Michael and the good Lord,*
*for loving me whether I'm*
*a beauty or a beast.*

✦  ✦  ✦

# The
# Bride
## and the
# Beast

# Prologue

## Scotland, the Highlands
### ✦ 1 7 4 6 ✦

GWENDOLYN WAS NINE years old the day she almost killed the future chieftain of Clan MacCullough.

She was hauling herself up a sturdy young oak, carefully testing each branch to make sure it would bear her weight, when his shaggy pony came into view.

She settled her backside into a well-worn hollow in the trunk and peered through the minty green veil of leaves, her heart skipping a beat. Aye, it was he. There was no mistaking Bernard MacCullough's regal bearing or the shock of dark hair that tumbled across his brow. He wore a scarlet and black tartan draped over his saffron shirt. A silver badge emblazoned with the MacCullough dragon secured the tartan, drawing her attention to shoulders that seemed to grow broader with each passing day. Below his short kilt, his long, tanned legs hugged the pony's flanks.

Gwendolyn rested her chin on her hand and sighed, content simply to drink in the sight of him as he guided the pony down the rocky path with a grace and mastery beyond his fifteen years. Although he rode through this pass every day, she never tired of watching him. Never tired of dreaming that one day he would look up and catch a glimpse of her.

"Who goes there?" he would call out, reining his pony to a halt. "Could it be an angel fallen from the heavens?"

" 'Tis only I, m'laird," she would reply, "the fair Lady Gwendolyn."

Then he would flash his white teeth in a tender smile and she would gently float to the ground. (In her dreams, she always had a pretty pair of gossamer wings.) Using only one hand, he would sweep her up before him on the pony and they would ride through the village, basking beneath the proud smiles of her mama and papa, the slack-jawed gazes of the villagers, and the envious stares of her two older sisters.

"Look! There's Gwennie at the top of that tree. And they say pigs can't fly!" A burst of raucous laughter jerked Gwendolyn out of her reverie.

As she looked down and saw the circle of children gathered around the tree, her skin began to crawl with an all too familiar dread. Perhaps if she ignored their taunts, they would just go away.

"I don't know why ye're wastin' yer time up there. All the acorns are down here on the ground." Ross, the burly son of the village blacksmith, slapped his knee, howling with mirth.

"Oh, do stop it, Ross," laughed Glynnis, Gwendolyn's

twelve-year-old sister. She twined an arm through his and tossed her flowing auburn curls. "If you'll leave the poor creature alone, I'll let you steal a kiss later."

Gwendolyn's eleven-year-old sister, Nessa, whose silky straight hair was a shade more gold than red, captured his other arm, pouting prettily. "Keep your lips to yourself, wench. He's already promised his kisses to me."

"Don't fret, lasses." Ross squeezed them both until they squealed. "I've kisses enough to go 'round. Although 'twould take more kisses than I've got to go 'round that sister of yers."

Gwendolyn couldn't stop herself from replying. "Go away, Ross, and leave me alone!"

"And what will you do if I don't? Sit on me?"

Glynnis and Nessa made a halfhearted attempt to smother their giggles with their hands. The rest of Ross's companions roared with laughter.

Then an unfamiliar voice sliced through their merriment. "You heard the lady. Leave her be."

Bernard MacCullough's voice was both smoother and deeper than Gwendolyn had imagined. And he'd called her a lady! But her wonder over that was quickly overtaken by mortification as she realized he must have heard the entire exchange. As she looked through the branches, all she could see of her defender was the top of his head and the polished toes of his boots.

Ross turned to face the interloper. "And who the bloody hell are ye to—?" His snarl died on a croak as he went red, then white. "I d-didn't realize 'twas ye, m'laird," he stammered. "F-f-forgive me." He dropped to one knee at the feet of his chieftain's son.

Bernard seized the front of his shirt and hauled him to his feet. Ross might have outweighed the boy by at least a stone, but he still had to crane his neck to look Bernard in the eye. "I'm not your laird, yet," Bernard pointed out. "But I will be someday. And I should warn you that I never forget an injustice done to one of my own."

Gwendolyn bit her lip to still its trembling, amazed that their taunts couldn't make her cry, but that his kindness could.

Ross swallowed hard. "Aye, m'laird. Nor will I forget the warnin'."

"See that you don't."

Although Ross was subdued as he led his companions from the clearing, Gwendolyn caught the smoldering look he shot the top of the tree. She would pay later for his humiliation.

Her ragged nails bit into the bark as she realized they'd done exactly as she'd demanded. They'd left her alone.

With him.

She pressed her cheek against the trunk of the tree, praying she would disappear right into it like some bashful wood sprite.

A matter-of-fact voice dashed her hopes. "They're gone. You can come down now."

She closed her eyes, dreading the contempt that

would darken his face if she accepted his invitation. "I'm really quite comfortable where I am."

He sighed. " 'Tisn't every day I have the privilege of rescuing a damsel in distress. I should think you'd want to thank me."

"Thank you. Now would you please just go away and leave me be?"

Defying him was her first mistake. "I'll not do it. 'Tis my land, and therefore my tree. If you don't come down, I'll come up after you." He planted one boot in the lowest crook of the trunk and reached for a dangling limb.

Already imagining how fast he could scale the tree with those long, limber legs of his, Gwendolyn then made her second mistake. She began to scramble higher. But in her haste she forgot to test each bough before she put her weight on it. There was a creak, then a crack, then she went plummeting toward the earth. Her last coherent thought was *Please, God, let me land on my head and break my neck.* But the fickle branches betrayed her once again by breaking her fall instead.

She had only a mercifully brief glimpse of Bernard's shocked face before she slammed into him, knocking him flat.

It took Gwendolyn a moment to catch her breath. When she opened her eyes Bernard was stretched out beneath her, his face only an inch from her own.

His eyes were closed, his stubby, dark lashes fanned out against the masculine curve of his sun-bronzed cheeks. Gwendolyn was so close she could even make out a hint of the whiskers that would soon shadow his jaw.

"M'laird?" she whispered.

He neither groaned nor stirred.

She moaned. "Oh, God, I've gone and killed him!"

If only the fall had killed her as well! Then the villagers could find them here, her body draped protectively across his, united in death as they'd never been in life. Unable to resist the heartbreaking pathos of the image, Gwendolyn buried her face against his breastbone and snuffled back a sob.

"Are you hurt, lass?" came a smoky whisper.

Gwendolyn slowly lifted her head. Bernard's eyes were open now, but not in the death stare she'd feared. They were a rich green, the color of emeralds spilling across a cache of hidden treasure.

As he gently brushed a leaf from her hair, Gwendolyn scrambled off of him.

"I've bruised naught but my pride," she said. "And you? Are you hurt?"

"I should say not." He climbed to his feet, swiping leaves and dirt from his backside. " 'Twould take more than a child landing in my lap to knock the wind from me."

A child? Gwendolyn could almost feel her braids begin to bristle.

He brushed a twig from his hair, eyeing her from beneath that wayward lock across his brow. "I've seen you at the castle before, haven't I? You live at the manor in the village. You're the daughter of my father's steward."

"One of them," she replied tersely, not wanting him to suspect that she lived for those days when her papa would take her to the castle while he conducted his business simply because she might catch a glimpse of Bernard bounding down the stairs or playing chess with the chieftain or sneaking up behind his mother to give her a teasing kiss on the cheek. To Gwendolyn, Castle Weyrcraig had always been a castle of dreams, a place of pure enchantment where even the most un-likely of wishes might come true.

"You've a baby sister, haven't you? And another on the way. I've met your two older sisters," he said. "A cheeky pair, aren't they? Always batting their eyelashes and wiggling hips they don't yet have." A bemused smile softened his lips as he took in her rumpled tunic and the faded knee breeches she'd pilfered from her papa's laundry. "You're not like them, are you?"

Gwendolyn folded her arms over her chest. "No, I'm not. I'm fat."

He looked her up and down in frank assessment. "You've a bit of extra flesh on your bones, but 'tis not unbecoming on a child your age."

*A child!* Somehow it galled her more that he'd called her a child again than that he'd agreed she was fat. How could she have ever thought she loved this arrogant lad? Why, she loathed him!

She drew herself up to her full four feet three inches. "I suppose just because you live in a grand castle and ride a pretty pony, you fancy yourself a man full grown."

"I've still got some growing to do. As do you." He wrapped one of her flaxen braids around his hand, drawing her nearer so he could lean down and whisper, "But my father believes me man enough to escort a most esteemed guest to our castle on this very night."

Gwendolyn jerked the braid out of his hand and tossed it over her shoulder, terrified he was going to tweak her nose or pat her on the head as if she were some drooling puppy. "And just who would that guest be?"

He straightened and folded his arms over his chest, looking smug. "Oh, that's one secret I could never trust to a mere slip of a girl."

Horrid boy. Wretched boy. "Then I'd best be on my way, hadn't I, so you can attend to your *manly* duties."

She started up the hill, absurdly pleased that he actually looked taken aback by her desertion. "If you'd like, I can give you a hint," he called after her.

She refused to flatter him with a reply. She simply stopped and waited in stony silence.

"He's a true hero!" Bernard exclaimed. "A prince among men."

Since Gwendolyn had thought the same thing about him only a few minutes ago, she was none too impressed. She started walking again.

"If that lad troubles you again, you'll let me know, won't you?"

Gwendolyn squeezed her eyes shut against a rush of longing. Only a short while ago, she would have given her eyeteeth for the privilege of claiming him as her champion. Now, gathering the tatters of her pride around her, she turned stiffly to face him and asked, "Is that a request or a command?"

As he rested his hands on his lean hips, she realized she'd once again made the mistake of defying him. "Consider it a command, lass. After all, someday I'll be your laird and master as well as his."

Gwendolyn tilted her nose in the air. "That's where you're wrong, Bernard MacCullough. For no man shall ever be my laird and master!"

She wheeled around and went marching toward the village, missing the smile that played around Bernard's mouth as he whispered, "I wouldn't be so sure of that, lass, if I were you."

# Part I

+ + +

Man is neither angel nor beast; and the misfortune is that he who would act the angel acts the beast. —Blaise Pascal

No beast is so fierce but knows some touch of pity.
—William Shakespeare

# Chapter One

## Scotland, the Highlands
### ✦ 1761 ✦

THE DRAGON OF WEYRCRAIG prowled the crumbling parapets of his lair, fighting the urge to throw back his head and unleash a savage roar. He'd been a prisoner of the daylight for too long. Only when the shadows of night cloaked Weyrcraig could he cast aside his chains and roam unfettered through the castle's maze of passages.

The darkness was his dominion now, the only kingdom left to him.

As he gazed upon the sea, the salt hanging thick in the air stung his eyes. But the chill bite of the wind failed to penetrate the armor of his skin. Since coming to this place, he'd grown numb to all but the harshest of provocations. A whispered endearment, a tender caress, the silky heat of a woman's breath against his skin had all become as distant and bittersweet to him as the memory of a dream.

A storm was breaking over the far horizon. The rising wind whipped the North Sea into a boiling froth, sending the towering waves crashing against the cliffs below. Lightning strung its web from cloud to cloud, shedding little light, but leaving the inky darkness even more impenetrable in its wake.

The approaching storm reflected his wildness back at him like the shards of a broken mirror. The distant rumble of thunder could have been the ghostly roar of cannons or the growl trapped in his throat. He searched his soul, but could find no trace of humanity. As a child, he had feared the beast that slept beneath his bed, only to come to this place and discover he was that beast.

He was what they had made of him.

He bared his teeth in an expression few would have mistaken for a smile as he envisioned them cowering in their beds, trembling to imagine his wrath. They believed him to be a monster, without conscience or mercy. He had made it clear to them that his demands were law, his will as irresistible as the siren song of the wind wailing through the lonely glens and rugged mountain passes.

The cowardly ease of their surrender should have brought him some satisfaction, but it only whetted his hunger, a hunger that gnawed a burning hole in his belly and threatened to devour him from the inside out. Whenever he was caught in its grip, he longed to hurl their meager offerings back in their faces and scorch them to ashes with the searing flame of his breath.

They were supposed to be cursed, but he was the one who felt the fires of damnation licking at his soul.

He was the one doomed to wander this shattered ruin of his dreams without even a mate to ease his loneliness.

As he searched the churning clouds, his gut clenched with a fresh hunger, keener and more piercing than any that had come before. He might never be able to satisfy his insatiable appetites. But on this night, he would no longer deny himself some tasty morsel to take the edge off his longing. On this night, he would seek to satisfy the primal desire that lurked in the belly of every beast—even man.

On this night, the Dragon would hunt.

Gwendolyn Wilder did not believe in dragons.

So when a desperate pounding sounded on the door of the manor, followed by a frantic shout of "The Dragon's on the rampage, he is—he's goin' to murder us all in our beds!" she simply groaned, rolled onto her stomach, and dragged the pillow over her head. She'd almost rather have been murdered in her bed than snatched from her dreams by the ravings of a blithering idiot.

She plugged her ears with her fingers, but could still hear Izzy stomping across the hall below, muttering a litany of curses invoking various parts of God's anatomy, some less holy than others. A nasty thud was followed by a whimper that made Gwendolyn wince. Izzy had undoubtedly kicked the hapless hound who had dared to trip her.

Gwendolyn rolled to a sitting position on the heather-stuffed tick, dismayed to find herself alone. She would rather have awoken with her youngest sister's elbow jabbing her in the ear than learn that Kitty was on the prowl.

She threw back the sheet, scattering a stack of Royal Society pamphlets across the timber floor. The sheet was pocked with scorch marks from all the hours she'd spent reading by candlelight beneath its shelter. Izzy had always sworn that someday Gwendolyn would burn them all to death in their beds.

Gwendolyn eyed the bed on the other side of the loft, and was not the least bit surprised to find it empty. Even the Dragon would have been hard-pressed to murder Nessa in her bed, since she was most frequently to be found in someone else's. Nor was Nessa always fastidious enough to require a bed. There were several strapping lads in the village who whispered that for a certain bonny Wilder lass, any haystack or mossy riverbank would do. As she threw a shawl over her nightdress, Gwendolyn could only pray that her older sister wouldn't meet a dire fate at the beefy hands of some jealous wife.

Gwendolyn reached the splintery railing of what had been a minstrel's gallery in the manor's finer days just in time to see Izzy hurl open the main door. Ham, the tinker's apprentice, stood framed in the doorway, his eyes gleaming with fear.

"The devil take ye, lad!" Izzy roared. "How dare ye

come poundin' on the door o' decent Christian folk at this hour!"

Although visibly shaken by the sight of the stout maidservant with hair wrapped in rags, Ham stood his ground. "If ye don't wake yer mistress, ye auld cow, the devil's goin' to take us all. He'll most likely burn the village to the ground if we don't give him what he wants."

"And just what would that be this time?" Izzy demanded. "Yer scrawny gizzard on a platter?"

Ham scratched his head. "No one knows for sure. That's why I've been sent to fetch yer mistress."

Gwendolyn rolled her eyes. She never thought she'd have cause to rue her love of reading. But with Reverend Throckmorton away, she was the only one who could decipher the Dragon's writing.

She might have crept back to bed and left Ham to Izzy's mercy had her papa not chosen that moment to drift into the hall. He floated out of the darkness of his chamber like a ghost of the handsome, vibrant man she remembered from her childhood, his ivory nightshirt hanging on his wasted frame and his fine white hair bristling around his head like the spores of a dandelion. Gwendolyn started down the stairs without thought, her heart clenching in her chest. She wasn't sure which was more painful—his helplessness or her own.

"Gwennie?" he called plaintively.

"I'm right here, Papa," she assured him, catching him by the elbow before he could stumble over the dog as Izzy had done. The dog gave her a grateful look.

"I heard such a turrible commotion," her father said, turning his rheumy gray eyes on her. "Is it the English? Has Cumberland returned?"

"No, Papa," Gwendolyn replied, gently smoothing a grizzled lock of his hair. Alastair Wilder sometimes forgot his own name, but he'd never forgotten the ruthless English lord who had robbed him of his sanity nearly fifteen years ago.

"Cumberland's not coming back," Gwendolyn promised him. "Not tonight and not ever."

"Are yer sisters safely abed? 'Twouldn't do to have their virtue stolen by those wretched redcoats."

"Aye, Papa, they're safely abed." It was easier to lie than to explain that since so many of the clan's young men had fled the village to seek their fortunes elsewhere, Glynnis would probably welcome a regiment of lusty English soldiers with open arms while Nessa welcomed them with open legs. It pained her to think of her sweet Kitty straying down that path. "You needn't fear Cumberland or his redcoats," Gwendolyn assured him. " 'Tis nothing but that silly Dragon again, making mischief at our expense."

A feverish tinge brightened his cheeks, and he wagged a finger at her. "Ye must tell them to do whatever he says. If they don't, 'twill surely be the ruin of us all."

" 'Tis just what I was tryin' to tell this stubborn auld . . ." Ham faltered as Izzy's eyes narrowed. "Um . . . yer maid here. If ye'll give Gwendolyn yer leave, sir, she can come with me and read the note the Dragon left for us. There's some that say 'tis written not in ink, but in blood."

Her father's fingers dug into her arm. "Ye must go with him, lass. And make haste! Ye may be our last hope."

Gwendolyn sighed. "Very well, Papa. But only if you'll let Izzy tuck you back into bed with a cup of goat's milk and a nice warm brick wrapped in flannel."

His face crinkled in a smile as he squeezed her hand. "Ye've always been my good girl, haven't ye?"

It was a familiar refrain, one Gwendolyn had learned by heart while her sisters were out romping in the sunlight and stealing kisses from blushing lads. She was a good girl, a sensible girl, the girl who had held the struggling family together after her father went mad and her mother died giving birth to his stillborn son a mere fortnight later. Neither of them ever spoke of the cold, rainy night shortly after that when a nine-year-old Gwendolyn had found him on his knees in the side yard of the manor, trying to dig up her mother's grave with his bare hands.

"Aye, Papa." Gwendolyn brushed a kiss against his cheek. "You know I'd do anything for you." She added under her breath, "Even slay a dragon."

There was a storm brewing over the sleepy little village of Ballybliss. Although the steep mountain walls would shelter the glen from the full brunt of its fury, a taut expectancy shimmered in the air. The scent of the coming rain mingled with the briny tang of the sea. As Gwendolyn hurried toward the bonfire that had been built in the heart of the village square, the wind plucked flaxen tendrils of hair from her woolen snood and made her nape tingle with foreboding.

She hugged her shawl around her as a gust of wind whipped the bonfire into a frenzy and sent a cascade of sparks whirling into the night.

Gwendolyn was not surprised to find her sisters on the fringes of the milling crowd. They loved nothing so much as excitement, and in its absence had been known to craft some fine melodramas of their own with their ceaseless round of scandals, tantrums, and heartbreaks.

Glynnis hung on the arm of the silver-haired tinker, her cheeks flushed and her lips glistening as if they'd been kissed both recently and thoroughly. Unlike Nessa, Glynnis never allowed herself to be compromised until *after* the wedding. She'd already sent two elderly husbands to early graves, inheriting both their cottages and their meager belongings.

Nessa perched on a bale of hay next to Lachlan the Black, the younger son of the village smith. From the lazy ease with which he was nuzzling her ear, and the hay scattered through Nessa's auburn curls, Gwendolyn deduced it was not their first tryst of the night.

It was sharp-eyed Catriona who spotted her. She came bounding off the lap of a freckled lad and ducked through the crowd until she reached her side.

"Oh, Gwennie, have you heard?" she cried, her

raven curls bouncing. "The Dragon has sent another demand."

"Aye, Kitty. I've heard. But I don't believe. And nor should you."

Her sister's nickname had always suited her. As a curly-headed moppet, Kitty had liked nothing better than to take long, languorous naps and sip fresh cream from one of the Staffordshire saucers that had belonged to their mother. It was her more recent habit of curling up in the laps of strangers that dismayed Gwendolyn.

"No one knows what the note says," Kitty confided, "but Maisie's mother fears the Dragon might be developing a taste for human flesh. And Maisie believes he wishes to mate with one of the village lasses." She hugged back a delicious shiver. "Can you imagine what it would be like to be ravished by a beast?"

Gwendolyn's gaze strayed back to Lachlan, who had as much dark, curly hair growing out of his ears as on his head. "No, pet. You'd best ask Nessa about that."

They were both distracted by the voices rising above the wind.

"I say we give him whatever he wants," came the wheedling tones of Norval, the village baker. Even in the firelight, his face was as pasty as an underdone yeast roll. "Perhaps then he'll go back to hell and leave us be."

"And I say we march upon the castle and burn it to the ground," roared Ross. The blacksmith's eldest son and Gwendolyn's longtime tormentor banged the wooden handle of his hammer on the ground. "Or do none of ye have the ballocks?"

His challenge met with nothing but awkward silence and averted eyes.

Ailbert the Smith stepped into their midst. While Ross was known for his bluster and Lachlan for his skillful wooing of the fair sex, their father was a man of action. His lanky form and stern visage commanded everyone's respect.

He held aloft the sheaf of vellum, allowing it to ripple in the wind. It would have been found in the same place as all the other messages had been—pinned by a single feathered arrow to the trunk of the gnarled old oak that stood sentinel over the village.

Ailbert's voice rang like a bell tolling their doom. "How much more will we allow this monster to take from us? He demands the best of our crops, our flocks, our finest whisky and wool. What will we offer him next? Our sons? Our daughters? Our wives?"

"Better me wife than me whisky," one of the Sloan twins muttered, tipping an earthenware jug to his lips. The lady in question drove her elbow into his ribs, and he spat half the whisky down his shirtfront. Nervous laughter rippled through the crowd.

"Oh, ye'll give him yer whisky, lad." As Auld Tavis shuffled forward, the merriment died. The stooped gnome had been an old man fifteen years ago; now he was ancient. He pointed a gnarled finger at Ailbert. "And if he wants to lay with yer wife, ye'll hand her over, too, and thank him when he's done." Tavis cackled, baring his shriveled gums. "Ye'll give him whatever he wants 'cause ye know bloody well ye brought it on yerselves and 'tis no more than ye deserve."

Some of the villagers were shamefaced, some defiant, but they all knew exactly what he spoke of. Almost as one, they lifted their eyes to Castle Weyrcraig, the ancient fortress that had cast a shadow over their lives for as long as anyone could remember.

As Kitty edged closer to her, Gwendolyn's own gaze was drawn to the castle. The gutted ruin perched on the cliff overlooking Ballybliss like some madman's folly—crumbling towers stretching toward heaven, winding staircases descending into hell, jagged holes blown through the heart of the ancient keep. Gwendolyn had striven to be practical in all things for a very long time, but even her imagination was stirred by its vision of doomed romance and dying dreams.

The villagers might pretend to ignore its grim reproach, but no one had forgotten that terrible night fifteen years ago when the castle had fallen to the English. Not even the barricaded doors of their cottages had been able to muffle the roar of the cannons, the screams of the dying, and the damning silence that had followed when there had been no one left to scream.

Although there were those who had always whispered that the castle was haunted, it was only in the past few months that its ghosts had begun to wreak their havoc on the village.

Lachlan had been the first to hear the eerie skirl of

bagpipes drifting down from the castle, although bagpipes had not been heard in the glen since the rebellion of '45. Soon after, Glynnis had spotted spectral lights flickering past the darkened windows that gazed down upon the village like soulless eyes.

Gwendolyn would have liked to claim that she had heard and seen nothing of the sort, but one bitterly cold February night when she was hurrying home from the apothecary's with a poultice for her father's eyes, an unearthly wail had frozen her in her tracks. She had slowly turned, transfixed by a melody that seemed to hearken back to another time. A time when Ballybliss and Clan MacCullough had thrived beneath the benevolent chieftainship of their laird. A time when the manor had rung with her father's piping and her mother's laughter. A time when all of their hopes and dreams for the future had rested upon the shoulders of one boy with a dazzling smile and eyes the color of emeralds.

The melody's piercing sweetness had made her heart ache and her eyes sting.

She had seen no flickering lights that night, but as she had lifted her gaze to the castle's battlements, she would have almost sworn she saw the shadow of the man that boy might have become had he lived. In the time it had taken to blink away her tears, he had vanished, leaving both him and his song no more than a wistful echo in her memory.

Soon after, Ailbert had found the Dragon's first demand pinned to the trunk of the old oak.

" 'Tis the curse," Ross muttered, robbed of his bluster by Auld Tavis's taunts.

"Aye, the curse," his father echoed, his stern face looking even longer than usual.

Lachlan tightened his protective grip on Nessa. "It don't seem fair somehow that Nessa and I should suffer. We was little more than bairns when the curse was cast."

Auld Tavis wagged a bony finger at him. "Aye, but the sins of the father shall be visited on the son."

Murmuring their agreement, several in the crowd signed furtive crosses on their breasts. The Crown might have outlawed their priests and tartans, but not even fifteen years of ironfisted English rule could make them relinquish their God. Gwendolyn doubted either Tavis or the villagers realized he was quoting Euripides, not Holy Scripture.

Gently nudging Kitty aside, Gwendolyn stepped into the circle of firelight and said firmly, "Pish, posh. There's no such thing as curses. Or dragons."

The crowd erupted in boisterous protest, but Gwendolyn refused to be daunted. "Have any of you ever seen this Dragon?"

After a moment of pensive silence, Ian Sloan exchanged a glance with his twin. "I heard his turrible roar."

Ham piped up. "I felt the ripple of his wings as he passed overhead."

"And I smelled his breath, I did," Norval added. " 'Twas like brimstone straight from the fires of hell. And the next mornin', my field was scorched bare."

"Scorched or torched?" Gwendolyn snatched the sheaf of vellum from Ailbert's hand. "If our tormentor truly is a dragon, then how does he write these ridiculous demands? Does he grip a quill in his talons? Employ a secretary?"

"Everyone knows he can change from dragon to man at will," an elderly widow insisted. "Why, he might even walk among us this verra night."

As neighbor edged away from neighbor, casting glances rife with suspicion, Gwendolyn briefly closed her eyes, struggling to remember that somewhere in the world mathematicians were studying Euler's *Analysis Infinitorum*, philosophers were arguing Adam Smith's *Theory of Moral Sentiments*, and beautiful women with powdered hair and silk slippers were whirling around gilded ballrooms in the arms of men who adored them.

She turned to Ailbert, hoping to appeal to the man's sense of reason. "I believe this 'Dragon' of yours is nothing but a cruel hoax. I think someone is taking heartless advantage of your desire to punish yourself for what can never be undone."

Ailbert's sullen face mirrored those around him. "No slight intended, lass, but we called ye here to read, not think."

Gwendolyn snapped her mouth shut and the creamy sheaf of vellum open, revealing the familiar arrogant masculine scrawl. "It would appear M'lord Dragon is hungry. If it wouldn't be too much bother, he would like a haunch of fresh venison, a jug of well-aged whisky . . ." Several of the men nodded their approval.

However devilish the Dragon's threats, they could not fault his taste in fine liquor. "and . . ." Gwendolyn faltered, her icy voice melting to a whisper. ". . . one thousand pounds in gold."

The gasps that greeted her words couldn't have been more horrified. It had been whispered for years that one thousand pounds had been the price that someone in the village had been paid to betray their chieftain to the English.

Ailbert sank down heavily on a tree stump, rubbing his gaunt cheeks. "And just how are we to come up with a thousand bloody pounds? Doesn't he know those English leeches have bled every last shillin' and ha'pence from our coffers with their fines and their taxes?"

"Oh, he knows," Gwendolyn said softly. "He's just toying with us, batting us around the way a cat bats around a fat, juicy mouse."

"Before he gobbles it down," Ross added glumly.

"And if we don't deliver the gold?" Ailbert lifted his pleading eyes to Gwendolyn, as if she could somehow temper the Dragon's threats with mercy.

As Gwendolyn scanned the rest of the missive, she briefly considered lying, but feared her eyes would betray her. "He says it will spell the doom of Ballybliss."

Never ones to miss an opportunity for melodrama, Kitty burst into tears and Nessa and Glynnis abandoned their respective lovers to throw themselves into each other's arms.

Ailbert rose from the stump to pace the clearing. "If

we can't give him the gold, there must be somethin' else we can offer the devil. Somethin' to make him leave us be for a while."

"But what?" Ross demanded. "I doubt we could scrape up ten pounds between the lot of us."

Suddenly Auld Tavis's singsong croak mesmerized them all.

*May the dragon's wings spell yer doom*
*And his fiery breath seal yer tomb.*
*May vengeance be upon yer heads*
*'Til innocent blood be shed.*

It was a chant the village children had learned at the knees of their parents. It was the curse the clan's own chieftain had laid upon them with his dying breath. It shouldn't have made Gwendolyn shiver, but it did.

"What are ye sayin', auld man?" Ross demanded, snatching Tavis up by the front of his tunic.

Ross's bullying failed to dim the sly twinkle in Tavis's eyes. "Every one o' ye knows this Dragon is none other than the MacCullough hisself returned from the grave to punish those who betrayed him. If ye truly want to rid yerselves of him, then break the curse."

As Ross lowered Tavis to the ground, Ailbert's eyes went cool and distant. "Innocent blood," he murmured. "Perhaps a sacrifice of some sorts." As his gaze slowly traveled the pallid circle of faces, his wide-eyed niece, Marsali, clutched her newborn babe to her breast.

"Oh, for God's sake!" Gwendolyn cried, wishing she had Izzy's talent for creative blasphemy. "Is this what the monster has driven us to? Contemplating human sacrifice?"

Ross, who had just fathered a baby girl of his own on the fourteen-year-old lass he was betrothed to, snapped his fingers, his ruddy face brightening. "Innocent blood. A virgin!"

Ross's eyes narrowed as he scanned the crowd. Most of the girls in Ballybliss wed shortly after they reached the age of twelve. His gaze briefly lingered on, then quickly passed over Glynnis and Nessa, before lighting on Kitty.

"Oh, no you don't!" Gwendolyn exclaimed, shoving her sister behind her. "You'll not make my baby sister fodder for some mean-spirited swindler!"

Kitty gently disengaged herself from Gwendolyn's grip. "It's all right, Gwennie. They couldn't feed me to the Dragon anyway because I'm not . . . I mean . . . Niall and I"—she ducked her head—"well, he said there'd be no harm in it."

Gwendolyn's heart sank. The freckled lad who'd been sharing his lap with Kitty flushed scarlet, then ducked into the shadows.

"Oh, kitten," Gwendolyn said softly, reaching to correct one of her sister's wayward curls. "Didn't I strive to teach you that you deserved so much more?"

"Don't be angry," Kitty pleaded, pressing Gwendolyn's palm to her cheek. "I just didn't want to end up like . . ."

*You.*

Although Kitty faltered, Gwendolyn heard the word as surely as if she'd said it aloud. Blinking back the tears that stung her eyes, she gently, but firmly, withdrew her hand from Kitty's grip.

She crumpled the Dragon's vellum in her fist, wishing she'd never been fool enough to leave her cozy bed. Even her father's fitful sanity was preferable to this madness.

Wheeling on Ross, she slapped the ball of paper against his chest, despising his smirk even more than when they'd been children. "Good luck finding a virgin in Ballybliss. You'd be more likely to find a unicorn. Or a dragon!"

As she turned away, a peculiar silence fell over the clearing, broken only by the sound of Kitty's sniveling. Even the wind seemed to be holding its breath.

Gwendolyn turned back to find herself facing a gauntlet of cool and assessing eyes. Faces she had known since childhood had closed into the forbidding masks of strangers.

"Oh, no," Gwendolyn said, taking an involuntary step backward. "Surely you don't think you're going to . . ."

Ross looked her up and down, assessing the generous curves that were such a stark contrast to the willowy grace of her sisters. "The Dragon could live on that for a while, couldn't he?"

"Aye," someone else muttered. "He wouldn't trouble us for a very long time if he could make a meal o' her."

"She might even eat him if she got hungry enough."

As Kitty's sniveling rose to a wail and Glynnis and Nessa began to shove their way through the crowd in a desperate attempt to reach Gwendolyn's side, the villagers began to advance on her, looking more like a mob with every step.

"Oh, no you don't!" she cried, beginning to take two steps for every one of theirs. "I'd make a dreadful sacrifice for your stupid Dragon because I'm ... I'm ..." She frantically cast about for a reason why they shouldn't feed her to a dragon that didn't exist. Shooting Kitty a burning glance, she blurted out, "I'm not a virgin!"

That startling revelation gave them pause. Even Glynnis and Nessa looked taken aback. "Why, I'm the most wanton strumpet in the village. You can ask any man here." Gwendolyn's shawl slipped from her shoulders as she flung a finger toward Nessa's latest beau. "I've even bedded Lachlan. And his father!" That desperate claim elicited a strangled gasp from Ailbert's dour wife. But the mob was in motion again as they exchanged disbelieving glances.

"And Glynnis's last two husbands! And Reverend Throckmorton!" Breathing a silent prayer of thanksgiving that the sweet little man wasn't around to hear *that* particular confession, Gwendolyn whirled to run. If she could only reach the manor, Izzy could doubtlessly hold off even the bullish Ross with nothing more than a rolling pin and one of her Medusa-like glares.

Gwendolyn had barely taken three steps when she crashed into the smothering softness of Marsali's ample bosom. As she slowly lifted her eyes to meet the woman's maternal smile, Gwendolyn realized it wasn't the men of Ballybliss she had to fear, but the women.

# Chapter Two

As THE VILLAGE WOMEN prepared Gwendolyn for the Dragon's pleasure, the sound of weeping nearly drowned out the rumble of the storm outside the shuttered windows of Marsali's cottage. Kitty bawled the loudest, while Glynnis sobbed into her handkerchief and Nessa used the hem of her gown to dab away each glistening teardrop before it could fall. It wouldn't do for Lachlan to see her with a reddened nose or swollen eyes. Gwendolyn's sisters' more passionate protests regarding her fate had quickly subsided when they realized they were both outweighed and outnumbered by Marsali and her cronies.

Gwendolyn gritted her teeth as Kitty emitted a particularly piercing wail. "You're so noble and brave, Gwennie! To sacrifice yourself for us all this way."

"Perhaps Lachlan will compose a song in your honor," Nessa offered. "His fingers are quite nimble on the strings of a clarsach." From the dreamy half-smile that broke through Nessa's gloom, Gwendolyn deduced they were quite nimble elsewhere as well.

"Aye, we shall never forget you," Glynnis vowed with a watery sigh.

"I doubt you'll have the chance," Gwendolyn said firmly, "since I have every intention of being back in my own bed come morning."

But Marsali and her mates had other ideas. Each time Gwendolyn tried to rise from the stool they'd set before the fire, they shoved her back down. They'd already dragged off her practical woolen gown and stuffed her into a white linen garment more suited to a virgin sacrifice.

As the other women tugged away the drab snood and unwound her coil of braids, Granny Hay peered into her face. "Her mother was such a beauty. 'Tis a pity the lass isn't comely like her sisters."

The old woman's words caused Gwendolyn only the faintest sting. She'd long ago resigned herself to being the smart sister in a family of legendary beauties.

Granny seized her lower lip and peered into her mouth. "She does have sweet dimples and bonny teeth, though," she said, baring her own yellowing stumps.

"And lovely golden hair," said Marsali, raking her grimy fingernails through the shimmering mass. Her own mousy brown locks hung in lank, unwashed strands around her face.

"If only she weren't so fat," snapped Ailbert's wife, still smarting from Gwendolyn's attempt to claim her husband as a lover. Gwendolyn had to bite her lip to keep from pointing out that the portly woman outweighed her by more than eight stone on a dry day.

" 'Tis just as well ye were chosen, lass," Marsali said gently, casting a doting look toward the cradle in the corner where her baby daughter slept, safe from the Dragon's greedy claws. "After all, ye're nearly twenty-five years old. Ye've little enough hope o' finding a husband at yer age."

"I'm younger than both Glynnis and Nessa," Gwendolyn pointed out.

"Aye, but Glynnis has already buried two husbands and Nessa can have her pick of any lad in the village."

"Perhaps Auld Tavis would take Gwennie to bride," Kitty suggested hopefully.

Gwendolyn shuddered. "No thank you. I'd rather be eaten by a dragon than gummed to death by that old scoundrel."

As Marsali spread Gwendolyn's hair around her shoulders in a gleaming mantle, a crack of thunder shook the cottage, making them all jump. Gwendolyn folded her hands in her lap to hide their sudden trembling.

"You needn't worry about Papa," Nessa assured her. "We shall look after him."

"The last time I gave you charge of him," Gwendolyn said, "his nightshirt caught fire when you went off with the butcher's nephew and left him sitting too close to the hearth."

Glynnis lowered her handkerchief. "But this time she'll have me to help her."

"You're the one who let him go charging off into the blizzard to fight invisible 'redcoats' wearing nothing but a short kilt and a claymore. He nearly froze to death before I could find him," Gwendolyn reminded her sister.

She twisted her hands together, fighting a flare of panic. It was painfully obvious that Kitty didn't need her anymore, but what would become of Papa if anything were to happen to her? It wouldn't take more than an hour for Izzy's short-tempered bellowing to reduce the confused old soul to tears.

"There's no such thing as a dragon," she mumbled beneath her breath. "I'll be home in time to spoon Papa's morning porridge into his bowl."

A loud crash shook the rafters, giving Gwendolyn a violent start. But it wasn't until she saw the mingled guilt and dread on the ashen faces of the other women, however, that she realized the crash was not thunder, but the clamor of fists pounding on the door.

They'd come for her.


Although they had bound her hands in front of her, Gwendolyn marched grimly along at the head of the mob, refusing to be dragged. The wind whipped her hair across her cheeks in stinging cords. Lightning crackled across the sky and thunder rolled and swelled like the hungry growl of some great beast's belly. Although she'd steeled herself for its arrival, she still flinched when the first cold drops of rain struck her face.

The fat drops made the mob's torches sizzle and sputter, and Gwendolyn could smell the stench of damp pitch.

Ross and Ailbert marched on either side of her, herding her along the steep, narrow path that twisted its way up the cliffside. Gwendolyn gazed straight ahead, until the forbidding shadow of Castle Weyrcraig fell over them.

The fortress crowned the cliff, eerily beautiful even in its decay. On this night there were no lights flickering through its hollow rooms, no ghostly wail of bagpipes to welcome them. Yet the place that had once been Gwendolyn's cherished castle of dreams had become the stuff of nightmares, filling her with dread. Ailbert swore beneath his breath and even Ross's beefy limbs betrayed him with a tremor. As they shoved her back into motion, Gwendolyn stumbled for the first time since they had seized her.

As they left behind the sheltering walls of the glen, the full fury of the storm broke over them. Rain lashed at Gwendolyn, plastering the thin linen robe to her body and soaking her to the bone. The wind set up a shrill howl as the driving rain extinguished the last of the torches, leaving them in near darkness. Hastening their steps, the villagers scanned the sky, as if expecting their doom to swoop down out of the churning clouds on wings of flame.

Ross gave her a harsh jerk, and Gwendolyn went down hard on one knee. She ignored the sharp pain and forced herself to keep moving, fearful the mob might trample her. Their panic had become a palpable thing—a metallic bitterness at the back of her throat. She didn't know whether to be terrified or thankful when the remnants of the iron gates that had been shattered by English cannon fire nearly fifteen years before emerged from the shadows ahead of them.

This time it wasn't Gwendolyn, but the villagers who faltered.

Until this night, all of the offerings to the Dragon had been left outside the gates. Except for a handful of lads bold or foolish enough to accept a dare from their less courageous peers, no one had passed between those gates since that bleak morning fifteen years ago when the villagers had carried the bodies of their laird and his family down the hillside.

For a moment, Gwendolyn believed she might be saved. Believed they would not dare to breach the unholy sanctuary of the castle courtyard.

But that was before Ross wrenched one of the gates right off its rusty hinges. Rain coursed like tears down Ailbert's gaunt cheeks as he shouted, "Let's have done with it, then!"

Gwendolyn began to struggle in earnest as they drove her through the gates. She had time to collect only a few scattered impressions—stone walls covered with damp lichen; a headless statue of a woman garbed in flowing marble; a set of broad flagstone steps leading up to a splintered door.

Once they'd dragged her into the heart of the courtyard, it didn't take Ross long to find a hole in the crumbling, weed-choked cobblestones. Lachlan handed him a sledgehammer and with one mighty swing, Ross drove a tall stake into the ground.

Ailbert secured Gwendolyn's hands behind her, cast a rope around her chest, waist, and thighs to bind her to the thick shaft of wood, then muttered, "May God have mercy on yer soul, lass."

"If you leave me here, it won't be *my* soul needing mercy, but yours," she bit off through her chattering teeth. "Especially if I perish from exposure and you return to find nothing but my bones."

"The Dragon'll be pickin' his teeth with 'em before the morn," Ross snarled.

Before she could spit in his face, the sky exploded. A forked tongue of flame descended from the heavens, followed by the thunderous crack of a serpentine tail.

" 'Tis the Dragon!" a woman screamed. "He's comin' for her!"

A mighty roar seemed to pour from the throat of hell itself. Its deafening clamor went on and on, sending the villagers fleeing into the night and leaving Gwendolyn at the Dragon's mercy.

Gwendolyn could not have said when she closed her eyes and began to scream. She only knew that the terrible roar died at the exact same moment as her scream.

She slumped away from her bonds, going limp with terror. The rigid stake pressing against her spine was the only thing keeping her on her feet.

It took her several long minutes to realize that the rain had died to a gentle patter, more melancholy than threatening. It took her even longer to screw up the courage to open her eyes.

When she did, she discovered that her only companion was the headless statue of the woman in the corner, looking as forlorn and abandoned as she felt. She swallowed around a knot of panic. At least she still had her head.

*For now.*

That little girl's voice came from somewhere in the past—from a time when she had believed that flickering will-o'-the-wisps haunted the marshes and bogs, that squat bogies could transform themselves into handsome men just long enough to lure innocent maidens to their ruin, and that a boy with eyes the color of emeralds might mistake her for an angel.

She searched the shadows, realizing with a start that she was not alone after all. Someone . . . or something . . . was watching her.

Although it cost her the very last crumbs of her strength, Gwendolyn forced herself erect, refusing to meet any monster, real or imagined, while cowering in terror.

"I don't believe in you, you know," she called out. Embarrassed by the hoarse croak that emerged from her throat, she tried again. "This is 1761, not 1461, and

I'm not some ignorant peasant you can intimidate with your superstitious nonsense!"

When only the whisper of the rain greeted her defiant words, she wondered if perhaps her sanity had snapped somewhere during that torturous journey to the castle.

She shook a sodden string of hair out of her eyes. "I'll have you know I'm a student of science and rational thought. Whenever Reverend Throckmorton journeys to London, he brings me back pamphlets from the Royal Society for Improving Natural Knowledge by Experiment!"

A gust of wind swirled through the courtyard, snatching away her words and raising the gooseflesh on her arms. *There.* In the corner to her left, something had moved, had it not? Even as she watched, some formless shape was beginning to separate itself from the shadows. Her entire body began to quake with a bone-deep chill that had nothing to do with the rain or the cold.

"You don't exist," she whispered, praying that if she said it often enough, it would be true. "You don't exist. You're not real. I don't believe in you."

Every instinct urged her to close her eyes and make the thing that was slowly emerging from the darkness go away. But the same damnable curiosity that had once prompted her to dip one of Izzy's hair rags in a flask of oil and light it—while Izzy was wearing it—wouldn't even allow her to blink.

In the end, it wasn't the stark ebony wings that rippled

around the magnificent breadth of his shoulders or the silvery smoke streaming from his nostrils that proved to be Gwendolyn's undoing. It was his face—a face more terrible and beautiful than any she might have imagined.

That face was the last thing she saw before her eyes rolled back in her head and she slumped into a dead faint.

# Chapter Three

As the man who called himself the Dragon gazed with stunned disbelief upon the offering the villagers had left for him, the lit cheroot tumbled from his lips and hissed to its death in a puddle of rainwater.

"I know you've earned a reputation for making women swoon," his companion remarked, stepping out of the shadows and cocking one sandy eyebrow, "but never before at the mere sight of you."

The Dragon began to circle the stake, his long, black cloak billowing around his ankles with each step. "What in the holy hell possessed them to bring me a woman? All I wanted was a haunch of venison and a jug of whisky to warm my bones on this miserable night."

"I'd be willing to wager she'd warm your bones." His friend appreciatively eyed the woman's full breasts and ample hips. "She's what my outspoken great-aunt Taffy, who was once the mistress of George I, would call a 'good breeder.' "

She appeared to be wearing some diaphanous length

of fabric that was more shift than gown. Rain had plastered the garment to her skin, leaving little to a man's imagination. The shadow of one dusky nipple peeped shyly out from between the sodden strands of honey gold hair that spilled over her breast.

Realizing with a start that he was ogling her just as avidly as his companion was, the Dragon took off his cloak and wrapped it around her, swearing beneath his breath.

She had slumped forward when she swooned. He gently tipped up her chin with one finger to reveal a jaw that was strong but compelling. A hint of a dimple graced her cheek. Her lips were full, her skin as soft and white as fleece.

"Bloody savages," he muttered, tugging at her bonds. "Leaving her trussed up like some sort of sacrificial lamb. I ought to fetch my pistol and shoot the lot of them."

"Then they might think you were displeased with their gift."

He shot his friend a dark look. It was beginning to rain in earnest again, forcing him to blink the raindrops from his thick lashes. The wet ropes resisted his efforts to untie them. When he saw the raw grooves they'd carved into the tender flesh of her upper arms, he swore again, more savagely this time. As he chafed her wrists, trying to massage the blood back into them, she moaned.

The last of the ropes fell away. As her knees crumpled, he scooped her up in his arms and started for the castle.

His companion abruptly sobered. "Do you really think that's wise? If she sees your face . . . ?"

He left the question unfinished, but the Dragon knew only too well the dangerous consequences of such folly.

He swung around, the golden waterfall of the woman's hair streaming over his arm. "What would you suggest I do with her? Leave her out here to drown in this storm like some abandoned kitten?"

A rending crack of thunder deafened him to his friend's response and sent a violent tremor through the woman's body. The sky seemed to split open at its swollen seams, unleashing another torrential downpour. The Dragon cradled the shivering woman against his chest and raced for the castle, left with no choice but to carry her into his lair.

Without going to the bother of opening her eyes, Gwendolyn stretched, all but purring with contentment. She never dreamed it would be so very cozy in a dragon's belly. On the contrary—in the flicker of eternity before that *thing* had come lumbering out of the darkness, she'd had ample time to imagine her flesh being seared from her bones by flame or stripped away by boiling acid.

She rolled to her side, pillowing her cheek against a fat, fluffy bolster. Compared with the prickly, heather-stuffed tick she shared with Kitty, it felt as if she were sleeping on a nest of feathers. The heady incense of sandalwood and spice enveloped her. Perhaps she wasn't in a dragon's belly after all, she mused, but in heaven.

She stiffened, coming fully awake. Even the meek Reverend Throckmorton had always preached more on the perils of hell than the pleasures of heaven. Up until that very moment, she wasn't sure she had believed in either. But neither had she believed in dragons.

She drew in a steadying breath before sitting up and opening her eyes. As her gaze surveyed her surroundings, that breath escaped from her lungs in a sigh of pure astonishment. This was surely a heaven more luxuriant and decadent than anything the pious minister had dared to imagine!

She floated in a shimmering pool of midnight blue satin. The rumpled bedclothes shrouded a whitewashed four-poster whose carved columns jutted upward in a fanciful swirl. Lit candles ringed the bed—not smelly tallow, but fragrant wax, melting in a cascade down the graceful arms of the standing candelabrum that cradled them. The tapers cast a flickering halo of light heavenward, drawing Gwendolyn's eyes to the mural painted on the rounded dome of the ceiling.

Nude women, both goddesses and mortals, frolicked in faded pastel meadows, the exuberant abundance of their rosy flesh making Gwendolyn feel as svelte as Kitty. There was Persephone, forsaking spring to surrender her heart to the lord of darkness; Ariadne guiding her lover from the monster's labyrinth; Psyche waking up in a bed of flowers while Cupid watched her from the shadows, his beautiful face forever hidden from her curious eyes.

Gwendolyn craned her neck, so beguiled by their shameless sensuality that she barely felt the sheet slide from her shoulder. She might not have noticed it at all had she not heard a sharply indrawn breath that was not her own. She glanced down, her skin prickling with shock as she realized that beneath the bedclothes, she was as naked as Psyche. Snatching the sheet up to her chin, she slowly lifted her head.

The luminous candlelight gave the bed the unholy glow of a sacrificial altar, but left the corners of the chamber veiled in darkness. Yet she knew she was not alone.

She wished she had paid more attention to Reverend Throckmorton's sermons. Perhaps she wasn't in heaven after all. Perhaps this decadent bower was a place of endless torment disguised as dark pleasures of the flesh.

Gwendolyn shook her tousled hair out of her eyes. "Only the worst sort of coward would spy on a woman from the shadows. I dare you to show yourself."

She heard a muffled footfall, and instantly regretted her challenge.

If this was hell, she was about to meet its overlord.

# Chapter Four

T HERE'S NO NEED TO BLANCH and cower beneath the blankets. I'm not a dragon or a monster. Simply a man."

Gwendolyn squinted into the corner and clutched the sheet to her breasts, the caress of that smoky baritone somehow more a threat to her virtue than her own nudity. She didn't know whether to be frightened or relieved when its owner stopped just short of emerging from his veil of shadows. The moody flicker of the candles kept her eyes from adjusting. She could make out little more than a dark figure leaning against the wall with indifferent grace.

"If I'm cowering beneath the blankets, sir," she said, "it's because some shameless libertine has stolen my clothes."

"Ah, but if I were so shameless a libertine, there would have been no need for me to steal them. You would have surrendered them willingly."

The clipped English bore no trace of a burr to soften

its mockery. Against her will, Gwendolyn was beset by an image of strong, masculine hands peeling the wet fabric from her naked flesh. She clenched her teeth to hide a shiver that had little to do with her fear. "You dare to accuse me of cowardice, yet you're the one hiding in the shadows, too craven to show your face."

"Perhaps it's not fear for myself that prompts my caution, but fear for you."

"Is your face so horrible to look upon? Will it drive me insane or turn me to stone?"

"It already made you swoon, did it not?"

Gwendolyn touched her fingertips to her temples and frowned, unable to summon up more than a hazy recollection of that moment in the courtyard—the smell of rain, the flap of wings, a silvery swirl of smoke . . . and his face. A face made all the more terrible by its utter impossibility. She struggled to capture the memory, but it melted away, more elusive than the stranger taunting her from the shadows.

"Who are you?" she demanded.

"The villagers of Ballybliss call me the Dragon," he replied.

"Then I shall call you charlatan. For only a charlatan would perpetrate such a cruel hoax."

"You wound me, my lady," he said, although the hint of laughter in his voice told her she had succeeded only in amusing him.

She sat up straighter, tossing a damp curl over her shoulder. "I'll have you know I'm no lady."

Her ears were so tuned to his movements that she

would have almost sworn she could hear him cock an eyebrow.

"At least not in the strictest sense," she amended. "My father possesses no title."

"Forgive my presumption. You don't speak in the crude tongue so common to these Highland savages, so I naturally assumed . . ."

"My mother was a lady. The daughter of a Lowland baron. She died when I was nine." Gwendolyn lifted her chin against a pain that time had done little to dull.

"Your lack of nobility is no lack at all to me, since I can assure you that I'm no gentleman."

She was unsure whether to take this as reassurance or warning. Gwendolyn dared a glance beneath the sheet before giving him a smile as sweetly mocking as she imagined his to be. "So I gathered. If you were, I'd still be wearing my clothes."

"And still be in imminent danger of expiring from consumption." His voice hardened. "Which leads me to a question of my own. Just how did you end up sopping wet and bound to a stake in the middle of *my* bloody courtyard?"

Gwendolyn stiffened. "Do forgive me for having the ill manners to disturb your precious solitude, M'lord Dragon. I can just picture you sitting with your cloven hooves propped up on the hearth, enjoying a nice warm cup of kitten's blood, when you heard the shouting of the mob. 'Damnation!' you must have growled. 'I do believe someone has left another human sacrifice on my doorstep.' "

He was silent for so long that Gwendolyn began to tremble. But his reply, when it finally came, was as dry as the rattle of dragon bones. "Actually, I was enjoying a nice glass of port when I heard the commotion. I had to swear off kitten's blood because it gave me dyspepsia." Gwendolyn was caught unawares by the dazzling flare of a match. Its flame died before she could blink, leaving her with the aroma of cheroot smoke and a glowing tip in the darkness. "So the villagers dragged you up the cliff in the pouring rain, bound you to that stake, and left you to die at my hands." He snorted. "And they have the nerve to call *me* a monster."

Gwendolyn focused on where his eyes should be, trying to hold his invisible gaze. "I don't see how you can condemn them when they were responding to your own greedy demands."

A cloud of smoke streamed from the darkness, revealing a flash of temper. "I asked for a haunch of venison and a jug of whisky, not a bloody woman."

"That's not all you asked for, was it?" she said softly.

His sudden stillness warned her to tread with care. "Why do you defend them when they care so little for you that they would cast you away as if you were of no more consequence than a sack of rubbish?"

"Because they're foolish, uneducated, and misguided, but you're nothing but a mean-spirited bully, preying on ignorant superstitions and terrorizing innocent people!"

The glowing tip of the cheroot vanished, as if he had stubbed it out in a fit of anger. "They might be ignorant.

But they're far from innocent. They've more blood on their hands than I do."

Up until that moment, Gwendolyn would have sworn her captor was English, but a faint burr had crept into his speech along with his passion, like moonlight stealing over the heather.

"Who are you?" she whispered again.

"Perhaps I should be the one asking that question," he suggested, his voice even more clipped than before. "By what name should I call you?"

Frustration emboldened her. "You refuse to tell me who you are, yet I have no lack of names to call you."

"Such as coward? Bully? Charlatan?" he offered.

"Blackguard. Knave. Scoundrel," she added.

"Come now," he coaxed. "I'd have expected more imagination from that nimble little tongue of yours."

She bit her bottom lip, tempted to let fly with a string of oaths that would have made Izzy blush. "My name is Gwendolyn. Gwendolyn Wilder."

She gasped as a gust of wind whipped through the chamber, extinguishing the candles. At first, she thought he'd gone, forsaking her to the darkness, but then he was there, surrounding her on all sides without ever once touching her. She breathed him in—the aroma of sandalwood and spice, as inescapably masculine as it was intoxicating. In that moment, she knew exactly where she was.

*His* lair. *His* chamber. *His* bed.

"Why you?" His whisper resounded with a strange urgency. "Why did they choose you?"

To Gwendolyn's ears, his words had the ring of deliberate cruelty. *Why didn't they choose someone prettier? Someone thinner? Someone more like Glynnis or Nessa or even Kitty?*

She closed her eyes, thankful he couldn't see her burning cheeks. "They chose me because virgins are even more uncommon than dragons in Ballybliss."

His hand brushed her damp hair, its treacherous tenderness reminding her without words that it could be more dangerous to be at a man's mercy than a monster's. "A thousand pounds. Is that the price they're putting on innocence these days?"

He didn't wait for an answer she did not have. There was another gust of wind, then more darkness. But this time Gwendolyn knew that he was gone. She hugged her knees to her chest and gazed up at the mural she could no longer see, feeling more alone than she had ever felt in her life.

The Dragon had never much cared for the taste of virgins.

Their flesh might be delectably tender, but wooing them required both charm and patience, two qualities he hadn't possessed in abundance for quite some time now.

As he wound his way into the depths of the castle, stepping over shattered stones and ancient bloodstains without a second thought, he cursed his ill fortune. He had never intended for his elaborate hoax to lure a woman into his lair. Especially not a woman as maddening as the one who now kept him from his bed.

When he had laid her back on those rumpled bedclothes, unwrapped his cloak, and started to peel the sodden linen from her icy flesh, he had thought only to warm her. But as each snowy inch of her skin was revealed, the detachment that usually served him so well had abandoned him. His own flesh had been gripped by a primal fever that curled low in his belly and made him burn to touch her. It had been torture enough when his eyes had lingered on the pale, generous globes of her breasts, but when he caught himself trying to steal a glimpse of the soft, blond thatch of down he knew he would find between her thighs, he had jerked the sheet up over her.

While he'd kept his candlelight vigil, waiting for her to regain consciousness, he'd had ample time to wonder if he'd truly become so much of a beast that he would be tempted to ravish an insensible woman.

He lengthened his strides and raked a wayward lock of damp hair out of his eyes. Not that there was actually anything "insensible" about his captive. As she'd warned him in the courtyard, she was the most sensible of creatures—a student of science and rational thought who devoured pamphlets from the Royal Society for Improving Natural Knowledge by Experiment. She didn't believe in dragons and she didn't believe in him. He couldn't very well take exception to that insult, since he didn't believe in himself, either.

If he had expected those big, blue eyes of hers to

well with tears while she pled for her freedom and her life, he would have been sorely disappointed. She had even dared to chide him for his greed. She might have shamed him if he still had a conscience.

He was shaking his head at her boldness when he rounded the corner to discover that he had little hope of drying out his own damp clothing because his lavishly appointed wing chair, his cozy fire, and his bottle of port had been appropriated in his absence.

The underground room had once served as an antechamber to the castle dungeon and a haven for its guards. Rusted axes, claymores, and broadswords adorned the dank stone walls, giving the room all the welcoming charm of a medieval torture chamber. But the room's grim ambience didn't seem to be troubling the man who reclined in the Dragon's chair, his stocking feet stretched toward the fire crackling on the stone hearth. He'd traded his damp frock coat for a scarlet and black tartan. A jaunty plaid bonnet adorned with a cockade of white feathers perched on his brow, the perfect complement to the bagpipes propped against his knee.

The Dragon paced to the hearth, earning a somnolent glare from the fluffy gray cat toasting himself on the hearthstones. He'd taken in Toby in the hopes that the massive feline would help reduce the rat population of the castle. But Toby and the rats seemed to have reached some sort of gentleman's agreement. The rats would flourish and Toby would sleep twenty-three hours a day.

The Dragon hadn't realized how exhausted he was until he had nowhere to sit. He swung around, ignoring the unspoken question in his friend's eyes. "If you keep marching around the parapets bleating on those pipes, Tupper, we're going to be found out for sure."

"On the contrary," Tupper replied, hefting his glass of port in a smug toast. "I'm quite a tolerable piper. I don't bleat at all. And the villagers think I'm a ghost."

The Dragon shook his head. "I can't imagine why you're so enamored of this accursed country and all of its ridiculous trappings."

"What's not to love?" Tupper exclaimed, the bogus burr he'd taken to affecting since their arrival in the Highlands growing thicker with each word. "The misty mornin's? The sparklin' burns that ripple through the glens? The quaint charm of its folk?"

"The fog? The chill? The damp?" the Dragon countered, backing closer to the fire.

Tupper slanted him a sly look that was decidedly at odds with his cherubic countenance. "Aye, but with a bonny lass to warm your bed, even the cold and the damp might be bearable."

"If you're referring to the 'bonny lass' I just left in my bed, I can assure you that the cold and the damp would make better companions on a lonely night than her frosty contempt."

His interest piqued, Tupper leaned forward in his chair and mercifully dropped the burr. "So what gruesome crime did this girl commit to deserve being fed to the likes of you?"

The Dragon sank down heavily on the edge of the hearth, ignoring Toby's growl of protest. "No crime at all. She's innocent."

Tupper snorted. "Perhaps in her eyes, but not in the eyes of the villagers. So what is she? A murderer? A thief?" A hopeful twinkle lit his brown eyes. "A harlot?"

"I should be so fortunate. At least I'd know what to do with a harlot. It's much worse than that. They intended her to be a sacrifice." The Dragon could feel his jaw stiffening as he struggled to form a word he'd had little cause to use in his dealings with the fair sex. "A *virgin* sacrifice."

Tupper gaped at him for a moment before throwing back his head and roaring with laughter. "A virgin? They've given *you* a virgin? Oh, that's priceless!"

"Not quite. The villagers seem to think she's worth a thousand pounds."

Tupper abruptly sobered. "I tried to tell you it was too soon to play that particular card. You should have given them time to fret over your demand. Time to start eyeing each other and wondering who among them might have that ill-gotten treasure buried in his cellar." His reproachful sigh ruffled the drooping plume of feathers on his hat. "But who am I, Theodore Tuppingham, the plodding son of a minor viscount, to gainsay a man who has stared down the mouths of the fire-spewing cannons at Louisbourg? A man who has been knighted by the Crown for valor and amassed a fortune using nothing more than his quick wits and his utter lack of care for his own life? I'm descended from a long line of sniveling cowards. All I have to do to inherit my title is outlive a papa given to gout and heart palpitations."

As Tupper waved the glass, splashing wine on the flagstones, the Dragon whisked it out of his hand. "You shouldn't drink port, you know. It makes you blather."

"And it makes you brood," Tupper retorted, retrieving the glass and draining it dry.

The Dragon buried his fingers in Toby's plush mane. A more amiable cat would have purred, but Toby's whiskers simply twitched in a regal sneer. "I'm at an utter loss, Tup. Whatever shall we do with her?"

Tupper settled back in the chair. "Has she seen your face?"

"Of course not. I may be a bloody fool, but I'm not an idiot."

"Then perhaps it's not too late for me to disguise myself as one of those rugged Highlanders and carry her back to the village."

"And what? Leave her in the square with a note pinned to her gown saying, 'Thank you very much for the delectable virgin, but I'd prefer a nice tasty strumpet'?" He snorted. "You might fool *them* with such a ruse, but it's far too late to fool her. She already believes I'm nothing but a greedy charlatan out to fleece the villagers of all their worldly goods."

"Couldn't you threaten her with your fiery wrath if she dares to expose you?" Tupper snapped his fingers. "What about my dragon-shifting-into-a-man-at-will rumor? I was particularly proud of that one."

"And it might have worked had they offered me some witless girl afraid of her own shadow." He shook his head, his exasperation tinged with reluctant admiration. "This one won't be so easy to fool. If we let her go, she'll bring the whole village down on our heads. And I'm not ready for that. Yet." As he rose to pace the chamber, Toby threw himself into a full-body stretch, taking up every inch of hearth the Dragon had vacated. "It seems I have no choice but to add abduction to my burgeoning list of sins."

"So you intend to keep her?"

"For now. But she must never see my face."

Tupper lifted the glass to his lips before remembering it was empty. "And if she does?"

The Dragon surveyed his friend, his lips twisting in a bitter smile. "Then she'll discover that there are darker things in this world than dragons. You must remember, Tup—the villagers just *think* you're a ghost. I *am* one."

# Chapter Five

WHEN GWENDOLYN AWOKE the next morning, she was both angry and hungry—a dangerous combination when she was in her best temper, which she most definitely was not at the moment. She'd had a restless night to brood over M'lord Dragon's high-handed treatment of her and it hadn't helped that every time she'd awakened, it had been with his scent in her nostrils.

She sat up, relieved that she was no longer in darkness. A buttery shaft of sunlight poured through a round iron grate set high on the wall. Last night, all of her senses had been enveloped by her captor, and she had not noticed the sound of the breakers striking the rocks far below. Now she realized that he must have carried her to one of the castle towers facing the sea, a tower spared the worst of the English cannon fire all those years ago.

She clambered out of the bed, wrapping the satin sheet around her as if it were one of the Roman togas garbing the demigoddesses on the ceiling. Her linen robe was lying in a soggy heap on the floor. Gwendolyn shook her head. She supposed it was too much to expect the Dragon to have enough sense to hang up the garment so it could dry.

As she circled the chamber, trailing the sheet behind her, a cascade of dust motes drifted through the air, tickling her nose. It was quickly apparent that the extravagant bed, the satin sheets, and the wax candles in their standing candelabrum were an oasis of luxury in a desert of barren neglect. A superior smile touched her lips. M'lord Dragon might be a beast at heart, but he certainly appreciated his creature comforts.

Faded wainscoting and peeling whitewash covered the paneled walls of the chamber. She poked her nose behind a moth-eaten curtain and found an ancient privy. Any ideas she might have had about escaping down its yawning shaft were banished after she dropped a loose bit of plaster into it and failed to hear so much as an echo of a splash. At least she was to be spared the indignity of asking M'lord Dragon to empty her chamber pot. Although, she thought with an evil grin, it might be worth sacrificing her dignity to insult his.

A wooden birdcage festooned with cobwebs hung in the corner, its occupant long flown—or so Gwendolyn believed until she stood on tiptoe to peep through the cage's bars and saw the tiny nest of bones huddled on its floor.

She backed away from the cage. There was something so pathetic, so betrayed about that fragile corpse. At one time, it had belonged to some merry, chirping creature who had trusted that someone would return to listen to him sing, to clean his cage . . . to feed him.

Gwendolyn whirled around, suddenly discovering what was missing from the chamber.

A door.

She circled the walls, tempted to beat against them as the hapless bird must have beat his wings against the bars of his cage when he realized no one was ever coming back. She could almost believe the Dragon had cast some dark enchantment upon her. Some diabolical spell that would allow him to come and go as he desired, but that would keep her his prisoner forever.

She sagged against the wall, shamed by her panic. What was it about this place? It was no longer the enchanted castle she had once believed it to be, yet it still possessed the power to awaken her every girlish fancy. Fancies she'd squelched during the years she'd spent caring for her father. She was even more ashamed to realize it was the first time she'd thought of Papa since last night.

Her only hope for him lay in his frequent lapses of memory. If his broken mind decided to go wandering in the past as it so often did, perhaps he wouldn't even miss her. The thought gave her less comfort than she had hoped.

She straightened. The solution to her dilemma was really quite simple. One of the panels had to be a door.

She began to circle the room again, this time using

her fingernails to pry at each panel in turn. She soon found herself back where she had started without having heard even a creak of encouragement. The Dragon might as well have chained her to a wall in the castle dungeon.

"God's toenails," she swore, slumping against the panel as her stomach growled in frustration.

The distant sound of singing drifted to her ears. Gwendolyn cocked her head, recognizing the words and melody of the familiar ditty, but not the voice of the singer.

*I love the fair hair o' me Jenny Claire.*
*The bonniest lady is she.*
*But to woo the lass,*
*I must kick the . . . um, rump*
*O' her braw brothers three.*

Gwendolyn winced. The song was not only atrociously off-key, but sung in a Scottish burr thicker than Auld Tavis's. As it deteriorated into cheery whistling, Gwendolyn pressed her ear first to one panel, then to another, until she was rewarded by the sound of approaching footsteps.

Still gripping the sheet in one hand, she looked frantically around for a weapon. All she could find was the birdcage. With a muttered apology to its lifeless occupant, she wrenched it from its chain, then pressed herself to the wall next to the panel, holding the cage over her head with her free hand. Let M'lord Dragon see how he liked being caught in his own trap!

The panel clicked, then swung inward. A man ducked through the opening. Without allowing herself time to lose her nerve, Gwendolyn slammed the bird-cage down on the back of his head.

He slumped into a boneless heap.

"Oh, no!" Gwendolyn cried out, not in regret but in dismay, as the tray he'd been carrying crashed to the floor along with him, spilling a basket of crossbuns and a pitcher of steaming chocolate.

She scrambled to rescue one of the crossbuns before it rolled under the bed, but could do nothing to stop the rich chocolate from seeping into the floorboards.

She blew the dust off the bun and sank her teeth into its crust as she surveyed her captive. M'lord Dragon didn't look quite so fierce lying facedown on the floor in a puddle of chocolate, now, did he? She nudged him with her foot, but he did not stir. She knew she ought to take advantage of his stupor and flee, but her curiosity had always been stronger than her fear. She could not leave this place without seeing the face of the Dragon just once.

Clutching the sheet to her breast, she knelt down and gave his limp form an ungainly shove. As he rolled onto his back, she retreated, stifling a squeak.

Her alarm was quickly replaced by another emotion—one it took her a moment to identify.

Disappointment.

*This? This* was the fierce beast who had terrorized

the village? *This* was the man whose smoky baritone had sent shivers cascading over her bare skin? *This* was the man whose spice and sandalwood scent had haunted her restless dreams?

A snore escaped his parted lips, fluttering the sandy hairs of his well-trimmed mustache. The hair on his head was equally pale and already thinning at the crown. Although he wore a tartan plaid draped over one shoulder of his frock coat, his full cheeks were fair and stained with the natural blush of a born and bred Englishman. His generous girth strained the pearl buttons of his double-breasted waistcoat. His nose was rounded, his mouth bland, his face decidedly pleasant.

Gwendolyn slowly backed away from him, chiding herself for being ridiculous. After all, what had she expected? Some handsome, brooding rogue with a devilish smile and piercing eyes? Some dark prince laboring beneath a terrible curse that could only be broken by a maiden's kiss? She ought to be relieved that the beast had turned out to be nothing but a man. And a very ordinary one at that.

Shaking her head, Gwendolyn backed toward the open panel. "Farewell, M'lord Dragon," she murmured. "For I doubt we shall ever meet again."

"I wouldn't be so sure of that if I were you." A pair of warm hands closed over her shoulders from behind, caressing the fluted arch of her collarbones. "On the contrary, my dear, I think we'd best be prepared to enjoy each other's company for quite some time."

# Chapter Six

"DON'T TURN AROUND," the Dragon commanded with the authority of a man accustomed to having his orders obeyed.

Gwendolyn was tempted to defy him, but the subtle pressure of his fingertips warned her that he was fully capable of enforcing his command, with or without her cooperation. She didn't relish the prospect of engaging him in a full-out brawl, especially while garbed only in a sheet that had an alarming tendency to slither down her body with a will of its own.

Out of a swirl of dizzying impressions, she struggled to form an image of him. He was taller than her by at least a head, maybe more. He had an aristocrat's hands, with lean, long fingers and neatly clipped nails. Black hair dusted the backs of those hands. As she breathed in his scent, now mingled with the tantalizing musk of cheroot smoke, she realized what a fool she'd been to have mistaken the man she'd bashed with the birdcage for the Dragon, whose mere presence made every nerve in her body tingle with awareness.

The other man sat up, groaning and rubbing the back of his head.

"The cheeky little chit ambushed me," he muttered, drawing a handkerchief from his breast pocket and using it to swipe chocolate from his cheek. "I never saw it coming."

"One rarely does where a woman is concerned," the Dragon said dryly. She could sense him eyeing the carnage of what was meant to be her breakfast. "I take it she has no great fondness for crossbuns and chocolate."

" 'She' has no great fondness for being locked up like an animal in a cage," Gwendolyn retorted, holding herself rigid in the vain hope that she would forget she was still in his arms.

His smoky chuckle caressed her nape. "Wouldn't it be more pleasant to think of yourself as a pampered pet?"

"Even the most pampered of pets has been known to tear out its master's throat if ill-treated or too long deprived of attention."

"I shall take your warning to heart, although I can assure you that it was never my intent to deprive you of my attentions." Before Gwendolyn could fully digest that rather alarming statement, he nodded toward his companion. "Shall I make the introductions, Tup, or will you?"

The man climbed to his feet, brushing crossbun crumbs and splinters of birdcage from his fawn knee breeches before sweeping her a sheepish bow. "Theodore Tuppingham, my lady, at your humble service. But I hope you'll call me Tupper. All my friends do." His eyes were the same earnest brown as those of a spaniel her papa used to hunt with when she was a little girl.

"Gwendolyn Wilder," she replied stiffly. "And I fear I can hardly consider you a friend, *Mr. Tuppingham*, as long as you and your companion insist upon holding me hostage."

"Now that we've concluded with the pleasantries . . ." The Dragon stretched out a hand. "Tupper, your cravat."

Tupper gave the ruffled stock draped around his neck a puzzled look. "Is it crooked?"

The Dragon's long-suffering sigh stirred Gwendolyn's hair.

"Oh!" Tupper exclaimed, whipping off the cravat and laying it across the Dragon's palm.

As Gwendolyn realized what he meant to do with it, she began to struggle in earnest. "If you toy with the blindfold," he murmured, folding the scrap of linen over her eyes, "I'll bind your hands. And that might make it a trifle bit more challenging to keep your white-knuckled death grip on that sheet."

Gwendolyn had no choice but to surrender to his will. It was mortifying enough that he'd seen her without her clothes; she wasn't about to let him make sport of her in front of the blushing Mr. Tuppingham.

It would have been easier to despise him if he'd been rough with her, but he seemed to take exquisite care to make sure the silky strands of her hair didn't get tangled in the blindfold's knot. Still, as he caught her arm and steered her toward the bed, his taut grip warned her that his patience was at an end. "Leave us, Tupper. I should like to have a word with Miss Wilder. Alone."

"There's really no need for you to be angry with her, lad," Tupper said. "If I'd have taken more care—"

"You wouldn't have ended up wearing the birdcage for a bonnet. You can stop hovering like a nervous nursemaid, Tupper. I've no intention of torturing or ravishing our guest. Yet," he finished darkly.

The dreaded click of the panel came too soon.

"Sit," the Dragon commanded as the back of Gwendolyn's knees came up against the bed.

Gwendolyn sat, her jaw set at a mutinous angle.

The measured tread of the Dragon's bootheels told her he had taken to pacing. "Surely you must realize, Miss Wilder, that your untimely arrival at Castle Weyrcraig is as great a misfortune to me as it is to you. If I could let you leave, I would. You're a distraction I don't need and can ill afford."

"Then why don't you just send me home? I can assure you that I'm needed there," she said, hoping it was still true.

"Because I'm as much a prisoner in this as you are. I refuse to let you destroy everything I've labored over for—" he broke off suddenly, purging the passion from his voice, "the past few months. You'll simply have to remain my guest until my business with Ballybliss is finished."

"Your 'guest'?" Gwendolyn echoed with a disbelieving laugh. "Do you always keep your 'guests' locked in a room without doors? And what 'business' could a man like you possibly have with a dying Highland village populated only by those too poor or too mule-headed to leave?" A new thought struck her. "Is it the curse? Did you and your Mr. Tuppingham hear about the curse and decide Ballybliss would be easy prey for your trickery?"

She could hear him slow in his pacing. "I seem to recall some vague mention of a curse." When he paused, she found it easy to imagine him tapping that insolent mouth of his with one elegant finger. "Ah, yes, I remember now. It seems the clan's own chieftain called down doom upon the heads of the good folk of Ballybliss with his dying breath. Tell me, Miss Wilder, just what did your clansmen do to deserve such a terrible fate?"

"It wasn't what they did. It's what they didn't do." Gwendolyn bowed her head, thankful that he couldn't see the shadow of shame in her eyes. "Our chieftain was a secret sympathizer with Bonnie Prince Charlie and his cause. When the prince needed somewhere to hide after his defeat at Culloden, the MacCullough offered him sanctuary at Castle Weyrcraig."

"A noble, if misguided, impulse."

Gwendolyn jerked up her head. "Misguided? I think

not. The MacCullough was a dreamer—a man of vision who dared to imagine a Scotland free of English tyranny, a Scotland united beneath the banner of its rightful king."

"But at what price, Miss Wilder? Even the most magnificent of dreams has a way of turning to ashes by the light of day."

Gwendolyn's passionate denial died in her throat. She couldn't very well defend her chieftain while entombed in the ruins of his dream. She bowed her head again, toying with a fold of the sheet. "The Duke of Cumberland somehow discovered the prince's hiding place. Charles escaped into the night, but Cumberland was determined to make our chieftain pay for betraying the Crown. So he and his soldiers dragged their cannons up the hill and opened fire upon the castle."

"And I suppose this is when the MacCullough's loyal clan rushed to their chieftain's defense, drums thundering and bagpipes howling the doom of any redcoat who dared to lift a sword against their laird."

"The clan didn't come to his defense," she said softly. "The MacCullough was forced to stand alone."

"No wonder he cursed them," the Dragon said with a cynical snort of laughter.

"They were afraid!" Gwendolyn cried. "Every man, woman, and child in that village knew why Cumberland's enemies called him The Butcher. They'd heard how he'd slaughtered the wounded at Culloden until the soil ran red with Scots blood."

"So the villagers of Ballybliss just huddled in their

cottages behind their bolted doors while their laird and his family were massacred." Somehow, the utter lack of emotion in his words made them even more damning.

"They believed Cumberland would spare them if they didn't interfere."

"And did he?"

"They weren't murdered in their beds. Their cottages weren't razed to the ground." The blindfold did not hide the blush creeping into her cheeks. "Their wives and daughters weren't raped and forced to bear the babes of English soldiers nine months later."

The Dragon began to pace again, the husky counterpoint of his voice mesmerizing her. "But what little gold they'd managed to hoard was confiscated by the Crown in the name of taxation. Everything that had bound them together as a clan was outlawed—their faith, their tartans, their weapons. The youngest and the strongest fled Ballybliss, while those who were left behind spent the next fifteen years looking over their shoulders, waiting for the doom they'd been promised to swoop down from the sky like some angel of vengeance and destroy them."

"How do you know all of this?" Gwendolyn whispered.

"Perhaps I am that angel." Before she could decide if he was mocking her or himself, he laughed. "Or perhaps I'm simply an opportunistic devil who bought a drink for some pathetic old Highlander in a run-down tavern somewhere. Perhaps he spilled all of Ballybliss's secrets in my ear, including the morsel that someone in your village might be hoarding the thousand pounds they earned for betraying their chieftain. Perhaps he even told me that the badge of the MacCullough clan was a flame-breathing dragon."

"Perhaps he did," Gwendolyn agreed, wanting desperately to believe him. "After all, no one blathers more than a drunken Highlander."

"You've never seen Tupper after a few glasses of port."

"Nor do I care to. Which is one of many reasons why I want you to let me go."

"So we're back to that, are we?"

An image of Papa's face, crumpled with confusion as he wondered why she hadn't come to dress him and feed him his porridge, drifted into Gwendolyn's head. "What of my family? Have you no regard for their feelings? Would you have them think I was dead?"

A disarming note of anger edged his voice. "Where was your precious family when that mob of savages made off with you?"

Tucked in their beds with a warm brick wrapped in flannel. Thanking her for her noble sacrifice. Promising to have their lovers write songs in her honor. Vowing never to forget her. Gwendolyn swallowed, her silence condemnation enough.

"Just as I thought," he said. "The way I see it, you're safer in my hands than in theirs."

Now that, Gwendolyn thought, was the greatest lie he had told. "What if I promised not to expose your little charade?"

She was unprepared for the sweet shock of his fingers cupping her cheek. "You'd be lying."

As he stroked his thumb across her bottom lip, she closed her eyes beneath the blindfold, seeking to deny the melting effect of his touch.

"Couldn't you pretend to believe me?" she whispered. "I can be very convincing."

"I'm sure you can," he murmured. "But I haven't trusted anyone for a very long time, and something tells me I'd be a bloody fool to start with you." He drew away, the clipped formality returning to his voice. "If you'll promise not to render him unconscious, I'll send Tupper up with more breakfast. Will there be anything else you require during your stay?"

Gwendolyn surged to her feet. She cast one corner of the sheet over her shoulder and thrust her chin toward the general direction of his last comment. "There will be much I require. I strongly suggest that you double your demands for food. As you can see by my appearance, I am a woman of hearty appetites, and I shall expect them to be well satisfied."

He seemed to have something stuck in his throat, making his reply sound choked. "I'll consider it my privilege. I just hope you'll find me up to the task."

"And surely you can't expect me to spend the remainder of my incarceration garbed in this—this—rag." He didn't have to know that the cool satin felt like bliss against her bare skin compared with the scratchy wool she usually wore.

"Most certainly not. You can remove it anytime you like."

"And I shall also require some amusements to brighten the long hours. I prefer the stimulation of books to the tedium of needlework. Dozens of them. I've been known to devour two or three a day."

"Ah, so we return to your hearty appetites."

If she hadn't believed he'd have her hands bound before she could get them to her face, Gwendolyn would have jerked off the blindfold purely for the satisfaction of shooting him a venomous look.

"Will there be anything else, Miss Wilder?" he asked. "I could arrange for some musical entertainment. A quartet of string musicians fresh from their triumphant performance at Vauxhall Gardens, perhaps?"

"I don't believe I'll be needing anything else." She waited until she heard him moving toward the panel before spitefully adding, "Yet."

Gwendolyn sank toward the thronelike bed, hoping to maintain her air of regal dignity. Which might have been possible if she hadn't misjudged the distance and plopped down onto the floor, landing in a puddle of cold chocolate.

Her captor's rich laughter poured through the room.

Gwendolyn furiously jerked off the blindfold, only to discover that the Dragon had flown.

✦ ✦ ✦

A short while later, Gwendolyn was perched on the foot of the bed, clinging to her soggy sheet and glaring at the panel when it crept open.

Tupper poked his head into the chamber like a timid turtle. "If you're going to bash me over the head again, miss, would you mind letting me put down the tray first? White flour and Swiss chocolate are rather hard to come by in this particular corner of the Highlands."

"You're safe for now, Mr. Tuppingham. I'm all out of birdcages."

"That's a relief. Although getting clobbered did take my mind off the headache I'd earned from imbibing too much port last night."

As he moved to set the tray on the bed, giving her a wide berth, they eyed each other warily. With his puppy-dog eyes and sandy cowlick, Gwendolyn supposed he looked harmless enough. But she couldn't afford to forget that he was one of Satan's minions.

"I gather your master won't be joining us." Gwendolyn gave one of the crossbuns a poke, pretending indifference.

"Oh, he's not my master. He's my friend," Tupper replied, offering her a delicate china cup.

She took it, savoring the aroma of chocolate wafting up from its depths. The first sip was sheer rapture. "I can't help but wonder how you came to make the acquaintance of such a"— she had to grit her teeth against the urge to bring her captor's parentage into question—"mysterious fellow."

Tupper chuckled. "It's a long story, and my great-aunt Taffy always said I talk too much. I wouldn't want to bore you."

"Oh, please do," Gwendolyn implored, gesturing at the barren chamber. "What else have I to do?"

When he appeared to be wavering, she offered him a crossbun, recognizing the kindred gleam in his eye. He wasted no time in plopping down on the opposite corner of the bed and tearing off a buttery hunk of the bread. Gwendolyn helped herself to a bun, in the interest of being companionable and encouraging him to confide in her. If she hoped to defeat the Dragon in his own lair, she would have to learn both his strengths and his weaknesses.

"We met in one of the gambling hells in Pall Mall two years ago," Tupper confessed, pausing just long enough in his chewing to brush a sprinkling of crumbs from his rumpled waistcoat.

"Why am I not surprised?" Gwendolyn hid the acid sweetness of her smile behind another sip of chocolate.

"I was alone in one of the back rooms preparing to shoot myself in the head—" At Gwendolyn's horrified gasp, he paused just long enough to give her a heartening smile. "As I was saying, I was in one of the back rooms preparing to shoot myself in the head when—" He paused again, his mouth hanging open. Gwendolyn leaned forward, praying the name on the tip of his tongue would come tumbling out. "—*the Dragon* came strolling in."

"And he stopped you?"

Tupper shook his head vigorously, speaking through a hearty mouthful of bun. "Oh, no. He simply pointed out that I'd neglected to properly tamp down my charge and was just as likely to blow off my foot as my head. He removed the pistol from my hand, used his own rod to do the honors, then handed it back."

Gwendolyn lowered her crossbun, her mouth falling open. "If he was determined to be so accommodating, why didn't he just shoot you himself?"

Tupper chuckled. "I was deep in my cups at the time, and I do believe it was his matter-of-fact manner that sobered me out of my self-pity. You see—the Marquess of Eddingham had just threatened to call in all my vowels after he discovered I wasn't good for them. He was intent upon ruining me. The scandal would have killed my father. Of course, that wouldn't have been such a tragedy, since the ill-tempered old goat has always considered me the most wretched disappointment of his life and his death would have made me a viscount. But all of his assets are tied up in entailed land, and a fat lot of good a title would have done me while I was rotting away in debtors' prison."

Gwendolyn shook her head. "Please don't tell me the Dragon paid off your gambling debts."

"Not exactly." A rueful smile played around Tupper's mouth. "But he did engage the marquess in a game of dice that went on until dawn." He shook his head. "I've never seen a grown man so close to tears as the marquess was when he realized he had no chance of recouping his losses. And I can assure you they were quite staggering. As the sun began to rise, my new friend turned around and handed me his winnings. I then handed them back to the marquess to pay off my debts in full. When he realized what we'd done, he tore up my vowels and hurled them in our faces, shouting that he hoped we choked on them."

"The Dragon didn't keep any of the winnings for himself?"

"Not so much as a ha'pence."

Gwendolyn stopped chewing. "So why would such a benevolent soul choose to prey upon villagers who have little more than the rags on their backs? Does he need the money to pay off his own gambling debts?"

Tupper let out a bray of laughter. "I should say not. Why, there are some who say he's one of the wealthiest men in—" He snapped his mouth shut, his mustache twitching guiltily. She could almost see his round, guileless face withdrawing into its shell.

He sprang to his feet and began to back away from the bed. "He warned me about you. He told me you were more clever than I am by half and I should take care to guard my tongue whenever I was around you."

Gwendolyn scrambled to her feet, narrowly averting disaster when she tripped over the hem of the sheet. "Surely you can't blame me, Mr. Tuppingham, for seeking to learn something of the man who has made me his hostage. Please don't go, I implore you!"

Tupper shook a finger at her. "He warned me about that, too. Told me if you couldn't outwit me, you'd probably try to charm me with those dimples and that pretty mouth of yours."

Gwendolyn was accustomed to being blamed for her intelligence, but no one had ever before accused her of being pretty or charming. "He said such a thing?"

Tupper fumbled in the pocket of his frock coat, drawing forth paper, pen, a flask of sand, and a bottle of ink. "He told me to leave these with you. Said you should make a list of everything you require."

He tossed the items on the bed and dove for the panel, leaving her alone once again. Gwendolyn recognized the stationery. It was the same expensive vellum the Dragon used for his demands.

She caressed the creamy sheaf between thumb and forefinger, lost in thought. Despite their recent encounters, she was no closer to divining the Dragon's true nature than she'd been last night. If she could just remember what she had seen in that courtyard. . . . But the memory continued to elude her, leaving her with nothing but the conflicting truths she'd learned since then. He was a gambler who gave away his winnings, a bully who took exquisite care not to pull her hair, a thief who had her completely at his mercy, yet had made no attempt to steal her innocence.

Sinking down on the bed, she brushed her thumb against her lower lip, just as the Dragon had done earlier. What in heaven's name was wrong with her? She was beginning to feel as witless as Nessa. Instead of being outraged by his impertinence, she was yearning for a mirror for the first time in her memory.

Shaking off the ridiculous longing, she uncapped the ink, dipped the pen into it, and began to scribble. If the Dragon was intent upon keeping her as his prisoner, then she would see to it that he paid dearly for the pleasure of her company.

# Chapter Seven

$\mathcal{A}$ WOMAN'S SCREAM ripped through the deserted streets of Ballybliss. When the villagers came spilling out of their cottages in their nightdresses and nightshirts, they found Kitty Wilder standing in the moonlight at the mouth of the village, gripping her chest as if the arrow still quivering in the trunk of the ancient oak had pierced her heart.

Three young lads tripped over their own feet in their rush to comfort her, but her sisters reached her first. As Glynnis and Nessa gathered the trembling young girl into their arms, clucking like mother hens, a dour-faced Ailbert reached up and pried the arrow from the rough bark. A hushed murmur traveled through the crowd. There was no need for the blacksmith to tell them that the ivory paper rippling from the arrow's shaft was not a flag of surrender.

For the past twenty-four hours, Castle Weyrcraig had yielded nothing but ominous silence. While many had expressed their hope that the curse had been broken and the Dragon was off to torment some other unfortunate village, none had dared give voice to their secret fear that they'd somehow compounded their past transgressions with a darker and even more damning sin. A warm spring sun had burned off all traces of last night's storm, making the madness that had seized them during their march to the castle seem more nightmare than reality.

But the consequences of that madness could no longer be denied—Gwendolyn Wilder was gone and her poor, mad father would spend the rest of his days waiting to hear a familiar footstep that would never come.

Clutching the paper in his fist, Ailbert led a grim parade through the narrow streets of the village, accompanied by Kitty Wilder's sobs. He marched right up to the stoop of the only cottage in Ballybliss maintained by the English Crown and began to pound on the door.

After several minutes, the door flew open, bathing them in a golden halo of lamplight. "G-g-good heavens, man, what is it?" stammered Reverend Throckmorton, his nightcap on backward and his wire-rimmed spectacles hanging askew from one ear. "The second coming?"

Ailbert did not speak. He simply thrust the piece of paper beneath the man's nose.

The reverend shooed it away. "And what's this? Another message from that beastly Dragon of yours?" He shook his head. "I strive to be a patient man, you know, but I've just returned from a grueling journey and I've no time for such pagan nonsense. Why don't you go wake that dear, sweet Wilder girl and let me get a decent night's sleep."

He was about to close the door in their faces when Ailbert wedged his foot between door and jamb. "We'd be much obliged if ye'd read this note for us. So obliged we wouldn't even think o' breakin' that lamp ye're holdin' in yer hand there and burnin' yer cottage to the ground."

The reverend gasped in outrage, then took the paper from Ailbert's hands. While the villagers crowded closer to hear his words, he adjusted his spectacles, tutting beneath his breath, "Bagpipe-playing ghosts. Dragons burning up your fields with their breath. Pointy-eared bogies stealing your babies and leaving their own. Is it any wonder you were such easy prey for the Papists?"

"We didn't come here for a sermon, old man," Ross snarled, hanging over his father's shoulder.

With an injured sniff, Throckmorton began to read. " 'Good folk of Ballybliss' "—the reverend started to interrupt himself, then obviously thought better of it— " 'although you've taxed my patience before, I've decided to give you a full fortnight to retrieve the thousand pounds I requested.' "

The pronouncement was greeted with fresh gasps and groans. Even the reverend looked taken aback. "A thousand pounds? Wasn't that the reward the Crown paid for the life of that traitor MacCullough?"

"That was naught but vicious gossip," Ailbert

muttered. "No one in this village has ever seen that much gold."

Throckmorton wisely returned his attention to the paper. " 'Until that time, I will have need of the following: five dozen eggs, a half-dozen rounds of cheese, ten steak and kidney pies, three dozen biscuits, twelve loaves of crispbread, five pounds of smoked haddock, a bag of onions, a sack of oatmeal, seven turnips, twenty-five apples, two dozen oatcakes, a side of moor venison, three pounds of fresh mutton, three dozen potatoes, a head of kale, fourteen . . .' "

When Throckmorton's recitation went on and on without so much as a pause for breath, Ailbert's mouth dropped open. He snatched the paper out of the minister's hand, then scanned it from right to left. He didn't have to know how to read to recognize that it was covered from margin to margin on both sides with the same carelessly elegant scrawl.

"There's a postscript," the reverend pointed out, lifting the lamp to squint at the back of the paper. " 'While your recent offering was much more delicious than I had anticipated,' " he read, " 'I should warn you that any more uninvited gifts will cost you not only a thousand pounds, but your miserable lives as well.' "

Ross rested his chin on his father's shoulder, his broad face crestfallen. "Can ye believe he has the nerve to ask for all that? Ye'd have thought he'd be full after he ate that Wilder lass."

Granny Hay shook her grizzled head. "P'r'aps she

only whet his appetite. Me puir Gavin was like that. The more he ate, the more he wanted." She sighed. "The priest swore 'twas his heart that gave out in the end, but I've always believed 'twas that last mouthful o' me haggis that done him in."

Reverend Throckmorton's horrified gaze traveled the glum circle of their faces. "God in heaven," he whispered, "what have you done?"

Kitty Wilder tore herself out of her sisters' arms, her face smeared with grimy tear tracks. "They fed my poor sister to that nasty old Dragon, that's what they've done! And they ought to be ashamed!"

"Hush, lass," Nessa crooned, tugging her back. "Gwennie sacrificed herself for all of us, and she was more than glad to do it!"

The reverend blinked his red-rimmed eyes in disbelief. "You gave that poor child to this Dragon of yours? Why, she was the only one among you who had even a pinch of sense!"

"Keep talkin' like that," Ailbert snapped, "and I'll be thinkin' the Dragon might like a nice juicy Presbyterian."

"He's a bit on the scrawny side," Ross noted, leaning forward until his bulk threw an ominous shadow over the stoop, "but we could always let Granny Hay take him home and fatten him up with a bit o' her haggis."

Without warning, the good reverend hopped backward and slammed the door in their faces.

Ailbert swung around, swearing violently. "I'd like to wring the neck o' the muttonhead who talked us into tryin' to break that blasted curse." It was at that precise moment that he spotted Auld Tavis on the fringes of the crowd, attempting to tiptoe away. "And there he is now!"

He gestured to his youngest son. Lachlan grabbed the old man by the scruff of the neck. In his billowing shroud of a nightshirt, Auld Tavis looked even more like a moldering corpse than usual.

" 'Twas only a suggestion," Auld Tavis said in a wheedling tone as Lachlan hauled him toward the stoop. "I meant no harm by it."

"I say we stone him!" Ross shouted.

Ailbert shook his head. "There's no point in that now. The harm's been done."

Lachlan lowered a relieved Tavis to the ground while Ross shook his head in disgust.

"But whatever are we to do?" asked Marsali, hugging her baby daughter to her breast.

Ailbert scowled down at the paper in his hand, his long face even grimmer than before. "Start gatherin' eggs and milkin' cows. There's a dragon to be fed."


Gwendolyn's second day in captivity began with a jarring thump and a muffled oath. She sat up in bed, shaking her tousled hair out of her eyes just in time to see the panel easing shut behind someone. Her first instinct was to throw something at it, but as her eyes adjusted to the pearly glow of dawn seeping through the grated window, her anger turned to amazement.

She almost threw back the sheet before remembering

that such a motion would leave her as naked and rosy as she'd been on the day she was born. Tying the rumpled and chocolate-stained silk around her with a clumsy knot, she clambered out of the bed and surveyed the chamber with disbelieving eyes.

While she had slept, someone had crept into her tower cell and transformed it into a bower fit for a princess. She supposed it shouldn't surprise her that M'lord Dragon would have an ambitious clan of bogies to do his bidding. She was surprised the pitter-patter of their hairy little feet hadn't awakened her.

She wandered the chamber, absently touching this item or that. Against the wall beneath the window leaned a table draped with a cloth of wine satin. A single chair invited her to sit and partake of the feast that had been spread upon it, a feast that made yesterday's breakfast of crossbuns and chocolate seem little more than pauper's fare. Roasted apples, poached eggs, buttery crispbread, and oatcakes shared a platter, their appearance as delectable as their mingling aromas. Gwendolyn pinched off a taste of the crispbread, but for the first time in her life, food failed to hold her interest.

The hearth had been swept clean of its mouse droppings and cobwebs and laid with a tidy nest of logs. A pewter tinderbox perched on the mantel. The wax tapers in the standing candelabrum had also been replaced.

On a smaller but higher table, Gwendolyn discovered

a ceramic basin, a pile of clean rags, and a pitcher of warm water. She leaned nearer and sniffed, half expecting the water to be scented with sandalwood and spice. But it was a sweetly floral fragrance that drifted to her nose.

She poured some water into the basin and splashed a little of it on her face, but it failed to startle her from the waking dream her life had become.

That dream grew even sweeter when she spotted the books stacked in the corner. They were old, their covers cracked and their bindings frayed, but as far as Gwendolyn was concerned that only made the words cocooned between their musty pages more precious. There was Volume II of Swift's collected works, a first edition of Pope's *The Rape of the Lock*, Daniel Defoe's *Roxana*. But none of those novels thrilled her soul as much as a copy of Colin Maclaurin's *Treatise on Fluxions*, which looked as if its spine had never once been cracked.

Gwendolyn sat down on the floor, drawing the books into her lap. She might have sat there all day, content to leaf through their faded pages, if a splash of color in the opposite corner hadn't caught her eye.

She slowly stood, the books tumbling from her lap. An ancient leather trunk squatted against the wall, its lid propped open to allow its bounty to spill free. Gwendolyn drifted toward it as if beckoned by an unseen hand, the dreamlike haze surrounding her deepening with each step.

Before she was even aware that she had moved,

she found herself kneeling like an unworthy supplicant before a sacred altar. Unable to resist the tempta-
tion, she plunged both hands into the trunk, bringing
forth two fistfuls of pink-and-white-striped poplin and
a quilted petticoat with a frilled hem. A white muslin
dress trimmed in cherry ribbon emerged next, followed
by yards and yards of pleated taffeta in a hue that perfectly matched her eyes. She was already holding the
elegant sacque gown against her sheet-clad bosom
when she suddenly awoke from her daze.

She let the gown slide from her fingers. Such pretty
things were never tailored for great girls like her. They
were made to fit willowy beauties like Glynnis and
Nessa. A wistful smile touched Gwendolyn's lips as she
imagined Kitty's squeals of delight if she were to be
presented with such a dazzling array of finery.

Gwendolyn knew she ought to slam the lid of the
trunk down, but she could not resist tucking her hands
into the plush softness of a sable muff. Such finery had
probably been commonplace for Gwendolyn's mother
in her youth. But Leah Wilder had never expressed a
word of regret when she'd given up such luxuries to
marry the brash young steward of a Highland chieftain,
taking with her only a loyal young kitchen maid named
Izzy. When Gwendolyn's papa would vow to provide
her with a fortune of her own someday, her mother
would simply throw her arms around him, kiss his
cheek, and proclaim that his love and her precious little
girls were the only treasures she would ever need.

Gwendolyn blinked away a mist of tears. How had the Dragon come by such beautiful things? she wondered, trailing a velvet choker over her palm. How many other towns had he plundered before setting his greedy sights on Ballybliss? And was he deliberately mocking her by offering her a feast of finery?

She started to close the trunk, but hesitated, her gaze caught by a quilted petticoat.

Stealing a guilty glance around as if to make sure she wasn't being watched by invisible eyes, she unknotted the sheet, stepped into the petticoat, and drew it up over her hips. It hung there as if it had been tailored for her, even requiring a stubborn tug of its silk ribbons to secure it in place. She studied but then rejected an underbodice of blue silk, fearing she would need a lady's maid to untangle its web of laces.

She took up the sacque gown once again. She had no desire to stretch the taffeta or split the seams of the exquisite garment. Sucking in a deep breath, she dropped the gown over her head. It settled around her in a shimmering cloud, inviting her to slip her arms into the elbow-length sleeves that flared into pleated bells at the cuff.

Gwendolyn slowly extended her arms, marveling at the gown's flawless fit. Even without a corset to bind her waist, it wasn't the least bit snug or inclined to split its seams. She spun around, feeling as graceful and airy as the swirl of taffeta around her ankles.

The cherry rosettes adorning the bodice of the

white muslin gown seemed to wink at her, and before she knew it, she was casting aside the sacque gown and slipping into the muslin. She tried on gown after gown until she finally sank into an exhausted heap, clutching a lace apron, a lavender silk bag on a ribbon, and six pairs of shoes fashioned from brightly colored morocco.

She swept her gaze across the chamber, torn between elation and despair. What peculiar magic was the Dragon working? She'd hardly been beneath his spell for more than a day and he'd already transformed her into a vain and frivolous creature who scorned books in favor of gauze and ribbons.

Without warning, the echo of his smoky baritone flooded her mind. *Wouldn't it be more pleasant to think of yourself as a pampered pet?*

Perhaps that was exactly what he intended to make of her. She told herself that she would do well to remember that no matter how luxurious, the tower was still her cell and she was still his prisoner. He could shower her with extravagant offerings, but none of them could compare with the one gift he refused her—her freedom.

He came to her in the night.

Gwendolyn awoke from a sound sleep with the uncanny certainty that she was not alone. He did not stir or betray himself with so much as a whisper of a breath, yet his presence was as undeniable as the ever-present murmur of the sea against the rocks.

This night was not moonless like the night of their first meeting, and she could make out the faintest glimmer of his eyes in the ghostly light filtering through the grate. He appeared to be cocked back in the chair by the table, his long legs stretched out before him.

Gwendolyn sat up, thankful that she had chosen to don the most modest nightdress in the trunk and a prim cap to cover her hair. She refused to betray how much his presence unsettled her. "Good evening, M'lord Dragon. I would have thought you'd have more pressing things to do than spy on me while I sleep. Such as swooping down from the sky and carrying off innocent children in your talons."

"I never much cared for children. They generally turn out to be more of a bother than they're worth."

"I was rather hoping you'd decide the same thing about me."

"I haven't yet determined what your worth might be, although I suspect it's far beyond the value you place upon yourself."

Gwendolyn frowned, beset by the strange fancy that the darkness only allowed him to see her more clearly, to penetrate deeper beneath her skin until she was as vulnerable to him as when she'd been garbed in nothing but the sheet and her pride.

"So why have you come?" she asked, icy composure her only defense. "Did you think perhaps to bask in my appreciation for all the rare gifts you've bestowed upon me?"

"Did they please you?"

"Do you care?"

She could almost hear the pensive frown in his voice. "Oddly enough, I find that I do."

"The clothes are beautiful," she confessed, toying with the satin ribbons at the nightgown's throat. "But I can't help but wonder how you came by such a treasure trove of ladies' finery."

"They once belonged to a woman I knew."

"A woman you loved?" Gwendolyn asked, unable even as she spoke the words to fathom what compelled her to give voice to such a bold and improper question.

"Deeply," he responded without hesitation.

Hoping to hide the curious pang his words gave her, Gwendolyn laughed. "I was surprised to discover the gowns were a perfect fit. Of course, unlike most women of your acquaintance, I have no need of bustle or panniers to support the weight of the skirts," she added, referring to the padded frames and broad hoops that made it so difficult for ladies of fashion to negotiate carriages and doorways.

His voice was devoid of amusement. "Has it ever occurred to you that most of the women of my acquaintance wear those torturous devices to make themselves look more like you? Softer, fuller . . . more inviting of a man's touch?"

Gwendolyn couldn't have answered his question if she had wanted to. She could barely breathe. She could only be thankful that she wasn't still wearing only the sheet, for it would have surely slipped from her limp grasp.

He continued, paying her distress no heed. "Truth be told, I might not even have noticed that you had a bit more flesh on your bones than is considered strictly fashionable if you weren't compelled to point it out with such damning regularity."

When Gwendolyn found her voice, it was a ragged whisper. "I discovered long ago that it spared others the trouble."

"How very convenient," he said, without mercy or pity. "I'm sure it also spared you the trouble of risking your own feelings as the rest of us mortals are forced to do."

Gwendolyn sat up straighter, hoping he couldn't see the sheen of tears in her eyes. "Have you forgotten, sir? You're no mortal. You're a monster."

She was prepared for some witty retort. She was not prepared for him to come striding toward her out of the shadows, revealing fragmented glimpses of his face.

He reached the bed, casting them both in shadow, and she felt the callused pad of his thumb stroking her cheek, caressing away the single tear that had spilled from her eyes. "Has it occurred to you, Miss Wilder, that we're both mythical creatures of a sort—I a dragon, and you a maiden? From the dawn of time, maidens have been endowed with miraculous powers. They can charm unicorns, break curses . . ." Although she would have thought it impossible, his voice grew even huskier. ". . . bring a man to his knees. But it remains to be seen whose is the greater power—yours or mine."

The last thing she expected was for him to lean down and lay his lips against hers. His kiss was dry, even chaste, but it set off a wistful yearning deep in her soul. When he drew away, she wanted to grab his shirt and pull him back.

Not wanting him to slip away into the darkness, she scrambled to her feet, using the bedpost to steady herself. "If my powers are truly so great, sir, then such a kiss should have turned you from beast to man."

He paused at the panel, his face still wrapped in a veil of moonlight and shadow. "Ah, but you're forgetting that it was *I* who kissed *you*. To free me from my dark enchantment, *you* would have to kiss *me*."

Leaving her with that bold challenge, he vanished into the night that had spawned him.


The Dragon stood at the highest point of Castle Weyrcraig, gazing out to sea with the eyes of a man who received little comfort from its soothing ebb and flow. Past the point where the breakers licked the shore, the inky waters were as smooth as a woman's skin, but the Dragon was not fooled by their deceptive calmness. Sharp crags and submerged rocks that could tear a man's heart from his flesh lurked just beneath those gentle swells.

His hands closed over the stone embrasure, all that

separated him from the great abyss of nothingness beyond. He watched as the moon flirted with the clouds, creating luminous pockets of light in the night sky, and wondered just how long it would be before he would shy away from even that much illumination.

Circumstance had driven him to become a nocturnal creature, but he'd been a bloody fool to think he could ease his restlessness by watching his captive sleep.

She had breathed like a child, deep and even, her stern jaw softened by the tantalizing hint of a dimpled smile. Tendrils of gold had caressed the rosy softness of her cheek, escaping from that ridiculous cap she must have unearthed from the trunk. She'd thrown one leg outside the sheet, causing her nightgown to ride up to the curve of her thigh.

When she had first awakened, he was afraid he wouldn't be able to speak, because his mouth had gone dry with desire.

He had known he should flee before the moonlight betrayed him, yet he had lingered—mocking her, taunting her, pushing her until those beautiful, proud eyes of hers had glazed over with tears. Risking both the moonlight and his pride, he had gone to her.

But that bit of lunacy had been nothing but a mild derangement compared with the madness that had possessed him to touch her lips with his own. To steal a taste—no more than a sip really—of a nectar he'd denied himself for far too long. It had been all he could do not to bear her back against the mattress and sink his tongue into the melting sweetness of her mouth.

His burning eyes searched the sky, but found no more solace than the sea had offered. He was already beginning to fear that he had lied to her. Because her kiss, willingly offered, wouldn't change him from beast to man, but might instead unleash his lust and brand him a beast forever.

# Chapter Eight

WHEN GWENDOLYN AWOKE the next morning, there was a bogie stretched across her feet.

She had slept fitfully during the long and restless night, and it took her a bleary moment to realize her legs weren't paralyzed by exhaustion, but by dead weight. She opened her eyes and saw ragged whiskers, tufts of woolly gray hair, and yellow eyes narrowed to malevolent slits. Shrieking, she went bounding out of the bed.

Before she could flatten herself against the door panel, the thing had disappeared. But the swinging sheet draped over the foot of the bed left little doubt as to its hiding place.

Gwendolyn pressed a hand to her chest and struggled to catch her breath, wondering if she was losing her mind. Men and monsters had plagued her sleep throughout the interminable night. In one hazy dream after another, she had stretched out her arms to invite the Dragon into them, never quite knowing or caring if he meant to kiss her or eat her. She might have believed their midnight encounter only a dream if she hadn't sworn she could still taste him every time she flicked her tongue across her lips.

"There's no such thing as a dragon," she muttered beneath her breath. "And there's no such thing as a bogie, either."

Despite that bold declaration, she pulled a folded parasol from the trunk before approaching the bed.

She slipped to her knees, the parasol vibrating wildly in her trembling hand. She had regained just enough of her sanity to wonder if the intruder might not be some monstrous rat.

Fearing the thing would charge her if she lifted a corner of the sheet, she swept the parasol beneath the bed, gingerly poking as she went. An inhuman growl drifted to her ears, raising the gooseflesh on her arms.

Gwendolyn slowly rose and backed away from the bed. Whatever the thing was (and she was no longer sure she wanted to know), she was trapped in the tower with it. Her shriek had failed to rouse any hint of a rescue. She briefly considered jumping on the bed and screaming at the top of her lungs, but she was afraid her voice might whip the creature into some sort of bloodthirsty frenzy.

She looked frantically around the tower. Her previous searches for an escape route had yielded nothing but a grated window she had no hope of reaching. But that was before M'lord Dragon had so kindly provided her with a table. And a chair to put atop it.

Gwendolyn did exactly that. Moments later, both she and the chair were perched precariously on the table. If she could loosen the grate from her position on the table she might be able to climb up on the chair and squeeze through the circular window.

At first she feared the rusty iron would prove immovable. But several determined pokes with the parasol turned the ancient mortar into dust. Twitching back a sneeze, she gave it one last violent stab.

She grabbed for the teetering grate, but it slipped from her fingers, landing somewhere outside the window with a clanking loud enough to wake the dead. Or the undead, she thought, shooting the bed a nervous glance.

She stood on tiptoe and peered down through the window, relieved to discover that her only way out wasn't a direct plunge into the churning sea. In fact, the view provided her with more cause for hope than she had expected—not three feet beneath the window was a narrow walkway ringed by a stone parapet.

Her heart began to race. If she could reach the walkway, it might be possible to scramble down one of the shattered stairwells to the ground. And if she could reach the ground, she could make a run for the village, escaping M'lord Dragon's clutches forever.

She hesitated, tempted to steal one last yearning look at the gifts he had given her. She was determined to take nothing of him with her but the nightdress she wore and the memory of a kiss so sweet she might spend the rest of her life wondering if she had only dreamed it.

She studied the window. She'd wiggled her way out of tighter spots in her day. As a child, she'd once hidden in the hollow trunk of an elder until night fell while Ross and his cronies combed the woods, intent upon making her the donkey in their boisterous game of Pin-the-Tail.

Leaving the parasol on the table, she clambered up on the chair. She stretched both arms through the window and grasped the roughened stone of the outer wall, hauling herself up until her toes just barely grazed the highest rung of the ladder-back chair. The rising sun shimmered against the distant swells, offering her a breathtaking view. The sea was calm this morning, the breakers whispering tender words to one another instead of roaring. The briny tang of the sea poured over her, washing away the seductive aroma of sandalwood and spice.

Her confidence buoyed, Gwendolyn began to wiggle in earnest. She had just started to shimmy her hips through the hole when she heard it.

*Thump. Thump. Thump.*

She froze. In her eagerness to be free of M'lord Dragon, she'd nearly forgotten about the beast beneath the bed. But it seemed he hadn't forgotten about her.

She could almost see herself from his point of view—a juicy morsel with its feet flailing helplessly in midair as it dangled half in and half out of the window. She sucked in a deep breath and shoved with her arms in a frantic effort to dislodge her hips. They refused to budge. Not only could she not move forward—she couldn't move backward, either.

The ominous *thump-thump* of the thing's padded feet crossing the floor ceased. Gwendolyn stopped wiggling and held her breath, hearing a foreboding rattle as it leapt from floor to table, from table to chair. She squeezed her eyes shut and clenched her teeth, waiting for the most enormous rat in all of Scotland to sink its razor-sharp little teeth into her ankle.

Something brushed her dangling toes—a plush warmth, as soft as lamb's down. Her eyes flew open as another sound reached her ears, a sound as soothing and unmistakable as the murmur of the sea—a deep-throated purring.

She was so intent upon its rumbling music that she wasn't aware the tower door had been thrown open until a droll voice said, "It's just as I've always said, Tupper. This chamber surely has the most exquisite view in all the castle."

# Chapter Nine

THE LAST THING THE DRAGON expected to see when he flung open the tower door was Miss Wilder's generous, but shapely, derriere flawlessly framed by the ring of the window.

He had finally sunk into a dreamless sleep near dawn, only to be awakened by a woman's muffled shriek. He had rolled over and dragged the bolster over his head, assuming it was only an echo from one of the many nightmares that had plagued him since he'd come to this place. But then a raucous clanging had driven him bolt upright on his makeshift pallet.

Fearing his captive had met some dire fate of her own making, he'd quickly pulled on his shirt and breeches and raced up the stairs, meeting an equally frazzled Tupper on the second landing. He'd been so intent upon reaching her that he hadn't given a thought to shielding his face.

It appeared Miss Wilder had indeed met a fate of her own making, but it was not nearly as dire as he'd feared. At least not for him and Tupper.

Her legs emerged from the ruffled hem of her nightdress, dangling above the makeshift ladder she'd fashioned from table and chair and providing them both with a rather shocking glimpse of creamy female calves. The Dragon looked back to find Tupper's guileless brown eyes as round as cinnamon biscuits.

Resisting the urge to clap his hands over them, he took his friend's elbow and steered him from the chamber. "Why don't you go around to the walkway and see what you can do from that end."

Tupper struggled to peer over his shoulder. "This end looks to be much more intriguing. Wouldn't it be better if I—"

"—did exactly as I requested?" the Dragon finished for him, giving him a none too polite shove toward the stairwell.

Although he jutted out his bottom lip like a sulky child, Tupper obeyed. The Dragon turned back to the chamber. Even more remarkable than Miss Wilder's dilemma was the sight of Toby balancing himself on the top rung of the chair just so he could butt his big, woolly head against the soles of her feet. The Dragon cocked his head, listening in disbelief. The cantankerous beast was actually purring!

The cat gave a disdainful twitch of its whiskers, then yielded before him as he approached the table.

Gwendolyn simply hung there, her stillness a sign that she knew he was there.

"I do believe you forgot your parasol, Miss Wilder," he called out, running one finger down the frilly umbrella. "I'm afraid you'll find it far more difficult to float to the ground without it."

"I was hoping to dash myself to death against the rocks," she replied, her voice muffled but audible. "Then I wouldn't be forced to endure any more of your stinging witticisms."

The Dragon's lips curved in a reluctant smile. "Shall I attempt to pull you back in?"

"No, thank you. I was headed the other way."

"So I gathered."

He removed the chair and deftly vaulted up on the table. Her pale feet scissored at the air, vainly seeking purchase. He wrapped his hands around her ankles to still them.

"There now, Miss Wilder. Don't be afraid. It's all right. I've got you now."

Gwendolyn feared that, for that very reason, nothing would ever be all right again. The Dragon's voice was a more comforting rumble than the cat's purring, but it was a lie. The warm palms curled around her bare ankles promised security, but delivered only danger. Her mortification swelled as she remembered with a flush of horror that she'd neglected to don any drawers before slipping into the nightdress. If those strong, lean fingers of his should stray . . .

"Tupper is coming around the other way," he

informed her. "He'll have to go all the way down to the ground and climb back up over some broken stones, so it may take him several minutes to reach you. Perhaps if I got a good grip on your legs . . . ?" His hands inched toward her calves.

"No!" Gwendolyn shouted, squirming violently. "I'd prefer to wait until Mr. Tuppingham arrives, if you please."

"While you're waiting, would you care to explain how you came to find yourself in your current . . . um . . . predicament?"

She sighed. "When I woke up, there was some sort of animal sitting on my feet."

"That could have only been Toby here. The rascal must have slipped into the room last night while your door was ajar."

Gwendolyn did not want to think about the Dragon's nocturnal visit and that tantalizing mingling of their breaths that shouldn't have been a kiss, but was.

"Do you have a fear of cats?" he asked her.

"On the contrary, I'm actually quite fond of them." She was not about to confess that she'd mistaken the cat for a goblin. "I thought he was . . . a rat."

The Dragon laughed. "If I woke up to find a rat that weighed nearly two stone sitting on my feet, I'd leap out the nearest window, too." Gwendolyn's breathing took on a ragged edge as he began to absently trace a pattern against her skin with the very tip of his finger. "I think I should try to pull you back through myself. Tupper doesn't seem to be making any progress."

"No, I think I hear him coming now," she called out cheerfully, although what she actually heard was the distant sound of stones crashing and a smattering of curses.

Naturally he ignored her wishes and wrapped his arms firmly around her thighs. It took only one sharp tug from those muscular arms to bring her sliding into his embrace.

Gwendolyn found herself enfolded from behind in a vise of velvet and steel. His arms were wrapped around her waist, his hips pressed to the softness of her backside. The trailing tails of his hem warned her that he'd neglected to fasten his shirt. If she turned, her cheek would be pressed against his chest, skin to skin.

But he would never allow that. It took her a dazed moment to realize that he was as much a prisoner as she was.

"Now I seem to be the one in the predicament," he said dryly.

"What's wrong, M'lord Dragon?" she asked. "Haven't you any blindfolds in your pocket?"

"I'm afraid I took them out to make room for my manacles and cat-o'-nine-tails."

"Perhaps you can persuade Mr. Tuppingham to loan you his cravat again."

"I just might do that if the bumbling oaf ever arrives. . . ."

They both heard him then, still distant enough to make most of his oaths mercifully inaudible.

Taking advantage of their situation, the cat jumped

up on the table and began to wend his way through the maze of their ankles.

"I do believe Toby has taken a fancy to you," the Dragon remarked. "I've never heard the grumpy old monster purr before."

As the cat butted his head forcefully against Gwendolyn's leg she said, "Given his girth, I'm surprised I didn't mistake him for a mastiff."

The Dragon unfolded one of his arms from her waist, only to trail the knuckles of his free hand along the curve of her collarbone. She felt a shiver of dark anticipation.

"I'm gratified to learn that it was Toby who frightened you," he murmured in her ear. "I feared it was me you sought to escape."

"Could you blame me if I had?"

"No," he said lightly, "but I would have anyway."

Gwendolyn had forgotten she was wearing the prim nightcap until he gave it a gentle tug. Her hair came spilling around her shoulders in a silken cascade. As he buried his face in it, Gwendolyn closed her eyes against a rush of longing.

"If you'll let me down, sir, I'll promise not to peek at your face," she whispered. "If it's some sort of battle scar or tragic birthmark you seek to hide from my eyes, I shall respect your desire for privacy. And I can assure you that I'm a woman of my word."

"You almost make me wish I were a man of mine," he muttered, tenderly raking away a handful of hair to expose her nape.

Gwendolyn might have been able to bear it if he'd simply touched her with his fingers. But it was his lips he laid against that vulnerable swath of skin. They lingered there, moist and warm, caressing her with melting sweetness. Gwendolyn would never have dreamed that being devoured by a dragon could be so unbearably delicious. It tempted her to offer up every morsel of her flesh for his pleasure.

As his mouth drifted away from her nape to graze the column of her throat, her eyes fluttered shut and her head fell back in unspoken surrender.

Cupping her jaw in his hand with an irresistible combination of tenderness and strength, the Dragon tilted her face just enough to allow him to touch his mouth to hers.

Gwendolyn might yet be a virgin, but she no longer possessed a maiden's mouth. The Dragon claimed it for his own, breaching the softness of her lips with a swirling tongue of flame. It licked to life a thousand kindred flickers along every inch of her flesh. Her breasts tingled and swelled. He tightened his arm around her waist, molding his hips to her backside.

Even if he had dared to turn her in his arms, she didn't think she could have opened her eyes. Her lids seemed weighted by an enchantment more powerful than any spell or curse. It wasn't so much the magic of his kiss that bewitched her, but the mundane—the rough, tender texture of him; the sweet, salty flavor of him. When her tongue flicked out to taste him in turn, he groaned deep in his throat and drew her even closer.

"I say, old fellow, am I too late to rescue the damsel?" Tupper's jovial voice came from the window, breaking over them like a dash of cold water.

"No," the Dragon said grimly, as he reached up and jerked off the cravat hanging loose around Tupper's neck. "You're just in time."

After Tupper had finished repairing the window grate in Gwendolyn's chamber, he emerged from the castle's shadows to find the Dragon pacing the courtyard where they had first found her. Despite the morning sunlight streaming over the crumbling walls, his friend's countenance was as black as midnight. Smoke streamed from his finely hewn nostrils as he took a long drag on the cheroot tucked in the corner of his mouth.

Tupper gave the tip of his mustache a nervous tug. "I didn't mean to interrupt your little tryst. I pray you'll forgive my lack of discretion."

The Dragon snatched the cheroot out of his mouth. "*Your* lack of discretion? It's not *your* lack of discretion that troubles me—it's mine. What must she think of me? Every time I find myself alone with her, I fall upon her like the beast she thinks I am. Have I been so long without a woman in my bed that I have to prey upon the first innocent who has the misfortune to cross my path?" He flung the cheroot away and resumed his pacing. "Is it any wonder I'm not fit company for civilized folk?"

Tupper fell into step beside him. "That's not precisely

true, you know. My great-aunt Taffy is quite fond of you. She says you put her in mind of this magnificent, high-strung stallion her father owned when she was a girl." Tupper shook his head, sighing sadly. "Of course, they eventually had to shoot the poor fellow in the head after he took three fingers off one of the grooms."

The Dragon paused in his pacing to give him a withering look. "Thank you for sharing that. I feel so much better now."

He covered the remainder of the courtyard in three long strides, forcing Tupper to scamper to keep up with him. "You really shouldn't berate yourself so," Tupper tried to console him. "It wasn't as if you had tossed her nightdress over her head and were having your way with her on the table. You simply stole an innocent kiss. What harm can there be in that?"

The Dragon couldn't very well explain to his friend that the kiss had been anything but innocent and that he feared the harm had been done to him, not her. That shy flick of Gwendolyn's tongue against his own had stirred his blood more deeply than any bold embrace of a London bawd ever had. He had thought to give her a taste of dragon's breath, but it had been he who'd ended up burning for her.

He came to a halt in front of the statue that still reigned over the ruins of the courtyard. Aphrodite, the Greek goddess of love, seemed woefully out of place in this courtyard where no love had dwelled for nearly fifteen years. If her head hadn't been blown off by one of Cumberland's cannonballs, he mused, he might very well have heard a mocking ripple of her laughter on the wind.

"I must be away from this place," he said softly, running a hand along the bared curve of the goddess's shoulder. "Before I lose my own head."

"We did give the villagers a fortnight to come up with the gold," Tupper reminded him.

"I know we did," the Dragon said, turning his back on Aphrodite's ravaged beauty. "But that doesn't mean we can't hasten them along, does it? Light some smoke pots in their fields. Flash some torches in the castle windows. Play the bloody bagpipes until their ears bleed. I want them at each other's throats until they're begging to bring me the bastard who's been hoarding that gold all these years."

Tupper snapped off a smart salute. "You can trust me to put the fear of God into them."

The Dragon swung around, his face set in such ruthless lines that even Tupper took a hasty step backward. "It's not God they have to fear. It's me."

# Chapter Ten

TUPPER CREPT THROUGH the Highland night, his stealthy footsteps guided by the dappled light of the rising moon. As he picked his way over a shelf of loose rocks, taking care not to dislodge a single one, his pulse quickened with exhilaration.

He'd never cared much for danger, but he thrived on drama, something that had been in short supply in his life until he'd met the Dragon in that gaming hell two years ago. It had been as much boredom with his aimless existence as fear of scandal that had prompted him to put the mouth of that dueling pistol against his temple. Although neither of them had brought up that night since then, he suspected that the Dragon knew he would have never had the courage to pull the trigger.

Had it not been for his friend's intervention, he'd either be rotting away in debtors' prison or drinking himself to death in his elegantly appointed London town house with nothing to look forward to but the occasional romantic entanglement with a bad actress and the legacy of gout and dyspepsia bequeathed to him by his father. The viscount's one attempt to purchase him a commission in the Royal Navy had ended in disaster when Tupper had gotten seasick on his very first voyage and cast up his accounts all over the braided coat of an admiral who just happened to be one of his father's oldest friends. Although his seasickness had eventually ebbed, his father's contempt never had.

Tupper almost wished his father could see him now—dressed all in black, creeping through a forest thicket without so much as stirring a leaf or snapping a branch. For the first time in his life, he was a man with a mission. As the foliage began to thin, forcing him to dart from tree to tree, he marveled that his footsteps were no longer plodding and clumsy, but fleet and full of purpose.

As he leapt a narrow ravine, his black cloak rippled behind him, making him feel as if he could take flight. He hoped the Dragon didn't mind that he'd borrowed the cloak. He felt it added a badly needed note of élan to his disguise.

Leaving the copse of trees behind, he started across a meadow littered with stones, counting on the rocky ledge at its outskirts to hide him from the village tucked into the glen below. He scanned the thick grasses, seeking a good place to light the smoke pot tucked beneath his arm. Its brilliant flare and billowing smoke would rouse the villagers from their beds, making them believe the Dragon had made another strike against them.

Therein lay the beauty of their scheme. The denizens of Ballybliss were so superstitious and so plagued by guilt that he had only to plant the seeds of fear in their fertile imaginations to convince them that some terrible supernatural force was at work in their lives. Then, if the milk curdled or the baby howled with colic or the cat coughed up a furball, it was surely the Dragon's doing.

Tupper positioned the smoke pot on a fat hummock of grass and drew a tinderbox from his pocket, chuckling beneath his breath. If the villagers were so foolish as to mistake sulfur for brimstone and smoke for dragon's breath, then they deserved their sleepless nights. He struck a flint against the tinder, then bent to touch its flame to the smoke pot's fuse.

"Is that you, Niall? When I woke up, you were gone. Why did you leave me all alone in the forest?"

As the lilting cadences of the sweetly female voice caressed his ears, Tupper straightened, the flame sputtering to its death. He slowly turned to face the woman who had caught him at his mischief.

"You're not Niall!" she exclaimed accusingly, taking a step backward.

"No, I'm not. If I were, I would have certainly never left you all alone."

She faced him in the moonlight, a fey wood sprite with skin as fair as cream and a tumble of dark curls. Her skirt was stained with grass, her hair tousled, her bodice misbuttoned, but her dishabille only made her more appealing. She looked like a wayward child playing at being a woman.

A woman whose rosebud of a mouth was still swollen from another man's kiss, he reminded himself.

She put her hands on her hips, and eyed him boldly. "I've never seen you in Ballybliss before, sir. And I know all of the men who live there."

Tupper had to clear his throat before replying. "I was afraid you were going to say that."

She looked down with embarrassment at her garments. "I hope you don't think I always go around looking like this. I just . . . took a bit of a tumble."

Tupper dragged his gaze away from the soft swell of her breasts, his tongue growing more tied by the minute. "I've been known to take a bit of a tumble myself on occasion. Once I drank too much port and tumbled right off my horse into the lap of a lady who was riding through the park in her phaeton."

"And did this lady think you were *falling* in love with her?"

It took Tupper almost a full minute of basking in the warmth of her sparkling brown eyes to realize that this beauty, this Highland rose, was flirting with him. *Him*. Theodore Tuppingham, the plodding son of a minor viscount.

"If she did," he replied, "then she showed it by screaming for a constable and beating me about the head with her parasol."

A merry half-smile curved the girl's lips as she took

in his black silk shirt with its full sleeves and fall of lace at the throat and cuffs, his clinging knee breeches, the shiny jack boots that pinched his toes abominably but gave him a dashing air that was well worth any suffering he had to endure, and the elegant folds of his cloak.

As her gaze traveled back to his face, her smile began to fade. "Why, I know who you are." Her eyes widened to luminescent pools as she began to back away from him. "You're the Dragon!"

Tupper was about to deny it, but the glow of awe in the girl's eyes stopped him. In his entire life, he had never had a woman look at him like that.

Before he even knew what he was going to do, he had sucked in his stomach, puffed out his chest, and said, "Aye, lass. I *am* the Dragon."

He wouldn't have been surprised had she fled the meadow screaming in terror or recoiled with disgust to discover that the Dragon was a balding, slightly paunchy Englishman. But what she did instead was hurl herself into his arms.

"You!" she shrieked, pummeling his chest with her small fists. "You're the wretched beast who ate my sister!"

As one of those fists connected with his newly concave stomach, his chest deflated with a mighty *whoosh*. Desperate to silence her before she roused the entire village, he dragged her against his chest and clapped a hand over her mouth.

"I didn't eat your sister," he hissed in her ear. "She's alive and well, and I can prove it. She even told me about you. You must be the youngest—Catriona. But she calls you something else. Um—Katie? Cat?" As he frantically searched his memory, she dug her sharp little teeth into his palm hard enough to draw blood, and he jerked his hand away.

"Kitty," she spat, squirming more like an outraged tiger than her cuddly feline namesake.

"Kitty! Of course! How could I have forgotten? You're Kitty and your sisters are Glenda and"—he snapped his fingers—"Nellie! You live in the manor in the village with your father, who's several cards short of a full hand of whist!"

Kitty ceased to struggle, but continued to glare up at him. "It's Glynnis and Nessa. And Papa has never cared for whist, only faro. He cheats atrociously, but Gwennie says we must allow him to win because it makes him laugh." She clung to his ruffled shirtfront, her eyes clouding as she began to absorb the full import of his words. "Gwennie . . . ? Could it be? Is she really alive?"

"She's alive and well," Tupper said gently, covering Kitty's hands with his own. "She's staying at the castle as my guest and she has beautiful clothes, ample food, and all the books she cares to read."

Kitty sagged against him, the silky sweep of her lashes fluttering as if she might weep. Tupper feared he might burst into sobs himself if he was forced to watch a tear tumble from those beautiful eyes of hers.

But she stilled the quivering of her delicate chin and slanted him an oddly sultry look from beneath the fringe of her lashes. "Who would have thought that

Gwennie would end up being your mistress instead of your meal."

"I can assure you that she hasn't been either," Tupper hastily protested, stepping away from her. "I haven't compromised your sister. Her virtue is as intact as it was the night she was left at the castle." Remembering the fiery kiss he'd witnessed between Gwendolyn and the Dragon only that morning, Tupper wasn't sure how much longer he would be able to make that claim.

Kitty sighed and shook her head. "That's a pity. If ever a lass was in need of a thorough compromising, it's our Gwennie."

Shocked by her frankness, Tupper turned away to hide his blush, cursing his fair complexion.

"So you're the Dragon." She looked him up and down with brazen regard, making him regret that he hadn't had time to suck in his stomach again. "Is it true that you can change from man to dragon at will?"

"Only on Tuesdays and the second Sunday of each month."

As she drew nearer, he began to back away from her, unnerved by the predatory glint in her eye. "And have you developed a taste for human flesh, as Maisie's mother says?"

Tupper jerked his guilty gaze from her mouth to her eyes, having been wondering at that precise moment what her lips might taste like beneath his. "I honestly don't think I'd fancy it. Underdone roast beef gives me indigestion." His back came up against a tree, making further retreat impossible.

She leaned toward him, her little pink tongue darting out to moisten her lips. "My friend Maisie swears you're possessed with a fierce hunger to mate with one of the village lasses."

He was, but he hadn't known it until that very moment. His gaze flicked back to her lips, a denial dying in his throat. He'd already done the Dragon's ferocious reputation enough harm for one night. Perhaps a sacrifice of his own scruples was in order.

"Far be it from me to cast aspersions upon your friend or her mother," he murmured, closing his eyes and leaning down with every intent of stealing a kiss.

When his lips met only air, he opened his eyes to find Kitty scampering away from him.

"Where are you going?" he cried out.

She spun around, looking more like a fairy than a wood sprite beneath the gossamer caress of mist and moonbeams. "I have to tell Glynnis and Nessa that Gwennie is alive and that I've met the Dragon! Do you know how jealous they're going to be? Glynnis is always playing 'lady of the manor' because she's had two husbands and I've had none and Nessa is always mocking me because she has all the juiciest tales. Now I've one of my own to tell!"

Envisioning the wrath of the real Dragon when he discovered Tupper's foolishness, Tupper cast about in desperation for some way to stop her. "Wouldn't it be better to have a secret than a tale? A secret that can remain just between the two of us?"

She cocked her head to the side, plainly intrigued by his proposal.

"Just think of it, Kitty," he said, moving toward her. "You're the only one in Ballybliss who knows my true identity. Can't I coax you into keeping that secret for just a little while longer? Surely the responsibility of guarding such a treasure would lift you in your own esteem, if not your sisters'."

She poked at the ground with her toe, a petulant cast to her lips. "Gwennie always said I couldn't keep a secret. She says I blather too much."

Tupper smiled. "A friend once said the same thing about me. But perhaps you've just never had one worthy of keeping. Come now, be a good lass and promise not to tell."

She slanted him a provocative look. "I might be able to do it. But only if you'll make me a promise of your own."

Tupper swallowed, hoping she wasn't about to ask him to show her his wings, breathe fire, or deliver Gwendolyn to her doorstep. "Very well."

"Meet me," she boldly demanded. "In this very meadow. Tomorrow night after the moon rises."

Tupper slowly nodded, convinced he was getting the sweeter end of this bargain. "Until then, dear lady, you must remember that you hold my fate in your gentle hands." He brought one of those hands to his lips, a gesture he'd watched the real Dragon use to great effect on any number of women.

When she responded with a gratifying shiver, he

drew off his cloak and wrapped it around her shoulders. She tipped her head back, her eyes drifting shut and her lips parting in invitation. Shaking his head ruefully, Tupper leaned down and brushed her brow with a chaste kiss.

When Kitty opened her eyes, she was alone in the meadow. She gazed up at the moon, utterly bewildered by the Dragon's desertion. Most of the lads of her acquaintance, including Niall, would have had their hands up her skirt a dozen times over by now, yet this Dragon fellow hadn't even tried to stick his tongue in her mouth.

But he had kissed her hand, called her a lady, and wrapped her in his cloak.

Kitty hugged the warm folds of the garment around her, wondering if she would ever see him again.

# Chapter Eleven

For the next few days after Gwendolyn's miserably botched escape attempt, the Dragon was nowhere to be found. Yet his presence was as inescapable as the muffled roar of the sea.

Although she would awaken from a dream-tossed sleep and search the shadows only to find herself alone, each day Tupper would deliver some new treasure from the Dragon's magical and seemingly inexhaustible trove—a gilt hairbrush and comb inlaid with mother-of-pearl, a first edition of René de Réaumur's *History of the Insects* bound in calfskin, a round wooden tub filled with scented bathwater.

The village, her sisters, even her beloved papa were all beginning to pale in the Dragon's shadow, like ghosts from another lifetime. It was as if she had existed not for days, but for centuries as his pampered thrall.

Her only company consisted of Tupper and Toby, and neither of them was very forthcoming about her mysterious captor. Tupper entertained her with stories about his spirited great-aunt Taffy and entertained himself by coaxing her to reveal some of Nessa's tamer amorous adventures and Glynnis's schemes to catch a new husband. He grew especially attentive whenever Kitty's name was mentioned, although he always seemed to stammer some excuse to leave whenever Gwendolyn brought up Niall, the freckled rogue who had stolen her sister's innocence. Toby simply rolled himself into a massive ball of fur at the foot of her bed and napped the long hours away.

Gwendolyn envied him his indolence. She found herself restlessly pacing the chamber for hours on end. Although Tupper continued to bring her delicious meals prepared from the finest offerings the village could provide, more often than not she found herself without an appetite, pushing the food from one side of her plate to the other.

One morning Tupper shoved his way through the panel door, staggering beneath the weight of a tall, sheet-wrapped burden. Gwendolyn jumped out of the bed, unable to disguise her childlike anticipation, an anticipation she hadn't felt since the Christmas morning before her mother had died. All that was visible of this new treasure was a pair of gilded feet that looked like the talons of a dragon curved around twin balls of gold. Tupper rested it next to the table with a grunt of relief, then fished a folded piece of stationery from his waistcoat pocket and handed it to Gwendolyn.

While Tupper mopped the sweat from his brow, she

slid her fingernail beneath the drop of bloodred wax sealing the stationery. A single sentence was scrawled across the creamy vellum: *I wish only that you might see yourself as I do.*

"Shall I?" Tupper beamed as he prepared to whisk away the sheet.

"No!" Gwendolyn cried, suddenly guessing what lay beneath it.

Although Tupper appeared baffled by her refusal to unveil the Dragon's gift, he was tactful enough to make no further mention of it. Late that evening, long after he had delivered her supper and gone, Gwendolyn tossed down her book, disgusted with herself for rereading the same paragraph for the eighth time. It was impossible to concentrate when her thoughts kept wandering back to the Dragon's last visit and her gaze kept being drawn to his latest gift.

She couldn't sleep. She couldn't eat. She couldn't read. If it hadn't been so absurd, she'd have thought she was suffering from lovesickness. Heaven knows she'd seen the signs of it often enough in Nessa: the fitful mooning, the listless appetite, the desolate sighs.

But how could she be falling in love with a man whose face she'd never seen? A man who was nothing to her but a smoky voice, a seductive touch, a ravishing kiss?

She brushed a finger against her lips, plagued by an old fear. Perhaps she was as vulnerable to the temptations of the flesh as Nessa was. She'd always fancied herself immune to such enticements, yet it had taken no more than one kiss from the Dragon's lips to melt her will and make her yearn for his touch.

She shifted her gaze from the Dragon's gift to the plate she'd left abandoned on the table, feeling the familiar urge to down what was left of her supper in a single swallow.

Instead, Gwendolyn slowly rose from the bed and approached the Dragon's shrouded offering. Before she could lose her courage, she reached up and snatched away the sheet.

A full-length mirror of pure hammered silver stood before her, cradled in a frame of ornately carved mahogany. Gwendolyn might have paused to admire its beauty had she not been captivated by the woman reflected in its polished sheen. Candlelight glinted off the golden tumble of her hair. A dressing gown of pure Oriental silk draped her lavish curves. Her cheeks were flushed, her eyes luminous, her lips moist and parted. She didn't look like the plump, square-jawed sister of three legendary beauties. She didn't look like the captive of a ruthless madman. She looked like a woman waiting for her lover.

Her hands shaking, Gwendolyn tossed the sheet back over the mirror, convinced that it must be as enchanted as the man who had given it to her. Not only was she aching for the touch of a stranger, but she was in danger of becoming a stranger to herself as well.

✦ ✦ ✦

Later that night, Gwendolyn sat upright in the bed, unable to say what had awakened her. There was no need for her to search the shadows for the Dragon on this night. The light of a full moon streamed through the grate, bathing the deserted chamber in spectral brightness. She sniffed the air, but failed to detect so much as a lingering whiff of cheroot smoke.

She cocked her head to listen, but all she could hear was the muffled roar of the sea. She rose and padded toward the window, drawn by its siren chant.

The Dragon might have ordered the grate replaced, robbing her of any hope of freedom, but by climbing up on the table and standing on tiptoe, she could still gaze out over the spectacular vista of moonlight and water and drink the salty air into her parched lungs.

Gwendolyn's breath caught in her throat. A sailing ship was cutting through the whitecapped waves, heading straight for the castle. With its billowing sails glowing alabaster in the moonlight, it looked no more substantial than a ghost ship laden with the spirits of the dead.

She blinked in wonder, half expecting the vessel to vanish before her eyes.

"Drop anchor, lads!"

The very mortal cry was followed by a mighty splash and the sight of a longboat being lowered into the water.

"Hey!" Gwendolyn shouted, curling her fingers through the grate. "Help! I'm up here! Somebody please help me! I'm being held prisoner!"

As she continued to shout, bouncing up and down

on her toes in her desperation to be heard, the shadowy figures manning the longboat began rowing toward the caves carved into the cliffs below the castle, leaving a shimmering trail of silver in their wake. Gwendolyn craned her neck to watch the boat until it drew out of sight, then collapsed into a kneeling position on the table.

She could shout herself silly, but it wouldn't bring deliverance. Because they were *his* men. And that was *his* ship.

The ship explained how he had claimed Castle Weyrcraig for his own without a soul in Ballybliss being any the wiser. It explained how he had managed to smuggle all of his decadent luxuries into the castle—the ornate bed, the feather-stuffed tick, the wax candles . . . perhaps even the mirror that reflected only what he wanted her to see. And it explained how he would make his escape once he'd milked the village of the last of its gold and its pride.

Gwendolyn had once dreamed of just such a ship. A ship that would carry her far away from Ballybliss to a world where musty old libraries held vast troves of leather-bound treasures. A world where tapestry-draped drawing rooms rang with witty conversation and daring ideas. A world where a man might look at a woman in appreciation for more than just her heart-shaped face or the dainty size of her waist.

And suddenly she knew whose world it was. It was *his* world. The Dragon's world.

Gwendolyn jumped down from the table and began to pace the chamber, blind to everything but her growing fury. He might not even bother to free her before he went. The villagers already believed her dead. What difference would it make to them if she was eaten by a dragon or moldered away in this lavishly appointed prison? He might just leave her here to rot in the gown of one of his discarded mistresses, while he returned to that elegant world of balls and drawing rooms—a world she would never know.

Her hands shaking with reaction, Gwendolyn found the tinderbox and lit each of the candles in turn. She was angry with her faceless captor, but she was even more furious with herself for being fool enough to fall beneath his spell.

She looked around the tower. Thanks to her host's lavish generosity, there was no lack of objects with which she might bash him over the head the next time he swaggered through that panel door. But he seemed to be avoiding her company as studiously as he'd once sought it.

Her gaze fell on her half-eaten supper. So M'lord Dragon thought he could woo her favor with generous gifts and pretty words scribbled on expensive stationery, did he? Well, perhaps it was time she taught him that Gwendolyn Wilder was made of sterner stuff than that.

Tupper marched into the dungeon antechamber and lowered the tray to the table. The Dragon continued to make notations in the leather-bound ledger that lay open before him. His handwriting might be an impassioned scrawl, but his columns of figures were as neat and precise as those of any maiden aunt.

"I told you I wasn't hungry, Tup," he said, flipping a page without looking up. "But this drafty old mausoleum has got me chilled to the bone. My cloak seems to have gone missing. Have you seen it?"

"Can't imagine where it's gotten off to," Tupper replied, clearing his throat nervously before shoving the tray on top of the ledger. "But apparently, you're not the only one who isn't hungry."

The Dragon surveyed the tray's untouched contents for a long moment before shifting his gaze to Tupper. "Is she ill?"

Tupper shook his head. "She doesn't appear to be. But this is the sixth meal she's refused."

"Two days," the Dragon muttered, shoving himself away from the table. "Two days with no food. What manner of game is she playing?"

"A dangerous one, if you ask me," Tupper offered. "I couldn't help but notice how wan her color was this evening. And she stumbled once and would have fallen had I not caught her elbow."

The Dragon raked his hair from his brow with tense fingers. Lack of sleep was doing little to improve his mercurial temper. His first instinct was to grab the tray, go straight up to the tower, and force her to eat, even if he had to shove the food down her throat one bite at a time.

Deciding that was his second instinct as well, he rose and reached for the tray.

Tupper stayed him with a hand on his arm. "The sun is just setting," he warned. "It's not full dark yet."

Swearing, the Dragon sank back into his chair. He had chosen his role and now, like any nocturnal predator, he would have to wait until dark fell to confront his quarry.

"Where are you going?" he snapped, scowling at Tupper's retreating back.

"Off to terrorize the villagers, you know. I thought I'd skip the pipe playing tonight and make an early start of it."

"An early start and a late finish, I presume. You've been attacking your duties with commendable enthusiasm lately. I didn't hear you come in until well after midnight last night."

"You know what they say," Tupper said, beaming an angelic smile as he backed out the door. "The devil's work is never done."

"No," the Dragon murmured, his eyes darkening with determination as he plucked a sugar biscuit from the tray and popped it into his mouth. "I don't suppose it ever is."

Gwendolyn had been expecting the Dragon, but she still jumped when the panel door went crashing against the opposite wall, awakening her.

She huddled against the headboard, her heart pounding in her throat. The moon had yet to sail over her window and she could discern little more than a shadowy figure looming out of the darkness. The rasp of his breathing warned her that if he had been a real dragon, fire would have come shooting out of his nostrils to singe the stray tendrils of hair that had escaped her nightcap.

He strode over to rest something on the table, then turned to face her. Even in the dark, his regard was nearly as palpable as a touch. She couldn't shake the sensation that his eyes could pierce the darkness—could plainly see the pulse fluttering in her throat, the uneven rise and fall of her breasts.

Gwendolyn should have known he'd force her to be the one to break the tense silence. "Good evening, M'lord Dragon. To what do I owe the honor of this visit?"

"Your own foolishness. Tupper tells me you haven't eaten in two days."

She lifted her shoulder in an elegant shrug. "You needn't trouble yourself, sir. As I'm sure you can see, it will take more than a few missed meals for me to waste away."

He strode toward the bed. Gwendolyn had believed herself beyond cowering before him. She was wrong.

She wasn't sure what heinous act of villainy she expected him to commit, but it certainly wasn't scooping her into his arms as if she weighed no more than Kitty and carrying her to the table. He sank into the chair, cradling her in his lap.

"Open your mouth," he commanded, his firm grip making squirming difficult, if not impossible.

Gwendolyn's first muddled thought was that perhaps he intended to kiss her even more thoroughly than he'd done before. It wasn't his mouth that touched her lips, however, but the smooth, cold bowl of a spoon.

"Open wide and try a taste, won't you?" he murmured, a husky note of pleading in his voice.

Gwendolyn couldn't remember the last time she'd been urged to eat. She'd always been more likely to hear "Save that last biscuit for Kitty, won't you?" or to have Izzy rap her across the knuckles with a wooden spoon as she reached for another helping of oatmeal. The piquant aroma of cinnamon reminded her of how hungry she was. It broke her heart to resist him.

"I'll not do it," she muttered between clenched teeth, shaking her head like a truculent three-year-old.

They were both only too aware that he possessed the strength to force that spoon between her teeth if he so desired. But as it turned out, that wasn't his desire at all. The spoon vanished, replaced by the beguiling warmth of his breath against the corner of her mouth.

That tender whisper of breath was followed by the faintest graze of his lips against hers. Her lips seemed to soften of their own volition, and when he took advantage of that softness by sliding his tongue between them, she moaned at the shock of it.

Before Gwendolyn could clear her dazed mind, he'd replaced his tongue with the spoon and poured a mouthful of melting warmth down her throat. She sputtered, but he covered her mouth with his own again, forcing her to swallow the delectable concoction.

The bread pudding was sweet, but not nearly as sweet as the teasing swirl of his tongue against hers.

She shoved against his chest, forcing him to break the kiss. But when she opened her mouth to utter an outraged protest, he simply dipped the laden spoon between her lips again, as if she were a baby bird who had tumbled out of her nest and he the naturalist intent upon saving her.

Before he could lift the spoon again, Gwendolyn managed to gather the wits he'd so skillfully scattered. "If you put any more of that *stuff* in my mouth without my leave, I'm going to spit it in your face."

"Come now, you wouldn't wish to wound Tupper's feelings, would you? He fancies himself quite the chef, you know. I should have let him try out his new recipe for haggis on you," he said, referring to the Highland staple of sheep's stomach stuffed with herbs.

"Tupper may be a fine chef, but you, sir, are a miserable bully."

"Only when I'm forced to deal with a stubborn child."

Gwendolyn struggled to escape his embrace, her temper flaring. "Which am I to be, M'lord Dragon—a pampered pet or a stubborn child? Or does your perception depend on how malleable a slave I am to your whims?"

His arms tightened around her. "You know nothing of my whims. If you did, you'd stop squirming in that maddening manner."

Gwendolyn did just that. The darkness that enveloped

them seemed to heighten her every sense. It magnified the ragged cadence of his breathing and the shudder of his heartbeat beneath her palm. Every breath she drew was rich with the aroma of sandalwood and spice. The crisp hairs spilling from the open throat of his shirt tickled her fingertips. But it was the rigid warmth of his lap beneath the softness of her bottom that sent a tremor of panic shooting through her. She tensed, going as stiff as a puppeteer's marionette.

"Now," he said, his voice deadly serious, "are you going to eat or do I have to kiss you again?" His breath grazed her flaming cheek, warning her that he had every intention of making good on his threat.

"I'll eat," she snapped, opening her mouth.

"You certainly know how to deflate a man's opinion of his charms," he said ruefully as he fed her a heaping spoonful of the pudding.

Gwendolyn's knowledge of male anatomy might have been limited to what she had overheard Nessa and Glynnis discussing, but as far as she could tell, his charms showed no sign of deflating. She swallowed. "Most men don't feel compelled to offer their kisses as a threat of punishment."

"Why, I've known ladies in the past who considered them a reward!"

"Were you holding them captive at the time or is that a more recent diversion for you?"

"I can promise you that none of them were quite as diverting as you." He used the spoon to dab a drop of pudding from her lower lip.

It made her wild to be so near him, yet unable to make out more than a shadowy mask of his features. It should have been unbearably awkward to be cradled on a stranger's lap. But somewhere between their first encounter and this one, he had ceased to be a stranger. He might have been nothing more than a phantom woven of shadow and texture, but those shadows and textures were becoming as familiar to her as the feel of her papa's wispy hair between her fingers or the sound of Kitty's breathing in the dark.

"I saw the ship," she blurted out, desperate to distract them both from the way each mingled breath seemed to draw their lips closer together.

It was his turn to stiffen. "Ah, and was that what spoiled your appetite?"

"Aye, it was. Because I still can't fathom why a man of your obvious resources would seek to steal from those who have so little."

"Perhaps I don't consider it stealing. Perhaps I simply consider it relieving them of something that was never rightfully theirs in the first place."

"If you're talking about the thousand pounds, it doesn't exist! It never did."

That infuriating note of amusement returned to his voice. "And why should I believe you, Miss Wilder? Only a short while ago, you didn't believe dragons existed."

"I still don't. And you've yet to prove me wrong."

"Then perhaps I don't believe in maidens, either. Are *you* willing to prove *their* existence?"

Gwendolyn had no answer for such a provocative challenge. She could only tip back her head to study the gleam of his eyes in the darkness.

He captured one of the golden tendrils that had escaped her nightcap and twined it around his finger, his voice deepening to a husky whisper. "Having you here . . . like this . . . do you have any idea what it does to a man like me?"

"Makes your legs go numb?" Gwendolyn ventured.

He was silent for a long moment, then a harsh bark of laughter escaped him. Still laughing, he swooped her up and strode to the bed. He didn't so much lower her to the mattress as toss her on it. She scrambled toward the head of the bed, believing for a breathless instant that he might actually be planning to join her.

Instead, he sank down beside her and splayed his palms against the headboard, pinning her between his arms. "Eat, Gwendolyn Wilder," he commanded, lowering his face to hers, "for if you don't eat every morsel on that tray, I'm coming back with Tupper's haggis. Then you'll be sorry you didn't choose my bloody kisses instead!"

A moment later, he was gone, leaving Gwendolyn to wonder if she wasn't already sorry.

# Chapter Twelve

THE NEXT DAY DAWNED with an oppressive heaviness. Gwendolyn dutifully ate every bite of her meals beneath Tupper's watchful eye, although the food tasted like sawdust in her mouth. She wasn't sure her poor beleaguered heart could withstand another of the Dragon's midnight visits.

Throughout the interminable day, even Tupper seemed distracted. Instead of chattering as he usually did, he spent most of his time looking longingly at the door, as if he were the prisoner instead of her. After choking down some woodcock and a warm bowl of cullen skink, Gwendolyn finally shooed him away, convinced she'd rather retire early than endure another moment of his pained attempts at conversation.

She had risen from the table to blow out the last of the candles when the first haunting strains of bagpipe music drifted through the grate. Shivering in the darkness, she climbed into the bed, leaned against the headboard, and hugged her knees to her chest. Although she now knew that the fingers that played upon the pipes were only too human, the mournful wail still stirred her own ghosts of sadness and regret.

For a wistful moment, the raw beauty of the music allowed her to forget the Dragon and remember instead a tall, slender boy with an unruly lock of dark hair that had insisted upon tumbling over his emerald green eyes. This castle had been his home, and if someone hadn't betrayed his father to Cumberland, he might still reign here as lord. She gazed up at the shadowy nymphs cavorting on the ceiling, wondering if he had ever slept in this very chamber.

Had he lived, she might have had to watch from the shadows while he took another woman to be his wife—the noble daughter of some neighboring chieftain or one of the prettier village lasses, perhaps even Glynnis or Nessa. She might have had to smile through her tears as his dark-haired, green-eyed son rode his own pony past the tree that had been her haven as a girl. But her pain would have been a small price to pay for the joy of watching Bernard MacCullough grow to manhood as the hope and pride of his clan.

Gwendolyn touched her cheek, startled to find it wet with tears. She didn't mourn just for that lost boy, but for the girl who had loved him. The girl who had roamed the forest glens and the winding corridors of this very castle, pining for a glimpse of him. Sometimes it seemed as if both of their lives had ended in the moment that first cannonball tore through the heart of the castle's keep.

The piping died on a plaintive note. She curled up on her side and drew the sheet to her chin, wondering what that boy would have thought of the woman she had become.


Gwendolyn was dreaming.

She ran through the maze of the castle corridors, a child again. She could hear the boy, but she could not see him. He stayed just ahead of her, dancing down the winding stone staircases, clearing the landings in one leap with the fleet grace of a cat. His laughter drifted back to her, bold and teasing, but no matter how hard she begged him to stop, he kept running, refusing to believe any harm could come to him.

She darted a frantic glance over her shoulder, shaken by the growing rumble of the cannons. If she couldn't catch him soon, it would be too late. But she was too fat. Too slow. Her short, plump legs were no match for his long, limber ones. Before she could turn one corner, he was rounding the next.

*Gwendolyn!* He sang out her name, urging her not to give up the chase.

The cannons were growing louder still, their sporadic booming shaking the floor beneath her feet. Couldn't he hear them? Couldn't he feel them?

As she plunged down the main staircase, she caught a glimpse of him sprinting into the great hall, his scarlet and black tartan rippling behind him like wings.

Hope spilled through her chest. If she could just

grab that tartan, she could hold him fast. She could throw her arms around him and keep him safe forever.

Her feet struck the flagstones at the foot of the stairs. A deafening roar shook the castle. She fell to her knees, clapping her hands over her ears.

When she finally dared to open her eyes and lower her hands, the cannons had fallen silent, leaving an eerie hush in their wake.

She slowly climbed to her feet, the yawning archway of the great hall beckoning her forward. Her voice cracked as she called out his name.

Her only answer was the whisper of the dust sifting down from the ceiling. She wanted to believe the stubborn boy must be hiding, that he was probably choking on his own laughter as he prepared to spring out at her from some shadowy corner.

But then she saw the scarlet and black bundle lying on the floor of the great hall. She knelt to gently brush her hand across the wool, expecting to find it damp with blood just as it had been in a hundred other dreams. But the wool was dry, her fingers unstained.

Those fingers began to tremble as she reached to tug back a corner of the tartan. Instead of resisting her pull as it usually did, the garment wafted up around her, leaving her gaping in astonishment.

The tartan was empty. The boy was gone.

The Dragon jerked bolt upright on his pallet, sweat sheening his muscular torso despite the chill in the air.

They were coming. He could hear them—the clattering hoofbeats; the rumble of wagon wheels on the rutted road that led to the castle; the cacophony of voices, cursing and shouting orders; the scattered musket fire. He leapt to his feet, his breath coming short and fast, and dragged on his discarded shirt.

He staggered blindly up the stairs, not bothering to light a candle or lamp. He emerged in the gatehouse, bewildered to find the cavernous room dark and deserted instead of teeming with men preparing for battle. He groped his way to the chapel, praying that he would find someone there, but his questioning cry came back to him as a hollow echo. It seemed that even God had abandoned him.

As he ran past a recessed window, a dazzling flash of light nearly blinded him.

He was too late. They'd already touched a torch to the first fuse.

The Dragon came to a halt in the main entranceway of the castle, his chest heaving and his hands clenched into fists. Never again would he cower in the dark, waiting to hear the damning whistle of that first incoming cannonball. Never again would he trust his fate to a deliverance that would not come. He wrenched open the main door and stumbled into the night.

He strode to the center of the courtyard and flung his arms wide, inviting the bastards to blow his bones into splinters. Squeezing his eyes shut, he threw back his head and let loose a roar that seemed to come from the very depths of his soul. But even that anguished howl was no match for the booming crash that shook the earth beneath his feet.

The crash faded to a rumble. The Dragon opened his eyes, surprised to find himself still standing. Rain poured over him, plastering his shirt and breeches to his body and washing away the last traces of the madness that had seized him.

"Oh, God," he whispered, sliding to his knees.

Had he known there was a storm coming, he would not have let himself sleep. If Tupper had been there, his friend would have tried to distract him with some witty anecdote, a game of chess, a glass of port, anything to take the edge off this torturous wildness that threatened his soul.

The Dragon buried his face in his hands. He could stand on the deck of a ship and withstand without flinching the cannons fired at his orders, but here in this accursed place, even the harmless blustering of thunder could drive him to the brink of insanity.

He lifted his head just as a flash of lightning revealed that he was kneeling at Aphrodite's feet. The last storm had brought him Gwendolyn, he remembered, a more welcome distraction than any Tupper could provide. He was shaken to realize how badly he longed to go to her at that moment.

He rose, his bones aching. Fighting the lash of the wind and the rain, he made his way toward the castle, determined to seek the only solace he deserved.

✦ ✦ ✦

Gwendolyn jerked awake.

At first she mistook the pounding of her heart for the ghostly echo of the cannons in her dream, but that was before a flash of lightning was followed by a clap of thunder. Gusts of wind pummeled the tower, howling their frustration when it refused to crumble before their force.

She hugged herself to still her trembling. She almost wished the Dragon were there, almost wished for the sweetness of his kiss to wash away the bitter taste of the nightmare. But a dazzling flare of lightning proved she was alone.

Finally the wind began to die down. She cocked her head as a curious banging reached her ears, too rhythmic to be thunder. She nearly shrieked when Toby landed on her feet with a muffled thud.

"Where on earth did you come from, big fellow?" she asked, stroking her fingers through his ruff. "I would have sworn Tupper let you out when he left."

The cat's only reply was a rumbling purr. Gwendolyn climbed out of the bed and began to feel her way around the wall. Between each flicker of lightning, the chamber went dark as pitch.

She fumbled for the panel door, but her hand met only air. The banging she had heard was the panel thudding softly against the opposite wall, still caught in the powerful fingers of the draft that had wrenched it open.

The door was ajar. Gwendolyn was free.

# Chapter Thirteen

GWENDOLYN BACKED AWAY from the door, wondering if she was still dreaming. If she dared to pass through that portal, would she hear the ghostly tap of a boy's footsteps on the stairs? Would the mocking music of his laughter beguile her into giving chase?

She pinched the tender flesh on the inside of her arm—hard. Reassured by the sting, she took a deep breath and ducked through the opening.

She hadn't fully realized what pains had been taken to make her tower warm and cozy until she encountered the chill, dank air outside her room. She groped her way down the narrow, winding staircase, ducking beneath a stream of rain that poured right through a crack in the ceiling. A broken block of stone snagged her nightdress. She jerked the hem free, then stumbled down three steps, the clumsy motion bringing her face-to-face with . . .

Nothing.

A ragged wound had been torn in the north wall,

exposing a dizzying vista of storm-tossed whitecaps. Fading flickers of lightning danced in the moonless sky, illuminating the craggy face of the cliffs and the sheer drop to the rocks below.

Gwendolyn scrambled backward, pressing herself flat against the opposite wall. Were these the terrors the Dragon had braved to come to her side in the dark of night?

At first she feared she wasn't going to be able to pry herself off the wall. But by steadying her breathing and squeezing her eyes shut, she managed to inch her way past the yawning gap and creep to the gallery below.

At the far end of the gallery was a flight of broad, stone stairs.

Gwendolyn started down the stairs, still not convinced that she wasn't dreaming. In this dream, her footsteps were not slow or plodding. Instead, she seemed to float down the stairs, the ruffled hem of her nightdress drifting behind her.

As she reached the entranceway, a cool, rain-scented breeze played across her skin. The splintered door that led to the courtyard hung half off its hinges in an invitation Gwendolyn could not ignore.

She hastened toward the door, trying to imagine the joy that would light her papa's face when she threw herself into his arms. She hesitated, unable to bring his dear, familiar features into focus. A troubling thought plagued her. What if he hadn't even missed her? When the Dragon had first made her his prisoner, she had believed her father's madness to be a blessing. But now she wasn't so sure. What if Papa simply squeezed her hand, called her his "good girl," and shooed her off to bed? Then there would be nothing left for her to do but crawl beneath the covers with one of Reverend Throckmorton's pamphlets, worry about Kitty, and wait for Nessa to return from the arms of her latest lover.

Gwendolyn slowly turned. The yawning archway of the great hall seemed to beckon her forward, just as it had in her dream.

She took one step, then another, her pulse racing with a strange mixture of fascination and dread.

The great hall had once been the heart of Castle Weyrcraig, and it was that heart that had been broken by Cumberland's attack. A cannonball had shattered a vast portion of the roof, freeing the clouds to scud across its ragged canvas. The rain had nearly stopped, and the moon had begun to peep shyly through the veil of clouds, as if to make sure the storm was truly gone and it was safe to come out. Tattered banners fluttered from the massive crossbeams that hadn't been splintered by the blow, the scarlet dragons that danced on their fields of black faded to the hue of dried blood. A massive stone hearth crowned the far wall, its hand-carved mantel draped with cobwebs.

Gwendolyn drifted into the hall, feeling barely more substantial than the ghosts who must surely haunt this place. She could almost hear the echoes of their laughter, their voices raised in song as they lifted their goblets in a victory toast to the might and majesty that had once been Clan MacCullough.

She shook off the fancy. It wasn't the ghosts of those long-dead warriors who haunted her, but the ghost of the woman who had once striven to make this drafty hall a home. Gwendolyn remembered the MacCullough's wife as a stout, good-natured soul who laughed a great deal and adored her only son. Her sweetly feminine touch was everywhere. A settee framed by ornate gilt scrollwork sat below a shattered looking-glass, cotton batting spilling out of its frayed silk cushions. In lieu of gloomy tapestries, the walls had been festooned with French linen in once ethereal pastels of pink and blue. A fluted Corinthian column lay toppled on its side in a puddle of rainwater.

As Gwendolyn traversed the hall, she had to pick her way through a field of broken pottery. She bent to pick up a shard of fine porcelain, smoothing her thumb over its lustrous surface. She had spent her life yearning for such beautiful things, and she could not help but mourn their destruction and the broken fragments of the dreams they represented.

She was turning it over in her hand when her foot came up against a disembodied head. She nearly screamed before realizing it was the marble head of the statue in the courtyard—Aphrodite, her shapely lips curved in a knowing smile that both pitied and mocked.

That was when she saw him.

He sat, as always, in shadow. But on this night, it

seemed that even the shadows weren't enough to hide him. He slumped in the center chair of a long mahogany table, his head buried in his folded arms. A crystal decanter with less than an inch of whisky remaining in its bottom rested before him, along with a silver tinderbox and a candle he hadn't bothered to light. He wore no coat or waistcoat, just a white shirt with its sleeves shoved carelessly past his elbows. From the way the fine linen clung to his powerful shoulders, outlining every sinew and muscle, Gwendolyn guessed he must be soaked to the bone.

He was oblivious to her presence. All she had to do was tiptoe away and she would be free of him forever. But before she could turn and do just that, thunder boomed in the distance, sending a shudder through his rigid muscles.

Before she even realized what she was going to do, Gwendolyn had crossed to his side and gently laid her hand on his shoulder.

He lifted his head without looking at her, shedding droplets of rainwater. "Good evening, Miss Wilder."

"How did you know it wasn't Tupper?"

"Tupper knows better than to sneak up on me in the dark. He might inadvertently get his throat cut." Gwendolyn swallowed. "But then again, his throat isn't nearly as bonny as yours."

The whisky hadn't yet slurred his speech, but it had softened the clipped consonants and flat vowels, giving his words a disarming lilt. Before she could withdraw her hand from his shoulder, he caught it and held it fast, his thumb gliding across her palm. "Nor are his hands so soft. Perhaps you're only a dream," he murmured, rubbing the back of her hand against his cheek. "Pray tell, would the prickly Miss Wilder have enough pity in her heart to come to me in my dreams with her soft hands and her skin smelling of sleep?"

The delicious warmth emanating from his touch only made Gwendolyn feel more prickly. "I don't believe that men in drunken stupors are capable of dreaming."

The Dragon laughed harshly. "Perhaps you're not a dream then, but a ghost. The white lady of the castle sent to warn me to leave this place before it costs me my eternal soul." He turned his head to look at her, his expression masked by shadows. "Ah, but the ever-practical Miss Wilder probably doesn't believe in ghosts, does she?"

Unnerved that he should have echoed her own dream so precisely, Gwendolyn said softly, "I used to think I didn't. But when I stand in a place like this, I'm not so sure."

She felt oddly bereft when he relinquished her hand and rose, seeking the deeper shadows of the hearth. The damp chill of the hall seemed to seep into her bones.

He looked up at the splintered rafters. "Have you ever wondered how they must have felt that night? Betrayed by one of their own. Abandoned by those they trusted to defend them. All they could do was huddle in the darkness with their own meager weapons and wait for that first cannonball to fall from the sky."

"They could have fled into the night with Bonnie Prince Charlie," she reminded him, wondering as she often had why they hadn't done just that.

His chuckle held little humor. "That might have saved their lives, but it would have cost them their precious pride." He traced the motto engraved over the mantel with his forefinger. " 'Wrong or right . . .' "

" '. . . a MacCullough always stands to fight,' " Gwendolyn finished for him. There was no need for her to read the motto. Its hateful words were carved into her heart.

"Were there children, do you suppose?" he asked lightly, swiping his finger through the thick layer of dust on the mantel.

Now Gwendolyn was the one who turned away, seeking to hide from the moonlight. "There was a child. A boy."

"Only one. That's unusual, is it not? I thought these Highland lords bred like rabbits."

Gwendolyn shook her head. "His wife was able to bear him only the one child. But unlike most men, he never reproached her. Instead, he treated her as if she'd given him the rarest and most precious of gifts—a son. An heir who would lead the clan once he was gone." Her voice trailed to a murmur. "I don't believe the villagers ever recovered from his loss."

The Dragon snorted. "From what you've told me

about the good folk of Ballybliss, I doubt that anyone shed a tear for him."

Gwendolyn swung around to face him. "I did!"

Unable to bear his silence, she drifted over to the jagged remains of a window. "I was little more than a child when he died, but I suppose I was half in love with him even then." A rueful smile touched her lips. "Silly, wasn't I, thinking a lad like that might spare a thought for a great, awkward girl like me?"

"Your only folly was fancying yourself in love with someone who was little more than a child himself."

"Ah, but you didn't know him. He was quite an extraordinary lad—strong and kind and noble. It was apparent even then what manner of man he would grow up to be."

The Dragon sounded oddly subdued. "A paragon of goodness, no doubt, given to uplifting the downtrodden, protecting the virtue of the innocent, and rescuing damsels in distress."

"He rescued me once. But I was proud and stubborn and instead of thanking him properly, I gave him a scathing set-down. I didn't realize it would be the last time I would ever see him alive."

She gazed out over the shattered ruins of the courtyard, but saw instead a sunlit path lined with weeping villagers, felt the rough bark as she dug her fingernails into the trunk of the oak, heard the mournful wail of the pipes as they heralded the death of all her dreams. "I saw them carry his body down the hill. I must have hidden in that very same tree and watched him ride through that pass a hundred times before, but that last time, he was draped facedown over the back of his pony. They'd wrapped him in the tartan he'd always worn so proudly."

Gwendolyn was aware that tears had begun to slip silently down her cheeks, just as they had done that day. Unaware that the Dragon had taken two halting steps toward her, his fingers curled into helpless fists at his sides.

Gwendolyn brushed a tear away with the back of her hand and turned to face him.

He stumbled around and braced both hands on the mantel. "I suggest that you leave me now, Miss Wilder. I'm lonely and I'm drunk. I've only been drunk for a few hours, but I've been lonely for a very long time, which hardly makes me fit company for discussing ghosts with a lady in her nightdress."

Gwendolyn was taken aback by his admission. She supposed she'd assumed that pangs of loneliness were reserved for plain women with lovely sisters.

"And where would you suggest I go, M'lord Dragon? Back to my cell?"

"I don't give a damn where you go," he ground out. "As long as it's out of my sight."

Gwendolyn couldn't have gone if there'd been another cannonball heading straight for the hall, not while there was a crack in the Dragon's armor that might provide her with a glimpse of the man inside.

"Shall I return to the village then?" She took another step toward him, thinking to lure him into the moonlight with her taunts. "Shall I tell them that their fierce Dragon is nothing but a man? A man who seeks to make others afraid of him, yet hides his face in shadows because he's more afraid of himself than they could ever be."

"Tell them whatever you bloody well like," he growled, his knuckles white against the mahogany of the mantel.

Gwendolyn crept nearer, lifting her hand, but not daring to touch the unyielding expanse of his back. "Shall I also tell them that you've shown me nothing but kindness? That you replaced my rags with garments fit for a princess? That you forced me to eat when I would have starved myself out of sheer stubbornness? That you've declined to devour their virgin sacrifice?"

He turned around. "Don't think I haven't considered it. Don't think I'm not considering it at this very moment!"

Hunger gleamed in his eyes, but he did not lay his hands on her. It was that, more than anything, that prompted her to touch her fingertips to his face. He inhaled raggedly as she gently explored his features, seeking the scar, the burn, the terrible deformity that had driven him to live in darkness and branded him a beast in his own eyes and the eyes of the world.

She had to ease aside a silky lock of hair to stroke a brow that was both strong and smooth. His eyebrows were thick and slightly arched, his lashes soft as feathers against her palm. She followed the arc of his cheekbone to the firm line of his nose. Her knuckles curved to caress a jaw lightly stubbled with a day's growth of beard. She was reaching to brush her fingertips against his lips when he caught her wrist, groaning.

She expected him to fling her hand away, not to bring her fingertips to his lips and press a kiss upon them. His lips were firm, yet soft. The tender urgency of their kiss sent a scorching sweetness melting through her veins.

He caught her by the shoulders and drew her against him in the darkness. "Would you sacrifice yourself to me, Gwendolyn? Would you sacrifice yourself to save this poor wretched beast that I've become?"

A strange calm stole over Gwendolyn as she gazed up into the shadows that composed his face. "You once told me what I had to do to turn you from beast to man."

Curling one hand around his nape, she drew him down and gently pressed her mouth to his.

# Chapter Fourteen

THE DRAGON STRUGGLED TO absorb the gift of Gwendolyn's kiss. It was too late to confess that he had lied to her, too late to warn her that her kiss could only weave an enchantment more dangerous than any that had come before. Instead of taming him, her kiss made him wild. Wild to kiss her. Wild to touch her. Wild to take her. He sucked in a shuddering breath as her mouth ripened beneath his, her lips parting in an invitation he no longer had the strength to resist.

Holding himself back so as not to frighten her, he wrapped his arms around her and swirled his tongue through the moist warmth of her mouth. She tasted of innocence and hunger, and it was precisely that shy ardor that made her kiss more affecting than any courtesan's caress.

"My sweet . . . my innocent," he whispered against the corner of her mouth. "You are a dream, aren't you? A dream come true."

Gwendolyn would have never believed the Dragon

capable of such gentleness. His mouth glided down the curve of her jaw, leaving a tingling trail of delight. He kissed the dimple in her cheek, then sought the one at the hollow of her throat before returning his mouth to hers.

This was no chaste brushing of lips, no misty mingling of breath. This was a kiss as sweet and dark as death itself. As he ravished her mouth with exquisite thoroughness, Gwendolyn had to cling to his shirtfront to keep from falling. He might have been the one drinking, but she was the one reeling, intoxicated more by his raw tenderness than by the whisky she tasted on his tongue. Although his breathing was as ragged as her own, she could feel his dragon's heart beating strong and true beneath her palm.

He did not break that bewitching kiss, not even when he bore her back against the table. Gwendolyn had thought to lure him into the moonlight. She had never dreamed that he would drag her deeper into the shadows or that she would go with him willingly, even eagerly.

The table pressed into her backside; he pressed himself into the softness of her belly, proving once and for all that he was no beast, but simply a man. A man who desperately wanted her.

"You're a bloody little fool. You should have gone when I told you to," he rasped even as he drew her more tightly against him.

Gwendolyn reached blindly for his face, finding his

hoarse reproach even more irresistible than his touch. He grazed her lips with his own, brushing them back and forth in a coaxing caress that made her heart double its already ragged rhythm.

He began to unlace the satin ribbons at the throat of her nightdress. Gwendolyn felt the tremor in his hands as he dragged the fabric down, exposing her shoulders.

"You have the softest skin," he murmured, feathering his fingers against her collarbone.

"Fat girls often do," she informed him, pressing her burning cheek to his chest. "It's their consolation for having so very much of it."

He cupped her face in his hands, his voice as fierce as his touch. "If you're not a goddess among women, then why is Aphrodite over there turning green with jealousy at the prospect of your unveiling?"

Gwendolyn laughed shakily. "Are you sure it's not just moss?"

As the Dragon buried his face against her throat to smother his exasperated chuckle, it was almost possible for him to believe that her yielding softness could fill all the empty places in his life. "If you won't believe the praise that spills from my honeyed tongue, I'll simply have to put it to another use."

Gwendolyn moaned deep in her throat as he did just that, sliding that honeyed tongue of his between her lips in a rhythm as ancient as that of the sea battering the rocks below the castle. A wicked thrill shot through her as he filled his hands with the softness of her breasts, his callused thumbs stroking her nipples to rigid attention through the crisp lawn of the night-dress.

She gasped into his mouth; he groaned into hers. His dragon's breath seemed to fill her, its tongues of flame igniting a raging fire low in her belly. Through the roaring in her ears, she could hear him murmuring her name, as if it were an incantation.

She could do nothing but moan her surrender as his other hand crept beneath the skirt of her nightdress, lingering to stroke the baby-soft skin of her inner knee. Ever since the morning he'd rescued her from the win-dow, Gwendolyn had taken great care to wear a pair of drawers beneath her nightclothes. Now she realized how foolish she had been to believe that thin layer of silk would shield her virtue. She should have known they'd present more of an enticement than a hindrance to a man like the Dragon.

It wasn't until she heard his ragged intake of breath that she remembered the slit in the silk at the cleft of her thighs. As those deft, aristocratic fingers of his brushed curls dampened by a desire she could no longer deny, her thighs went slack, inviting him—no—begging him to work his dark will upon her.

So this was it, Gwendolyn thought, her head falling back to loll helplessly against her shoulders. This was the unholy rapture for which Nessa and Kitty had traded their innocence and their pride. He lavished her mouth with kisses, all the while petting and stroking her until she was slick with a nectar thicker and sweeter than honey. Only then did he flick his thumb across the swollen bud at the crux of her curls. Only then did he press one finger deep into the aching hollow that had never before known the touch of a man.

Gwendolyn arched against his hand, pleasure spilling through her in a shimmering cascade that seemed to have no end. She almost cried out his name before remembering with a pang of dismay that she did not know what it was.

He was a stranger. A stranger looming over her in the darkness with his face masked by shadows and his hand up her skirt.

Feeling suddenly sick with shame, Gwendolyn shoved at his chest. "No," she cried, breaking away from his embrace.

He followed her, stopping at the very brink of the shadows. "What is it? Did you think I would force you? For God's sake, Gwendolyn, even *I'm* not that much of a monster!"

Gwendolyn clutched the arm of the settee, fighting to steady her breathing. She didn't want to cry in front of him; she wasn't a pretty crier like Glynnis or Nessa. "You don't understand. It's not you. It's me!" She hung her head. "I should have warned you. The women in my family all seem to possess a terrible weakness of the flesh."

A relieved laugh escaped him. "Oh, is that all? I can assure you, sweeting, that what you just experienced was utterly normal. There was nothing terrible about it. Not for you and most certainly not for me."

Gwendolyn whirled around to face him. "Do you know what the men in the village say about my sister Nessa? 'Take care when ye toss up the skirts o' that Wilder lass—ye may find another lad already under there.' They wink and they nudge each other and whisper, 'Do ye ken what's bonnier than a Wilder lass on her back? Why, one on her knees!'" The Dragon watched her from the shadows, his stillness uncanny. "Nessa has given herself away until there's nothing left of who she might have been. And now my youngest sister Kitty has started down the same path. But how can I condemn her when I've proved I'm no different from either of them! I'm just as willing to offer myself to any silver-tongued rogue who plies me with kisses or praises the softness of my skin."

He was silent for a long time—long enough for Gwendolyn to begin to wonder if she'd wounded him with her words. "And just how many other silver-tongued rogues have you offered yourself to?"

Gwendolyn pondered the question for a moment, sniffing back a sob. "None. Only you."

"Why, you're quite the little strumpet, aren't you?" he said lightly.

"You can't deny that I let you commit unspeakable liberties!"

"Oh, I wouldn't call them unspeakable," he replied, anger restoring the clipped edge to his voice. "First you let me kiss your mouth. Then you let me touch those exquisite breasts of yours through your nightdress. And then you let me put my fingers—"

"Stop it!" Gwendolyn clapped her hands over her ears, unable to bear his deliberate mockery. "How could I have let you do any of those things when I've never even seen your face? When I don't even know your name?"

"That may be true," he said quietly, "but for just a moment there, I would have sworn you knew my heart."

Gwendolyn's chest shuddered with the effort of choking back her tears. She wanted nothing more than to run into his arms, but she was as trapped by the moonlight as he was by the shadows. As long as he refused to reveal his identity, the expanse of floor that separated them would remain as uncrossable as the chasm of nothingness separating the tower from the sea. Fearful that she might try anyway, she spun around and ran from the hall.

Fingers of moonlight streamed through the open door, beckoning her toward freedom.

Gwendolyn ran up the stairs, leaving the Dragon to his shadows. She did not see him burst from the great hall, braving the light to come after her. Nor did she see him slump against the wall and rake his hands through his hair when he heard the sobs echoing down from the highest reaches of the castle.

# Chapter Fifteen

G OD'S FORESKIN!" Izzy bellowed, slamming a basin heaped with soiled nightshirts down on the kitchen table.

Kitty flinched and Glynnis snatched her breakfast of stale sugar biscuits and tea out of the path of the grimy water that came sloshing over the basin's edge. The hound napping on the hearth took one look at the maidservant's thundercloud of a brow and bolted from the room.

Kitty and Glynnis exchanged apprehensive glances, but wisely held their tongues as Izzy dumped the contents of the basin into a large iron kettle that was already steaming on the grate. Still cursing beneath her breath, she grabbed a wooden spoon and began to stir the laundry, looking like a wild-eyed witch brewing up a batch of toil and trouble.

Nessa came drifting into the kitchen, her eyes swollen and bleary from lack of sleep even though it was after ten in the morning. "For heaven's sake, Izzy, must you bellow and bang so? It's enough to wake the dead."

"The dead p'r'aps, but not ye." Izzy removed the spoon from the water long enough to shake it at her. "And I've every right to bellow and bang. I was up at dawn when ye and Kitty were just creepin' in after dallyin' all night with the menfolk."

Kitty blushed while Nessa sank into a chair and stretched, taking advantage of the graceful motion to steal a biscuit from Glynnis's plate. "Since Lachlan is the only lad I'm interested in at the moment, that would be *man*folk."

The maidservant rolled her eyes. "One man at a time, maybe. But there's always another one right behind him."

"Unlike Nessa," Glynnis pointed out, "I can be quite loyal. I never once strayed from the beds of either of my husbands."

"That's most likely what killed 'em," Izzy said. "Two puir auld men tryin' to do the job of a dozen strappin' lads."

While Nessa cackled with laughter, Glynnis sniffed and bit off a dainty piece of the biscuit. "Perhaps I should have taken my breakfast in one of my own cottages, Izzy. There's simply no point in trying to make polite conversation with you when you're in such a foul temper."

Izzy jabbed her spoon at the wall. "Ye'd be in a foul temper, too, young missie, if ye were locked in this manor day and night with that daft father of yers. I don't see how yer puir sister bore it all those years. If I were her, I'd've begged the Dragon to eat me!"

They shared a moment of somber silence in honor of Gwendolyn before Kitty said softly, "Papa mistook me for Mama yesterday. He kept clutching at my skirts and begging me to forgive him."

"As well he should," Izzy snapped, "since it was his own greed that killed the puir creature."

All three girls turned to stare at Izzy, having never heard such a thing pass the maidservant's lips before. For an elusive moment, her florid face seemed to be flushed by more than just the heat of the fire.

She averted her gaze, poking at the laundry with renewed violence. "I just meant because he had to go and try to get a son on her. After all, what man wouldn't be content with the lot o' ye?"

"What man indeed?" Kitty murmured, pushing her plate away.

Glynnis shifted her worried gaze to her youngest sister. "What ails you, kitten? You've been moping about for days. It's not like you."

"You're not breeding, are you, lass?" Nessa asked, reaching over to pat Kitty's hand.

Izzy groaned. "That's all we need 'round here. Another arse to wipe."

Kitty snatched her hand away from her sister's, her dark eyes blazing. "Of course I'm not breeding. How could I be when you taught me how to prevent it with my first monthly course?"

Nessa sank back in her chair and poured herself a cup of tea, eyeing her sister cautiously. "And I should think you'd be grateful for that."

"Why should I when you might have taught me something useful? Like how to mend stockings or polish the silver or manage a man's household."

"Trust me, Kitty," Glynnis said, arching one flawlessly plucked eyebrow. "You're better off knowing how to manage a man than his household."

"Aye," Nessa agreed. "It's not the silver most men want polished."

Kitty grew even more fierce. "Maybe every man isn't interested in *that*."

Glynnis exchanged a knowing look with Nessa. "If he has a heartbeat, he's interested."

"Don't tell me you've met a man who can resist your charms!" Nessa teased.

Kitty's ire subsided. "Perhaps he doesn't think I have any," she mumbled, gazing dolefully into her teacup.

Glynnis reached over to stroke her hair. "Don't be ridiculous. Why, everyone knows you're the bonniest lass in all of Ballybliss!"

"And if you think that's easy for her to admit, you're wrong," Nessa added, giving her older sister a feline smile.

Glynnis wrinkled her nose at Nessa before returning her attention to Kitty. "You haven't gone and done something foolish, have you, pet? Like falling in love?"

Letting out a pathetic wail, Kitty shoved the teacup

aside and buried her head on her folded arms. "Oh, why couldn't I have been the one the villagers fed to the Dragon?"

"Now why would that randy old Dragon want you?" Glynnis exclaimed, hoping to cheer her. "He only has an appetite for virgins!"

While Izzy snorted and Nessa joined Glynnis in her merry peals of laughter, Kitty burst into tears, sprang to her feet, and ran from the room.

Her sisters stared after her, their laughter fading. "What on earth do you make of that?" Nessa asked, frowning.

"I don't know," Glynnis replied grimly, rising to her feet. "But I intend to find out."

The Dragon sat with his back braced against one of the stone merlons at the pinnacle of Castle Weyrcraig. He couldn't remember the last time he'd watched the rising sun tip the waves with gold or felt a southerly breeze play across his brow. He turned his face to the sun, bathing in its grace.

Last night's storm had washed the world clean, leaving it smelling as fresh and pure as a newborn babe. He only wished his own sins could be washed away so easily.

Even with his eyes closed, he could still see Gwendolyn standing in the moonlight, her hair a tousled halo of gold and her cheeks flushed rose from the pleasure he had given her. It was as if one of the demigoddesses painted on the ceiling of the tower had tumbled to earth. But such gifts were not meant for the hands of mortal man.

Especially a man like him.

Remembering the wounded shame in Gwendolyn's eyes as she'd fled his arms, he lifted his hands to gaze at them. Even when they sought to give pleasure, they brought only pain.

A muffled footfall, followed by an awkward cough, warned him he was no longer alone. "When I went to check on Gwendolyn just now," Tupper said softly, "the panel was ajar. At first I thought . . ."

". . . that you'd find her in my bed," the Dragon finished, shooting his friend a wry look. "I hate to tarnish my reputation, but my powers of seduction aren't quite what they used to be."

"If that's true, then why didn't she run away?"

"Why don't you ask her?"

"I didn't wish to wake her. From the tearstains on her cheeks I deduced that she'd cried herself to sleep."

The Dragon's anger flared. "What's wrong, Tup? Bored with tormenting the villagers? Aren't they providing enough sport for you?"

"Actually," Tupper said, propping one booted foot on the stone embrasure between the merlons, "I'm finding their antics quite entertaining. Old Granny Hay took to her bed because she believed my piping was the wail of a banshee coming to claim her soul. One of the blacksmith's sons got into fisticuffs with one of the tinker's sons because they were both convinced the other's father was the one who betrayed the Mac-Cullough. And Ian Sloan nearly shot his wife when he awoke from a drunken stupor and mistook her for the Dragon." Tupper rolled his eyes. "Or so he claims."

"You're getting rather cozy with the good folk of Ballybliss, aren't you?" the Dragon remarked, studying his friend's face.

Tupper flushed. "How else am I to ferret out that thousand pounds?"

The Dragon turned back to the sea. There had been a moment last night when all of his grim plans had seemed to recede into the shadows before the tender sweetness of Gwendolyn's kiss. But that moment had been as elusive as the pleasure they'd shared. He had no future to offer her, only a past.

His eyes followed the path of a gull as it went wheeling down the rocky coast. "The ship is anchored in an inlet right beyond those cliffs, you know. Just waiting for my signal to come take us away from this place."

"Ah, but there's no r-rush, is there?" Tupper stammered. "After all, the villagers are just beginning to show signs of cracking. We mustn't be too hasty. Perhaps if we gave them another fortnight . . . ?"

The Dragon surged to his feet. "I don't have another fortnight to give them! I'm not even sure I have another night."

He paced the length of the parapet, raking his windswept hair from his brow. How could he explain to Tupper that the darkness that had sheltered him for so long was now his enemy? That he could no longer roam its shadows without fear? Fear that as soon as the gloom of dusk began to descend, he would betray his own will and make that long climb to the tower. Fear that he would no longer be content to lurk in the dark and watch Gwendolyn sleep, but would slip over to that bed and cover that delectable mouth and body of hers with his own.

He had not lied. He would never force her. But he could use all the sensual skills at his disposal to seduce her, which would make him even more of a monster than he already was.

He faced Tupper. "I'll give you one more night to scare some truth out of the villagers. If you have no luck, then we'll admit this has all been nothing but a miserable folly and we'll leave this accursed place on the morrow and never speak of it again. Agreed?"

Tupper's shoulders slumped. "Agreed." He was almost to the stairs when he turned and said softly, "You could tell her who you are, you know."

The Dragon spared his friend a pained smile. "If I knew, I just might do that."

*You could tell her who you are, you know.*

As Tupper traversed the moonlit meadow, his own words mocked him. He stumbled over a root, feeling every inch the bumbling oaf his father had always accused him of being.

*Stop slumping. Stand up straight. You're not half the man I was at your age.*

Perhaps his father had been right about him all along. After all, what sort of man would borrow another man's identity to impress a dewy-eyed young girl? He sighed, finding it only too easy to imagine the awe in Kitty's luminous eyes hardening to contempt when she discovered the truth—that he was nothing but a dull-witted sheep masquerading as a dashing wolf.

When cloaked in the shimmering scales of the Dragon, he could be eloquent and witty. He could whisk a bouquet of wildflowers out from behind his back and coax a blush into Kitty's creamy cheeks. He could lie next to her on a bed of sweetgrass and point out the constellations strewn like diamonds across the night sky, putting the classical education he'd obtained at Eton to good use for the first time in his life.

He could be the mysterious stranger he saw reflected in her eyes instead of a plain Englishman with thinning hair who blathered too much and blushed too easily.

As he leapt over a fast-running burn, his boot sank into the chill water, soaking it to the knee. Both of those men might very well be departing on the morrow, he thought glumly, and for that, he had no one to blame but himself. He had fooled himself into believing he could learn more about the villagers by wooing Kitty than by setting off smoke pots or letting out a savage roar whenever one of them strayed too far from his cottage in the dark of night.

If he was never going to see Kitty again after tonight, then why should he reveal his true identity? Why crush her romantic dreams? Why not leave her with her memories of the stolen moments they'd shared? At least then he could remain a hero in *someone's* heart.

Until Gwendolyn returned to the village after their ship sailed and told her sister what a fool he'd made of her.

Tupper stumbled to a halt and closed his eyes, knowing what he must do.

When he opened them, she was there, as ethereal as the wisps of mist rising from the dew-soaked grass. She wore the Dragon's cloak draped over her slender shoulders, just as she had done every night since their first meeting.

"Catriona," he said. "I'm so glad you came. There's something I must tell you."

She moved toward him, her shapely hips swaying. "I'm weary of you telling me things," she said thickly. "It's all you've done for the past week. Told me how bonny I am. Told me how my eyes sparkle like dewdrops on the heather. Told me how my lips were as ripe and pink as rose petals." Tupper stood paralyzed with anticipation as she cupped his cheeks in her hands and drew him down until those lips were only a breath away from his own. "Your friend was right. You do blather too much."

Tupper groaned as that succulent flower of a mouth budded beneath his, drawing him into a kiss as hot and irresistibly carnal as the weight of her small, firm breasts pressed against his chest. As every last droplet of blood in his body surged from his brain to his groin, he nearly let her drag him down to the sweet-smelling hummock of grass behind her. Nearly let himself accept the invitation she was so clearly offering.

It took more strength of will than he'd known he possessed to gently reach around and unfasten Kitty's slender arms from his neck. Struggling to catch his breath, he set her away from him. She would surely know he was a fraud now. The real Dragon would have never let himself get so flustered by a mere kiss.

A shock of dismay ran through him when he saw the tears glistening on her cheeks. "Nessa was right, wasn't she?" she cried. "You *can* resist my charms!"

Tupper reached for her, but she was backing away from him as if he had struck her. He stopped, fearful she would bolt altogether.

"Is that what you believe?" he asked, letting out a bark of disbelief. "That I haven't kissed you because I haven't wanted to?"

Kitty slowed her retreat, but skepticism still shimmered in her eyes. "Glynnis says you have an appetite only for virgins. That you'll never want a lass like me because I'm not—" She bit her bottom lip and shifted her gaze to the ground.

"Glynnis is right. That's exactly why I don't want to kiss you." Before her face could crumple, Tupper dared to draw nearer. "I don't want to kiss you because you deserve more than fumbling caresses and kisses stolen in the moonlight." He brushed a trembling teardrop from her cheek with his fingertips. "In truth, I would never do you such a grave dishonor unless I intended to make you my wife."

Tupper was nearly as surprised by his words as she was. He had never allowed himself to imagine returning to London with a little bit of Highland heaven to treasure for the rest of his life. He had never let himself dream that Kitty's lilting laughter or her graceful footsteps on the stairs might make his lonely town house a home.

A strange excitement buzzed along his nerves. Kitty was gazing up at him as if he'd dragged the luminous pearl of a moon down from the sky and slipped it onto her finger.

He threw back his shoulders and sucked in his stomach, unable to hold back a grin. "I suppose I'm trying to warn you, Catriona Wilder, that if you compromise my virtue with a kiss, you'll simply have to make an honest man of me."

Tupper had expected to see his own joy reflected on her face. But as she reached up to cup his cheek in her palm, a wistful sadness made her look older than her years. "You're already an honest man," she said. "A good man. A kind man. A decent man. Which is why I'm not worthy to be your wife."

Before he could fully absorb her words, she turned to go. The real Dragon might have been quick enough to catch her, but he was only Theodore Tuppingham, the plodding son of a minor viscount. He made a clumsy grab for her, but she had already melted into the mist, leaving him with nothing but an empty cloak that had never truly fit him.

 

Kitty ran through the forest, away from the sound of the Dragon calling her name. It had hurt to believe that he would not want her because she wasn't a virgin, but it was even more painful to learn that he wanted her anyway.

She dashed away her tears as she ran, dodging the slapping branches of alder and oak. Gwendolyn had tried to warn her, but she had refused to listen. After all, what did Gwendolyn know? She spent her days tending to the tiresome demands of their father while Nessa spent her nights accepting the flattery, the trinkets, and the rapt attentions of her many admirers.

What did it matter that those attentions seemed to wane as soon as they got what they wanted from her? There was always another lad just as eager for a saucy kiss or a quick cuddle behind the blacksmith's barn.

So Kitty had spent her innocence in a hasty, clumsy encounter that had been more painful than pleasurable, leaving her with nothing to bring to the bed of the man who wanted to make her his wife. The man she loved. A hoarse sob escaped her. She did love him—his plain face, his kind heart, his earnest brown eyes. And that was exactly why she couldn't marry him.

She stumbled to a halt, clinging to the weathered trunk of a birch. The Dragon's voice had faded, leaving her surrounded by the eerie creaks and croaks of the forest. A cool breeze chittered through the thin web of branches overhead. Kitty shivered. She'd been too blinded by tears to pay any heed to where she was running and now everything that should have been familiar to her seemed spooky and foreign.

A branch cracked in the darkness behind her. She spun around, her heart leaping into her throat. "Who goes there?"

The night whispered its secrets in a voice too low for her to hear, mocking her trepidation. She began to back toward the way she had come, hoping to retrace her path before the moon began its downward descent.

Before she could take three steps, a brawny arm snaked around her waist. A hand covered her mouth, stifling her startled yelp. She dug her fingernails into her assailant's hairy knuckles, shuddering at the suffocating heat of his breath in her ear.

"Sheathe yer claws, wee kitten, or I'll pull 'em out one by one!"

Only then did Kitty realize that it was Ross's meaty paw clapped over her mouth. Her eyes widened as Glynnis, Nessa, and Lachlan emerged from the darkness, their faces uncharacteristically somber.

Kitty lifted her foot and gave Ross's instep a vicious stomp. As he relaxed his grip, biting off a blistering oath, she scrambled out of his arms and whirled around to glare at him. "How dare you put your hands on me, you overgrown oaf?"

Ross took a threatening step toward her. "Ye'll let some beast paw ye, but ye're too good for the likes o' me?"

She expected Glynnis and Nessa to rush to her defense, but her sisters closed ranks around Ross with a reproachful look in their eyes.

"I don't know what you're talking about." Kitty looked from one to the other of them, seeking some sign that this was all a jest.

"We know what you've been doing," Nessa said.

"And who you've been doing it with," Glynnis added gently, the sorrow in her eyes more unsettling than all of Ross's blustering.

"All this time we thought the Dragon was some sort o' monster," Lachlan said. "But thanks to ye, lass, we now know he's just a man." A sneer touched his mouth, giving it a sinister cast. "A *mortal* man."

Kitty took an instinctive step backward. Her only thought was to flee—not to save herself, but to warn the Dragon.

"What are you going to do?" she whispered, hoping to buy them both some time.

In answer to her question, the forest came alive. Dark shapes came melting out of every tree, every bush, and every shadow just as the druids of old must have once done. But instead of bearing sacred stones and healing herbs, the villagers of Ballybliss were armed with crude cudgels, muskets, ropes, unlit torches, and all the daggers and claymores that had been buried in their backyards and hidden in their cellars since the

English had outlawed them. Some of them were still stained with the ancient blood of Clan MacCullough's enemies. Even old Granny Hay clutched a pitchfork in her withered hand, its jagged tines gleaming sharp and deadly in the moonlight.

As Kitty backed right into Ailbert's bony chest, Ross grabbed her by the elbow. "What does it look like we're goin' to do, lass? We're goin' to hunt us a dragon!"

# Chapter Sixteen

GWENDOLYN STOOD ON THE TABLE in the tower, clutching the cold iron bars of the grate as she watched the shadows rob the day of the last of its light. There was no longer any need for her to gaze longingly at the sea, dreaming of freedom. She had been granted that gift, only to discover that it wasn't what she wanted at all. Perhaps it never had been.

She climbed down from the table and began to pace the tower. Toby was stretched out on the bed pillows like some overfed sultan waiting for the dancing of the harem girls to begin. As he swiveled his head to follow her path, it was only too easy to imagine a hint of contempt in his arrogant golden gaze.

She had accused the Dragon of being a coward at their very first meeting, yet she'd spent the day huddled in this cell of her own making, ignoring the open panel. She could no longer even say exactly what she was afraid of. Him? Or herself?

He might cloak himself in shadows, but she had

spent the last fifteen years hiding behind a wall built with her own hands. The mortar binding its stones had been duty, pride, and virtue. She'd worn her duty to her father as a penitent wears his beloved hair shirt and taken as much pride in being plain and virtuous as her sisters did in being bonny. Even her hopeless yearning for a boy long dead had served only to protect her heart from the risks of living . . . and loving.

She picked up a copy of Manderly's *The Triumph of Rational Thinking* and riffled through its pages. The neat print with its tidy explanations and rationally drawn conclusions seemed to be no more than gibberish to her aching eyes. For once, logic had failed her, leaving her in the grip of an emotion that defied all reason.

She let the book slip from her fingers as she remembered her last sight of the Dragon. He had stood there on the brink of the shadows, a lonely ghost of a man, yet with more substance than anyone she had ever known.

*How could I have let you do any of those things when I've never even seen your face? When I don't even know your name?*

*That may be true, but for just a moment there, I would have sworn you knew my heart.*

She squeezed her eyes shut, wondering if he had been right. She might not know his name or his face, but she felt as if she knew his soul—his kindness, his tenderness, the generosity of spirit he sought to hide beneath his gruff exterior and mocking detachment.

Perhaps it was that glimpse of the man behind the mask that had frightened her so badly, driven her to say the words that would wound his pride and force him to set her free.

But she would never be free as long as her heart was still his prisoner.

Gwendolyn slowly turned to face the panel. She could slip into her nightdress, extinguish the candles, and climb into that inviting bed, but she knew instinctively that the Dragon would not come to her as he had done in the past.

If she wanted to set herself free, she would have to go to him.

Vaporous tongues of mist crept out of the glens and hollows, swirling like dragon's breath around the parapets of Castle Weyrcraig. The sea pounded at the cliffs below, roaring with mindless fury. The full moon cast an icy glow over the castle, chilling everything it touched and deepening the illusion that the ancient stones had been frozen in time.

Gwendolyn moved through the shadowy passages, refusing to be mired in the past for another moment. She was no longer a girl in search of a boy, but a woman in search of a man. A man woven not of myth and moonlight, but flesh and blood.

She cupped a hand around her candle flame to shield it from a violent gust of wind, not sparing so much as a glance at the gaping wound in the north wall of the stairwell or its shocking plummet into the sea. She sidestepped the fallen blocks of stone as if they were no more than a handful of pebbles scattered in her path.

The moonbeams streaming through the splintered remains of the entranceway door proved no enticement to Gwendolyn. She turned her back on them to scan the shadows, wondering just where a dragon might hide if he didn't wish to be found.

The great hall had been deserted by all but its ghosts. The crystal decanter still rested upon the table, the thimbleful of whisky in its bottom undisturbed.

Gwendolyn searched room after room—her haste growing along with her impatience—before finding her way to a dusty chapel. Except for a round window of stained glass set high in the nave above the altar, little of the sanctuary had survived the unholy wrath of Cumberland's cannons.

Picking her way around the splintered pews, Gwendolyn fought despair. What if the Dragon had gone? What if he'd slipped away to catch the ship she'd seen anchored offshore only a few nights ago?

"Please," she whispered, gazing up at the luminous circle of jewel-toned light.

Her eyes fluttered shut as a bone-deep conviction warmed her. If he was gone, she would feel it. He was still here within these walls. Somewhere.

She opened her eyes and hastened out of the chapel, her steps carrying her to the ramshackle structure that had once served as the castle's gatehouse. A faint reddish glow emanated from the dank stone stairwell in the corner, confirming what she should have already guessed.

The Dragon had gone to ground.

She waved the candlestick before her, making the shadows dance, but could see no end to the stairs. They looked as if they might wind all the way down into the heart of hell itself.

Gwendolyn lowered the candle, drawing in a shaky breath. It would be risky to beard the beast in his lair, but she had little choice. She wasn't sure how he'd react to being cornered, but if he lashed out at her, she only prayed her heart would be strong enough to survive the blow.

She began her descent, gathering the pleated taffeta skirts of the sky blue sacque gown close to keep them from brushing the glistening, lichen-furred walls. It was easy to believe that the narrow tunnel of stairs might open into the heart of a towering cavern. That she would find the Dragon curled up on a glittering nest of gold, diamonds, emeralds, and rubies. That he would lift his massive head, his iridescent scales shimmering in the mist, and breathe forth a blast of fire that would consume her to the bone.

Gwendolyn paused, forcing herself to shake off the fancy. If the Dragon had proved one thing last night, it was that he was no monster.

As she reached the foot of the stairs, the reddish glow deepened, beckoning her through an arched passageway that led to a stone antechamber. It was there that she finally found the Dragon, napping not on a nest of hidden treasure, but on a tousled heap of blankets and bolsters.

A rush of tenderness caught Gwendolyn unawares. The Dragon lay on his back, one arm outflung, his fingers curled into a loose fist. His face was turned away from the dying embers on the hearth. Although their faint glow did little to take the edge off the clammy chill of the chamber, he had kicked away the blanket that was supposed to be covering him, revealing one long, lean thigh encased in a pair of doeskin knee breeches and one stockinged foot. His shirt was open to the waist, exposing the gilded planes of a chest lightly furred with crisp, dark hair.

A drop of hot wax spattered on Gwendolyn's fingers. Her mouth went dry as she realized she held the power to expose his true nature within her trembling hands.

She hesitated. It seemed wrong somehow to spy on him when he was as defenseless as a child. But he'd suffered no similar qualms of conscience, she reminded herself sternly, when sneaking into her chamber to watch her sleep.

She slipped to her knees beside him and held the candlestick aloft.

His hand shot out, seizing her wrist. In a moment, he had sent the candlestick flying against the wall and switched positions with her. Gwendolyn gasped. It was one thing to be on her feet in his arms, but quite another to be on her back beneath him, the softness of her breasts colliding with the unyielding wall of his chest.

"Did you misplace something, Miss Wilder? Your common sense, perhaps?"

So she was to be Miss Wilder again, was she? Remembering how he had murmured her name against her mouth as if it were a sacred incantation, Gwendolyn felt a pang of loss.

"The only thing I've misplaced, M'lord Dragon, is my candle."

"Which is a blessed mercy, since you were about to set my hair afire with it."

"I suppose that now you're going to point out that I should be thanking you for not cutting my throat."

"Don't thank me yet. The night is still young."

Gwendolyn swallowed, transfixed by the predatory gleam of his eyes and the raw heat of his big, masculine body above hers. There was no hint of whisky on his breath, confirming her suspicion that he was more dangerous sober than drunk.

He rolled off her and dragged her to her feet.

"You're a most vexatious creature," he said, his purposeful strides carrying him to the hearth, where he used the iron poker to scatter all but a few stubborn embers. "When you're supposed to stay put, you try to escape. When you're supposed to escape, you stay put."

"Is that what you want? For me to go?"

He swung around to face her, the feeble glow of the embers casting him in silhouette. "What I want is of little consequence. You made that quite clear last night."

Even through the warmth permeating her body,

Gwendolyn could feel her cheeks heat. She was only too aware that she had tasted the pleasure he had apparently been denied.

"You should blush more often, Miss Wilder," he added softly. "It becomes you."

She touched a hand to her cheek. "How did you . . . ?"

"It's a well-known fact that dragons can see in the dark."

If he could see her blush, she thought, then he could see the care she'd taken with her appearance. He could see how she'd brushed her hair until it cascaded in shimmering waves down her back. He could see how she'd chosen the gown that would most flatter her curves. He could see how hard she had striven to see herself through his eyes.

"I suspected as much," she said wryly. "The shadows never did seem to afford me much protection where you were concerned."

"Is that what you felt you needed? Protection? From me?"

"More than you know." Yet even as she confessed her weakness, Gwendolyn drew nearer to him.

The wary gleam in his eyes deepened at her approach. "If you've come to bid me farewell before you hie back to that charming village of yours, I can spare you the trouble. I'll be leaving myself on the morrow."

Gwendolyn's heart lurched. "Without the thousand pounds you came for?"

"I've come to suspect that the cost of finding the gold may be more than it's worth."

"And just when did you make this discovery?"

She expected him to make light of her question, but when he finally replied, it was without a trace of humor. "Last night. When you tore yourself from my arms as if I were the vilest of beasts."

Gwendolyn shook her head. "We were both wrong last night, M'lord Dragon. It's not a maiden's kiss that has the power to change a beast into a man or a girl into a woman. As sweet as a kiss can be, there's something much more powerful."

"Don't!" he exclaimed harshly. "As much as I want you in my bed, I'll not have you compromise your precious virtue on my behalf."

"Is that why you think I came here tonight? To offer myself to you?" She took another step toward him.

"I must warn you that should you be so foolish, I don't know if I'll have the strength to refuse you. But I will have the strength to leave you on the morrow." He stretched out his hand as if it might have the power to stay her should his words fail to do so.

Gwendolyn caught that hand in her own. "I've come to offer you something more powerful than a kiss and more lasting than a touch." She pressed his palm to her breast, knowing he would feel the shudder of her heart beneath. "My love."

The Dragon couldn't have bolted in that moment had Gwendolyn flashed a torch in his face. With those two words, she had compromised something far more precious than her virtue, a treasure she had guarded her entire life—her pride.

"Don't be a bloody fool! How could you love a man whose name you don't know? A man whose face you've never seen?"

"I don't know," she confessed, bringing his hand to her lips. "But I do know that if you leave here on the morrow, you'll take my heart with you wherever you go."

As Gwendolyn's lips flowered against his knuckles, the Dragon groaned. He could almost feel the rugged scales that had armored his heart for so long cracking and falling away. He could not stop himself from breathing in the fragrance of her hair, weaving his fingers through its incandescent softness, lowering his mouth to hers.

He had once been fool enough to wonder who possessed the greater power—the Dragon or the maiden. But as Gwendolyn's lips parted beneath his own, entreating him to love her in return, his legs buckled, bringing him to his knees.

He wasn't even startled by the rumble of thunder in the distance. At least he thought it was thunder—his ears were roaring so loudly that it could have been thunder or cannon fire or simply the pounding of his heart as he surrendered it into Gwendolyn's hands.

"Kill the Dragon! Kill the Dragon!" The muffled chant sent a quiver of alarm through Gwendolyn's body.

"What in the bloody hell . . . ?" The Dragon cocked his head to listen. The chant was growing louder by the moment.

*Kill the Dragon!*
*Kill the Dragon!*
*We'll take his head.*
*Then he'll be dead.*
*And he'll trouble us no more!*

The Dragon swore beneath his breath, rose to his feet, then cupped Gwendolyn's face in his hands and pressed a fierce kiss to her lips. "Forgive me for interrupting our little interlude, my love, but I do believe we're about to receive some uninvited callers."

Before she could catch her breath, he grabbed her hand and went running up the stairs, dragging her along behind him.

# Chapter Seventeen

THE DRAGON HAD CALLED HER his love.

Gwendolyn stumbled along behind him, torn between terror and exhilaration. Even as her damnable common sense warned her that his words might have been nothing more than a mocking endearment, her heart sang with joy.

Which was why it was such a pity that they were going to die.

By the time they emerged from the dungeon stairwell into the gatehouse, the steady chant of the approaching mob had already disintegrated into shouts and howls. The Dragon pressed his back to the wall and wrapped one arm around her waist, dragging her against him.

"They haven't yet reached the castle," he murmured. "If we can make it to the battlements before they storm the courtyard, I can signal my ship to come retrieve us."

There was no need for explanation. As he brushed

his lips against her temple and gave her hand a heartening squeeze, Gwendolyn knew she would have followed him into hell itself. Hand in hand, they ran through the gatehouse, past the chapel, across the main entranceway of the castle. Although moonlight streamed through the splintered door, there was no time to steal a glimpse of his face, no time to do anything but run and try to choke air into her starving lungs. As they raced up the steps, a gray streak bolted past them. It took Gwendolyn a startled moment to realize it was Toby, moving at a clip much faster than his usual languid swagger.

They followed the length of the gallery until they reached a winding stone staircase identical to the one that led to Gwendolyn's tower. Even though he was now the prey instead of the predator, the Dragon seemed to anticipate every turn, every shattered block of stone, every gaping crack in the mortar that might have slowed their steps. They shot around the corner of the first landing, stumbling to a halt when they nearly ran head-on into Tupper.

His hair was disheveled and his black silk shirt torn in a dozen places. He wore only one boot and blood streamed from a shallow gash on his temple. "I was able to elude the villagers just long enough to signal the ship from the battlements!" he cried, doubling over to catch his breath. "The men should be sending the longboats even as we speak."

Recognizing that he was near exhaustion and hysteria,

Gwendolyn tore a strip of lace from her cuff and dabbed at his wound. "I don't understand, Tupper. How did this happen?"

The Dragon swept a narrow look over his friend. "Aye, Tupper. Perhaps you'd better explain to Miss Wilder how this happened." He stole a glance at the window, then at Gwendolyn. Although his face was still in shadow, the light of the torches bobbing their way up the cliff path was rapidly growing brighter. "And quickly."

"All my fault," Tupper gasped, straightening. "They followed Kitty when she came to meet me and—"

"Kitty?" Gwendolyn repeated. He winced in pain as she dropped the makeshift bandage and seized his elbow. "*My* Kitty?"

Tupper shook his head. "*My* Kitty. Or at least I had hoped she'd be mine, which is why I asked her to—"

"I don't give a damn whose bloody cat it was." The Dragon jabbed a finger at the window. "I just want to know why an angry mob is out there howling for my head."

Tupper shot him a sheepish glance. "It's not *your* head they want. It's mine. They think *I'm* the Dragon."

The Dragon's voice grew deadly quiet. "And pray tell me, Mr. Tuppingham, just how did they come to that particular conclusion?"

Tupper's cherubic countenance was at its most innocent. "I really wouldn't know. But they've been tracking me for hours. Hunting me like a fox. I would have been done for if I hadn't accidentally tumbled down a hill onto a ledge that was out of their reach. I believe that's when they decided to march upon the castle."

The Dragon slipped to the side of the window, still taking care to keep his face in shadow. The villagers were clearly visible now. Gwendolyn shivered as the air resounded with a Highland battle cry that hadn't been heard in that glen for over fifteen years.

The Dragon's voice was low and bitter. "If the bastards had been that zealous in defense of their chieftain, he might still be alive today."

Tupper tugged at his sleeve. "There's no time to dally. We must make haste. If we can make it to the caves before the mob rushes the castle, we might still be able to escape with our heads."

The Dragon swung around and clapped a hand on his friend's shoulder. "Good thinking, man. Let's go."

He reclaimed Gwendolyn's hand, but it took him several steps before he realized her feet weren't moving. He tugged at her hand. "Come, Gwendolyn. You heard Tupper. We have to make haste."

"I'm not going," she said softly.

"What do you mean you're not going? Of course you're going." His hands closed over her shoulders. "You must be mad if you think I'd leave you at the mercy of that bloodthirsty pack of wolves! They almost murdered you once before. I won't give them another chance."

Gwendolyn flattened her palms against his chest, her mind racing. "It's not me they've come for this time.

It's the Dragon. They think I'm dead. Perhaps the shock of finding me alive and well will buy you and Tupper the time you need to get to the longboat. I can even stall them while you're rowing out to the ship."

"I'll not leave you, damn it," he said grimly.

"You don't have any choice. If they find us here together, my life will be of no more value to them than yours." She gave his chest a violent shove. "Now, go, damn you! Before you get us all killed!"

The Dragon glanced out the window, then over his shoulder at Tupper, who stood on the third stair below him with head bowed, refusing to sway him with a look or a word. The light of the torches was growing brighter with each passing moment. If he lingered much longer, his masquerade would have all been for nothing.

Even before he cupped her face in his hands and ran his thumbs along her cheekbones as if he could brand their memory on his fingertips, Gwendolyn knew he was leaving her.

"I'll be back for you," he said fiercely. "I swear it on my life."

She touched his face, smiling through the tears that threatened to spill from her eyes. "You once told me that I made you wish you were a man of your word. Well, now you've gone and made me wish you were, too."

Before he could swear another oath he might not be able to keep, Gwendolyn tangled her hands in the rugged silk of his hair and dragged his mouth down to hers. It was a kiss like no other they had shared, a hot and salty-sweet communion forged from promises and regrets, broken dreams and unfulfilled desires.

They heard the crash of what was left of the courtyard gates being toppled from their moorings, followed by an alarmed cry from Tupper.

"Go!" Gwendolyn shouted, shoving the Dragon toward the stairs. "Before it's too late!"

Casting one last look at her, he plunged into the darkness of the stairwell, moving fast on Tupper's heels.

As the echo of their footsteps faded, Gwendolyn smoothed her hair, possessed by a strange calm. She knew that both the castle and her dreams might very well come crashing into flames all around her, but none of that mattered as long as she had a Dragon to defend.

As Gwendolyn materialized on the top step of the three broad flagstone stairs that descended into the courtyard of Castle Weyrcraig, the villagers fell back in amazement.

Gwendolyn believed they were simply surprised to discover her alive and uneaten. She had no idea what a vision she presented, with the color still high in her cheeks from the Dragon's kiss and her generous curves no longer shrouded in scratchy wool, but hugged by sleek taffeta in a hue that perfectly matched the blazing blue of her eyes. Her unbound hair tumbled down her back, its gilded waves catching sparks of fire and ice from the flickering torches and the frosty moonlight.

She stood there, her head no longer bowed, but held straight and high.

"Gwennie!" Kitty was the first to break the silence as she fought to tear herself from Niall's ruthless grip. "The Dragon told me you were alive! They tried to convince me I was a silly little fool to believe him, but I knew he would never lie to me."

Gwendolyn blinked in confusion before realizing that Kitty couldn't have been talking about *her* Dragon. Tupper's sheepish confession was suddenly beginning to make sense.

Nessa and Glynnis were gaping at her as if they'd never laid eyes on her before. Gwendolyn searched the crowd for Izzy, hoping to find at least one ally, but saw no sign of her. The loyal maidservant must have remained at the side of Gwendolyn's papa.

Ailbert separated himself from the crowd, flanked by his burly sons. "Step aside, lass. We've no quarrel with ye."

"Then it may surprise you to learn that I've a quarrel with you. After all, you were the ones who left me here to die in this very courtyard a little over a fortnight ago."

"Ye seem to have done all right for yerself," Ross snarled.

As his gaze lingered on the swell of her breasts spilling over the square-cut bodice of her gown, Gwendolyn suddenly recognized the contempt in his eyes for what it had always been—lust. All the times he'd tripped her, pinched her, called her cruel names, he'd simply been trying to punish her for making him want her.

"I suppose I've done better than you, Ross," she said gently. "Since I've never felt so small inside that I had to belittle others just to make myself feel bigger."

There were several gasps. Ross took a threatening step toward her, only to find himself restrained by his younger brother.

Lachlan tossed his dark hair out of his eyes, keeping one muscular arm wrapped around Ross. "Surely ye can't mean to defend this Dragon fellow!" he cried. "Why, he's been helpin' hisself to all the lasses in the village. Like young Kitty over there and God only knows how many others!"

"He wanted to make me his wife," Kitty wailed.

Nessa snorted. "If I had a shilling for every time I've heard that . . ."

"You probably do have a shilling for every time you've heard that," Glynnis retorted, sending an uneasy ripple of laughter through the townfolk.

Ailbert's gaze was no longer stern, but imploring. "Ye've always been a good girl, Gwendolyn Wilder. A sensible lass." At the sound of those familiar words on his lips, Gwendolyn felt a muscle in her jaw begin to twitch. "Surely ye must see that this scoundrel has made fools of us all, includin' ye. He's lied, stolen, and cheated us out of all the things that were rightfully ours."

"He had his reasons," she said, wishing she knew what they were.

"P'r'aps he did," Ailbert conceded. "Just as we've got our reasons for comin' here tonight. We've come for the Dragon's head, and it's his head we'll have. Now step aside, woman, before I'm forced to do somethin' we'll both regret."

Gwendolyn did not know whether she'd bought Tupper and the Dragon enough time to make it to the longboat, but her own time was running out. When Ailbert started forward, expecting her to stand aside and let him pass, she darted down the steps and grabbed the pitchfork out of Granny Hay's hands. Ignoring the old woman's startled cry, she jabbed the pitchfork at Ailbert's chest, forcing him to dance a merry jig to keep from being impaled on its tines.

"Damn ye, lass," he whined, retreating into the arms of the villagers. "Have ye well and truly lost yer mind?"

"I'd wager it's not her mind she's lost, but her soul." Ross's words sent a ripple of fear through the crowd. "Just look at her! Is that the same sweet Gwendolyn Wilder we all grew up with?"

As a hush fell over the villagers, Gwendolyn remembered that Ross had never been smart, but he'd always been cunning.

He swaggered forward, taking care to keep just out of reach of the pitchfork. "Why, the Gwendolyn we knew was fat and plain! She kept her head down and her nose buried in a book. She would've been perfectly content to spend the rest of her miserable life lookin' after that daft father of hers."

"My father is a hero!" Gwendolyn cried. "His sanity

was the price he had to pay for your father's cowardice and the cowardice of every man in Ballybliss!"

Ailbert blanched, but made no effort to defend himself.

Ross's sneer only deepened. "And what was the price you had to pay to win the Dragon's favor? Your virtue? Your mortal soul?" He swung around, appealing to his fellow villagers. "Just look at her—with her hair unbound and her breasts spillin' out of her dress as bold as any harlot's. She dares to defy us only because she knows the Dragon has given her the power to inflame the lust of every man here." Ross lowered his voice, forcing the villagers to strain to hear him. And strain they did, their eyes devouring Gwendolyn as they considered his words. "As she herself pointed out, she's been alone with the beast for o'er a fortnight. Why, there's no tellin' what ungodly acts he's taught her to perform."

Lachlan swallowed hard, his oversized Adam's apple bobbing from the effort. Even the stoic Ailbert had to draw a kerchief from his pocket and mop his brow, drawing a glare from his wife.

"The Dragon is no beast!" Gwendolyn shouted, hating Ross for making something so sordid of the tender encounters she and the Dragon had shared. "Why, he's twice the man you'll ever hope to be!"

"See!" Ross exclaimed. "It's exactly as I feared. The monster has bewitched her!"

"How could he have bewitched her," Kitty cried, "when you yourself admitted that he was only a mortal?"

Unexpected tears stung Gwendolyn's eyes. If she lived long enough, she was going to give her baby sister a great big hug.

Ross shrugged. "I could have been wrong about that, you know."

"Or perhaps *you* were bewitched," Gwendolyn suggested, inciting a wave of nervous laughter.

The laughter quickly died beneath Ross's sweeping glare. "I say we burn the lass."

"Aye, burn her!" his mother echoed, shooting Ailbert a triumphant look.

The crowd took up the cry, their shouts sending an icy chill through Gwendolyn. The stake they'd tied her to the night they'd left her at the Dragon's mercy was still rammed between the cobblestones in the center of the courtyard. It would be easy enough for them to bind her to it, pile some debris around her feet, and set it alight with their torches.

Gwendolyn backed up one step, then another, waving the pitchfork in a broad arc. If they rushed her, she was done for.

"The Dragon didn't bewitch me!" she cried, fighting to be heard over the rising din. "He's not a monster! He's a man! A kind and noble man!"

The villagers began to surge toward the steps, torchlight glinting off the blades of their weapons. Glynnis and Nessa hung back helplessly. Kitty finally succeeded in freeing herself from Niall only to be swallowed by the mob as she tried to reach her sister's side.

As Gwendolyn reached the top of the stairs, she

looked up into the moonlit sky. There was no echo of a roar to be heard, no winged shadow darting its way to her rescue. If she hadn't been so foolish as to believe in something as impossible as a Dragon, she wouldn't be standing here on these steps, waiting to be taken by the mob. But she didn't regret any of it, not a single kiss or touch.

As Ross moved in, flanked by his father and brother, Gwendolyn backed into the shadows of the doorway.

A strong arm circled her waist from behind, enveloping her in a warm cocoon. Gwendolyn breathed in a fragrant rush of sandalwood and spice, and exultation surged through her veins.

The Dragon had come back for her. Just as he had promised.

As he stepped forward, bringing them both into the light, the villagers fell back, gasping with shock. Gwendolyn could hardly blame them. The gleaming pistol in the Dragon's hand made all of their rusty swords and ancient daggers look like nothing more than the toys of petulant children playing at soldier.

When he spoke, it wasn't in a clipped English accent, stripped of emotion, but in a lilting burr, rolling with passion. "You'd best leave this courtyard now if you wish to leave it alive, for there'll be no beheading of dragons or burning of witches as long as a MacCullough is laird and master of Castle Weyrcraig."

# Part II

✦ ✦ ✦

How sweet I roam'd from field to
    field,
And tasted all the summer's pride,
Till I the prince of love beheld,
Who in the sunny beams did glide!

—WILLIAM BLAKE

# Chapter Eighteen

GWENDOLYN FROZE in the Dragon's arms, trying to absorb the shock of hearing a voice she'd thought never to hear again. Too many late nights and too many cheroots might have deepened its timbre to a stranger's smoky baritone, but its inflections were as familiar to her as the beating of her own heart.

Ross had paled as if he'd seen a ghost, but there was nothing spectral about the muscular arm wrapped around Gwendolyn's waist.

The hours seemed to swirl backward, returning her to that elusive flicker of time when she had first stood in this very courtyard only a fortnight ago. The Dragon had emerged from his hiding place, his cloak billowing about his broad shoulders, smoke streaming from his nostrils. Gwendolyn had watched, unable to look away, as his face—that beautiful, terrible, impossible face—had melted out of the shadows.

It was a memory her logical mind had refused to trust. A memory denied her until this very moment.

Gwendolyn slowly turned in his arms.

Instantly she saw how foolish she'd been to mistake Bernard MacCullough for a mere mortal. Despite the spark of devilment that lit his emerald green eyes, his face possessed the rugged purity of an archangel's. His strong brow was softened by a disheveled tumble of dark hair carelessly bound at the nape in a black velvet queue. His uncompromising jaw was compromised by the rueful humor of a mouth sculpted not for piety, but for pagan pleasures certain to tempt even the most virtuous of women.

His face bore no birthmark, no scar, no hideous deformity to mar its compelling planes, yet sun, wind, and dissipation had left their mark upon the boy he had been. Unable to stop herself, Gwendolyn touched her fingertips to the lines that furrowed his brow, the crinkles that fanned out from the corners of his eyes, the harsh grooves carved around his mouth. Instead of diminishing him, those hints of vulnerability only made him more beguiling.

She jerked her hand back, feeling betrayed to the very depths of her soul to discover that her beloved Dragon was no beast, but a beauty. She had always fancied herself smart, but he'd played her for an utter fool.

Unable to bear looking at him, yet unable to tear her gaze away, she began to back out of his arms.

He was no longer the slender boy she remembered. He was lean of hip, but taller and broader than she had ever envisioned him becoming. Although he was still bootless, and his shirt was hanging open over the impressive expanse of his chest, his dishevelment only seemed to emphasize the power coiled in his taut muscles. The loaded pistol fit into the cradle of his hand as naturally as if he'd been born to wield it.

As she continued to back away from him, seeking to escape the inescapable, he caught her wrist with his free hand, wary now not of the mob, but of her. His eyes darkened as they searched her face. "I couldn't leave you," he said, his voice low and urgent. "I had to come back."

It was almost more than Gwendolyn could stand, hearing the Dragon's voice emerge from that treacherous mouth of his. "At least I didn't have to wait fifteen years this time."

As she tried to twist away, Bernard yanked her against him, betraying a flash of temper. He spoke through clenched teeth, keeping one eye on the gawking villagers. "I'm deeply sorry if my being alive offends you, Miss Wilder, but we've more important matters to attend to at the moment. Such as saving our hides."

"And just what if I'm no longer sure yours is worth saving? What are you going to do then?" She glanced at the pistol in his hand. "Shoot me?"

She almost wished he would. She hadn't felt so humiliated since she'd tumbled out of that oak tree to land on his chest. She was beginning to wish she'd smashed him flat, sparing her the agony of falling in love with him, not once, but twice.

Before he could reply, Tupper came stumbling out of

the castle, rubbing his jaw. "Criminy, man, you didn't have to ambush me. If you'd have just asked nicely, I wouldn't have tried to stop you from jumping out of the longboat."

Gwendolyn looked down. Bernard's stockings and the lower half of his knee breeches were soaked with seawater and clinging to the already sinfully defined muscles of his calves and thighs.

"Dragon!" Every head in the courtyard jerked around as a lithe, dark-haired beauty came flying up the stairs to throw her arms around Tupper's neck.

"Kitty!" Although a blush stained Tupper's fair cheeks, he returned her embrace with touching fervency.

"Would that be your Kitty or his?" Bernard murmured in Gwendolyn's ear.

"I'm not sure anymore," Gwendolyn said stiffly, watching Tupper nuzzle Kitty's hair.

"How can that fellow be the Dragon?" Granny Hay jabbed a finger at Bernard. "I thought *he* was the Dragon."

"Don't be a fool," Auld Tavis croaked, shuffling to the foot of the steps. "Anyone can see that he's the MacCullough hisself returned from the grave to heap vengeance upon all our heads."

At the old man's dour pronouncement, several of the villagers sketched hasty crosses on their breasts while others began to retreat toward the courtyard gates. Until that moment, Gwendolyn had failed to fully comprehend why the villagers had been so taken aback by the Dragon's appearance. She, too, was shaken to realize that he had grown into the very image of his father.

"Ye're the fool, auld man!" Ailbert shoved Tavis back into the crowd. "Ye were with the rest of us when we climbed this very hill the mornin' after Cumberland's attack. The MacCullough was barely clingin' to life even then."

Gwendolyn stole a look at Bernard's face. Its rugged planes had been wiped clean of all expression. The effect was chilling.

"The MacCullough couldn't be alive." Ailbert wheeled on the villagers, the passion in his voice mounting as if he sought to convince not only them, but himself. "We saw him draw his last breath! Heard him utter his last words!"

"May the dragon's wings spell yer doom." Bernard's rich voice poured over the villagers, mesmerizing them where they stood.

*And his fiery breath seal yer tomb.*
*May vengeance be upon yer heads*
*'Til innocent blood be shed.*

He finished his recitation with an indifferent shrug of his broad shoulders. "Although my father always thought of himself as more of a scholar than a poet, it wasn't a bad effort." His glittering gaze swept the courtyard. "Especially when you consider that his life's blood was seeping from his heart at the time he composed it."

"Not the father, but the son," Granny Hay breathed, clutching at the tarnished crucifix she hid beneath her shift.

"But we found yer body, too, lad," Ailbert whispered. "All burned up in the corner o' the great hall. I wrapped it in a shroud myself, draped it o'er the back o' yer pony. . . . How . . . ?"

"Yes, how?" Gwendolyn demanded fiercely.

Bernard shot her a loaded glance before stepping forward.

"I suspect the body you found was one of Cumberland's scouts, mistakenly killed by the blast. By the time you discovered it, I was long gone. Taken prisoner by the English."

With those five simple words, Bernard described a fate beyond any of their imaginings. Gwendolyn tried not to envision what that innocent, bright-eyed boy must have endured at the hands of his father's enemies.

"It's a miracle!" Shoving aside anyone unfortunate enough to be in her path, Ailbert's wife came barreling up the steps. Throwing herself on her knees at Bernard's feet, she snatched up his hand and began to press adoring kisses on the back of it. "At long last, God has rewarded us for our patience! Our laird has come back to us!"

As Bernard retrieved his hand and wiped it on his breeches, she backed away, all but genuflecting. Although her performance set off a chain of agitated murmurs and halfhearted cheers, most of the villagers still looked more petrified than pleased. Except, Gwendolyn noted with a cynical snort, her older sisters. Glynnis's eyes held the unmistakable glint of avarice while Nessa was eyeing Bernard as if he were the most succulent of beef briskets and she'd had nothing but potatoes to warm her belly for a very long time.

"He's lying!" Ross stepped in front of his mother, his broad face ruddy with emotion. "Everyone knows the English took no prisoners. Not at Culloden and not here! He's an imposter, aye, that's what he is!" He gave Gwendolyn a contemptuous look. "And that whore over there is in league with him."

One minute Ross was sneering up at her; the next he was plastered against the courtyard wall, the mouth of Bernard's pistol jammed into the soft flesh beneath his jaw. Bernard's voice was low, but clearly audible to every soul in the courtyard. "It astonishes me that in fifteen years you still haven't learned how to address a lady. How many times do I have to warn you that I never forget an injustice done to one of my own?"

Ross's eyes widened as he gazed up into the implacable face of the man who had been born to have absolute dominion over his fate. "I never meant . . . I'm turribly sorry, sir. . . . F-f-forgive me . . . m-m'laird," he stammered much as he had on that summer day so long ago.

It shook Gwendolyn to realize that Bernard must remember that day as keenly as she did. But why shouldn't he? It had been his last day of freedom. The last day he had roamed these Highland hills as master of his own destiny.

A dagger of grief twisted in Gwendolyn's heart. As long as he had been a man without a past, she had been able to believe that they could share a future. But now that was impossible. The castle might have been spared the wrath of the mob's torches, but her precious Dragon had died a fiery death, burned to ashes along with the rest of her dreams.

Ignoring Tupper's and Kitty's quizzical stares, she slipped down the steps and tapped Bernard on the shoulder. He slowly turned, allowing an ashen-faced Ross to scramble away.

Gwendolyn was caught off guard by the way he towered over her. She forced herself to meet his wary gaze, although she was more than a little afraid of catching a disarming glimpse of the boy she had once adored.

"There's no need for you to defend me, *m'laird*," she said. "I'm not yours and I never will be."

Leaving the echo of her voice hanging in the stunned silence, Gwendolyn shoved her way through the crowd and out the gate, seeking to get as far away from him as her determined strides could carry her.

Gwendolyn sat on a rock, watching the tide come in. The waves were more subdued here, whispering instead of roaring. The chill spray misted her skin, but she was too numb to care. She wasn't even sure how she had ended up on this lonely stretch of beach. As soon as she had left the courtyard, she had broken into a run, only to realize that she had nowhere to run to. The village was as foreign to her as the castle had once been. She didn't seem to belong anywhere anymore.

So she had veered away from the main road and followed a winding footpath around the castle and down the cliff. Once she'd reached the rocky strip of sand, she had walked for a long time, trying to escape the shadow of the castle.

It was no longer a dragon's lair, but simply a crumbling ruin. Soon the gray light of dawn would creep over its burned-out chambers and shattered towers, ruthlessly exposing their ugliness. The night would be over, giving Gwendolyn no choice but to awaken from the beautiful dream she'd been living for the past fortnight.

She was gazing up at the cold and uncaring moon when she heard a soft footfall behind her. "You still haven't learned how to properly thank someone for rescuing you, have you?"

Gwendolyn rose and slowly turned to find Bernard MacCullough standing barefoot in the sand a few feet away. The wind tugged at his shirt and ruffled his dark hair.

"I'm surprised you didn't just let the villagers burn me," she replied. "Then you'd have been spared all of this awkwardness."

"I would have never left you at their mercy in the

first place, but I didn't want you to find out this way. When I began to fear that they might actually do you more harm than I could, I came back for you."

"So you returned from the dead just for me? I suppose I should be flattered. When were you planning on telling me who you really were?" Heat rose unbidden to her cheeks. "*After* I took you into my bed?"

He shook his head helplessly. "There were times when I ached to tell you. The first time I kissed you. The night of the storm . . . when you described the villagers carrying my body down the hill . . . when you cried for me."

"Those were just a few of the many tears I've wasted on you over the years. But you already know that, don't you? Because I poured my heart out to you. And you had the audacity to just stand there and listen while I babbled on and on about what a kind and noble boy you were and how much I'd always adored you." She turned her face away, sick with self-contempt. "How ridiculous you must have found me!"

"I've never found you ridiculous," Bernard said, daring to draw nearer. "All I could think was how disappointed you would be if you were to meet the man that boy had become." He reached to tilt her face toward him, but she jerked away. "I don't understand. You act as if you're more afraid of me than when you believed I was a stranger."

"I'm not afraid of you," she lied. "I just can't bear to have you touch me."

"Why not?"

"Because you let me fall in love with a man who never even existed. And you're not him!" Gwendolyn backed into the surf as all the hurt she'd been holding inside came spilling out. "You're not the Dragon! You smell like him and you sound like him, but you're not him, and I can't bear knowing that you're here and he's gone forever!"

Refusing to let him see her shed another tear for him, she dashed toward the cliffs, leaving him standing all alone in the moonlight.

Bernard stood with one foot on the rock Gwendolyn had abandoned, watching the sky melt from lavender to pink. He was reluctant to leave this place, knowing it might be the last time he would ever feel so close to her. He'd never once begged the English for mercy or his life, but as he had watched Gwendolyn flee from him, he had been a breath away from calling out her name. From imploring her not to go.

The Dragon would have gone after her. He would have stormed the village if need be and made her his captive again. He would have carried her back to the tower and made love to her until she couldn't remember her own name, much less his.

But Gwendolyn no longer believed in dragons. And it was her faith in him that had made the Dragon real. Without that faith, he was nothing but a heartless charlatan who had tricked an innocent woman into falling in love with an illusion.

The sun slipped over the horizon, striking the water with dazzling force. Once he would have shied away from the light, but now he welcomed its blinding rays.

His nights of hiding in the shadows were done. He'd spent fifteen long years denying his heritage. The time had come for Bernard MacCullough to reclaim what was rightfully his from those who had stolen it from him.

His clansmen were waiting to welcome home their long-lost son, and he had no intention of disappointing them. He might not be able to have the woman he wanted, but he would be damned if he would leave this place before getting what he'd come for.

The truth.

# Chapter Nineteen

Hope had returned to Ballybliss.

The village's twisting streets bustled with activity, their denizens rushing to and fro with an enthusiasm they'd never shown when seeking to appease the Dragon's appetites. Wagons loaded with lumber and goods rumbled their way up the cliff road to the castle almost hourly. The villagers no longer gave their gifts grudgingly, but with an almost pathetic eagerness, wrapping their humble offerings in faded hair ribbons and bits of string hoarded from Christmas mornings long past.

The lights that flickered in the windows of Weyrcraig after dark belonged not to ghosts, but to workmen willing to labor deep into the night to restore the castle's halls to their former glory. As word of Ballybliss's change in fortunes spread throughout the Highlands, many of the clansmen who had deserted the village years ago began to return. The streets rang with joyful cries as fathers embraced sons they hadn't seen in over a decade and mothers tearfully welcomed grandchildren they had never met.

For the first time in nearly fifteen years, Ballybliss was escaping the shadow of its past. And all because the prince of Clan MacCullough had come home to claim his kingdom.

As Gwendolyn hurried home from the market one morning, she stole a furtive glance at Castle Weyrcraig, wishing she could so easily escape the shadow it had cast over her life. Although more than two months had passed since she had last laid eyes on its master, she could sense him as surely as she had sensed him in the darkness of her bedchamber. Waiting. Watching. Biding his time.

He had proved his patience in the past two months by dropping all reference to the thousand pounds he had previously sought with such tenacity. Instead of cursing the Dragon's wiles, the villagers now chuckled over the cleverness of their young master, pretending not to care that his joke had been at their expense. Foolish and full of hope, they even dared to believe that he had forgiven them their terrible sin. Only Gwendolyn knew him well enough to suspect that his forbearance was nothing more than the calm before the tempest.

Ross was lounging on the steps of the village tavern. Before Gwendolyn could cross the street to avoid him, he sprang to his feet and swept her a bow. "And a good day to ye, Miss Wilder. Ye're lookin' right bonny on this fine summer mornin'."

Had it not been for his eager expression, Gwendolyn might have suspected him of mocking her. Since returning to the village, she'd worn nothing but drab woolen gowns with dingy aprons that did little to flatter her figure. She kept her hair wound into a rigid knot and secured in a homespun snood. Her head might ache and her eyes feel slightly crossed, but at least she didn't have to imagine the Dragon sifting his fingers through its unbound softness.

"Why, thank you, Ross. How very kind of you to notice," she replied with acid sweetness, deliberately stepping on his foot as she passed.

His pained grunt was still hanging in the air when his cousin Marsali emerged from the apothecary to thrust her squirming baby into Gwendolyn's face. "Have ye seen my wee angel lately, Miss Wilder? She's bloomin' into quite a beauty."

Gwendolyn drew a handkerchief from one of her packages and rubbed a smudge of dirt from the child's sallow cheek. "I do believe she's the very image of her mama."

Dodging the baby's bubble of spittle only succeeded in bringing her face-to-face with Ross's mother, who dropped into a curtsy so low her knees creaked and popped when she tried to rise. "And how would that dear father o' yers be, child?" she inquired with a simpering smile. "Verra well, I hope." After Gwendolyn had passed, she leaned over to one of her cronies and said in a whisper loud enough to wake the dead, "A pity the lass is taken. I always said she'd make a fine match for one o' my lads."

Gwendolyn hastened her steps, torn between shuddering and laughing. The villagers refused to believe that she wasn't their laird's mistress. Her stony silence on the subject of what had transpired between her and her captor during the fortnight she'd been missing only fueled their speculation. She couldn't leave the manor without one of them bowing and scraping at her feet, seeking to atone for the dark mischief they'd done her in the past. As amusing as their fawning was, it galled her that they believed she had ever belonged to Bernard MacCullough. Or that he might still care what became of her.

She sighed with relief when the back gate of the manor finally clanked shut behind her.

"Gwennie?"

"Aye, Papa, I'm right here." Gwendolyn rested her packages on the stoop, then hurried over to the side yard, where her father reclined in a chair beneath the dappled shade of an apple tree.

Kneeling beside him, she tucked the woolen lap robe around his wasted legs. He'd lost so much weight in the past few weeks that it hurt her eyes just to look at him. His ribs threatened to poke through the fragile parchment covering his chest, while his eyes seemed to sink deeper into their sockets with each passing day. It had been no strain at all for Izzy to heft him in her powerful arms and carry him outside. On warm summer days like this one, he liked to sit overlooking the stones that marked her mother's grave. It seemed to give him comfort, almost as if he could sense the presence of his beloved wife.

He clawed at Gwendolyn's arm, the faded blue of his eyes glistening with alarm. "I had a dream, child. I dreamt he came back for me."

"Oh, Papa," she said, shaking her head. "How many times do I have to tell you that Cumberland is far away from here? He'll never hurt you again."

"Not Cumberland. The Dragon! He's come back, hasn't he? To destroy us all."

A knot of mingled grief and fear tightened Gwendolyn's throat. "The Dragon's gone for good, Papa. He'll not trouble any of us again."

"But if he comes back, ye'll keep me safe from him, won't you, lass?" He squeezed her hand until she winced.

"Aye, Papa, I'll keep you safe. I swear it," she assured him, giving his wispy head a kiss.

He beamed up at her. "I knew I could count on ye. Ye've always been my good girl, haven't ye?"

He would never know that she was really a wicked girl full of sinful passions and shameful yearnings. A good girl would have been thankful that she hadn't succumbed to the Dragon's seductive wiles, but Gwendolyn sometimes awoke in the night, her cheeks wet with tears and her body burning with regret. Believing that she was back in the Dragon's lair, she would jerk into a sitting position and search the darkness for his shadow, only to be brought back to reality by the even whisper of Kitty's breathing.

Gwendolyn was almost relieved when Izzy emerged from the kitchen, carrying a basket of sopping-wet garments. If she could work herself into a state of exhaustion, she might be able to fall into a dreamless sleep tonight. Leaving her father dozing in the side yard, she began to string the clothes over the rope that stretched from the manor to the stone wall surrounding it.

Izzy had just shambled back into the kitchen with the packages when Glynnis and Nessa came sashaying out the rear door. Gwendolyn nearly groaned aloud. Her sisters were even nosier than the villagers. Each time she refused to answer one of their pointed questions about her time with the Dragon, they would pout and sulk for hours.

Warily watching their approach, Gwendolyn fished a biscuit out of her apron pocket and took a bite of it. Nessa and Glynnis exchanged a telling glance. They had both noticed Gwendolyn's healthy appetite since her return, although the timely arrival of her monthly courses had squelched any speculation that she might be breeding.

"You should have come with us, Gwennie," Nessa sang out. "Another one of the MacCullough's ships loaded with goods arrived from Edinburgh only this morning. We got to watch from the bluff while some of those burly young sailors of his rowed the whole lot over to the castle."

Glynnis clasped a hand to her breast. "I've never seen such beautiful things—gilded chimneypieces, fanlights of stained glass, settees upholstered in watered silk. Our laird must have truly impeccable taste."

"And not an ounce of thrift," Gwendolyn retorted, trying not to think of the absurdly extravagant bed the two of them had never shared.

Glynnis shrugged. "And why should he be thrifty when he owns an entire shipping fleet? One of his footmen told me that the Crown even knighted him for valor after he rescued some admiral or dignitary from the clutches of the French at Louisbourg."

"It was fortunate for the English that they decided to impress him into the Royal Navy instead of killing him," Gwendolyn said dryly. "But I do find it odd that we never heard about any of these heroic exploits of his."

"Ah, but that's because he was calling himself by another name," Nessa explained. "Bernard Grayson. Apparently, no one in England even knew he was a Scot."

Gwendolyn shook her head, draping one of her own homely dresses over the rope. "I'll never understand how he could have ended up fighting for the very country that destroyed his father." That was only one of the *many* things she would never understand about Bernard MacCullough.

Stealing a sidelong glance at Gwendolyn, Nessa nudged Glynnis. "Maisie's mother heard from one of the washerwomen that he was something of a scoundrel as well. Although he was welcome in some of the finest drawing rooms in London after he retired from the navy, she claims he spent most of his nights prowling through the gambling halls and bordellos."

Thinking how ridiculous her shy kisses and clumsy caresses must have seemed to a man of his experience, Gwendolyn gave one of Nessa's shifts a savage twist.

"Those days are most likely over now." Glynnis dragged the toe of her slipper in the dirt in an attempt to look nonchalant. "Since he's accumulated a fortune of his own and returned to claim his inheritance, 'twill be only a matter of time before he'll come looking for a wife."

"He'd best make haste if he hopes to catch you between husbands," Gwendolyn said, slinging a sopping-wet towel over the line and barely missing Glynnis's nose. "Then again, he might have enough silver in his pockets for your tastes, but not enough in his hair. You wouldn't want to marry a man who could outlive you, would you?"

"You can be his wife if you want, Glynnis," Nessa trilled. "For I have every intention of becoming his mistress."

As her sisters collapsed in a fit of girlish giggles, Gwendolyn groped in her apron for more biscuits. She was choking down the last of them when the garden gate clanked shut.

When she saw the man standing in the shadow of the wall, her heart did an odd little flip. But as he stepped from shadow to sunlight, she realized that it was simply Tupper, garbed in a sober black frock coat and knee breeches.

"Good day, ladies." He spared a polite bow for both of her sisters before turning his earnest brown eyes on Gwendolyn. "I was wondering if I might have a word with you, Miss Wilder. Alone."

"Why, certainly, Mr. Tuppingham," she replied, taking her cue from his stilted formality. Although he had been a frequent visitor to the manor in the past few weeks, he always seemed to make some excuse to leave whenever she appeared. She supposed he still felt guilty for his part in her abduction.

Glynnis and Nessa grudgingly took their leave, casting Tupper curious glances over their shoulders. They still couldn't quite believe that their baby sister had managed to snare such an exotic admirer.

Tupper drew off his hat and passed it from hand to hand, avoiding Gwendolyn's eyes. "I hope you'll forgive me for burdening you with this, but I didn't know who else to turn to. If Catriona's father were . . ." He hesitated, obviously at a loss.

"Sane?" Gwendolyn provided.

Tupper nodded gratefully. "If Catriona's father were sane, I would have gone to him. I realize you're not even her eldest sister, but you seem to be the one with the most . . ."

"Sense?" she offered when he hesitated again.

"Precisely! So it is with great trepidation that I find myself in the incredibly awkward position of standing before you today to beg for Catriona's . . . C-Catriona's . . ."

Sensing that he was about to lapse into a full-blown stammer, Gwendolyn suggested, "Foot?"

He gave her a reproachful glance. "I should say not. It's her hand I seek, in holy matrimony." Looking taken aback by his own boldness, he lowered his eyes and began to wring the brim of his hat in his hands. "Of course, I shouldn't blame you if you don't find me worthy of her."

"Don't be silly. I'd always hoped Kitty would marry a kidnapper's henchman."

Tupper looked so crestfallen that Gwendolyn immediately regretted her teasing. She gently pried the hat from his hands and smoothed out the brim before handing it back. Gazing up into his soulful brown eyes, she said, "Whatever I may think of your choice of companions, I can't deny that you'll make my sister a fine husband. Just when do the two of you plan to wed?"

A delighted grin broke over Tupper's face. "Since we're to be married on Scottish soil, there'll be no need to obtain a special license from the Crown. If it pleases you, we hope to be man and wife before the end of next week."

"That doesn't leave us much time." Gwendolyn frowned, her head already spinning with all there was to accomplish. "Kitty should have a new gown, although I suppose we could borrow the one Glynnis was last married in. And Izzy will have to prepare a ginger cake or some other such trifle for the guests. We won't be able to afford much extravagance, of course, but if we all sacrifice, we can . . ."

She trailed off as Tupper reached into the satin lining of his frock coat and drew forth a folded sheet of paper sealed with crimson wax. He held it out to her, looking even more nervous than before.

The creamy vellum was only too familiar. "If our laird is in need of some fresh venison," Gwendolyn said coolly, "I suggest he try the butcher's shop."

"It's not a demand this time," Tupper assured her, "but an offer."

Succumbing to his pleading look, she took the note and unfolded it, holding it between the very tips of her forefinger and thumb as if the ink itself might be tainted.

"So the MacCullough wishes to throw you and my sister a wedding," she said, feeling her mouth tighten as she scanned the scrawled missive. "And he's inviting the entire village to join in the celebration." She snapped the note closed. "It's a very generous proposal, but we've no need of his charity."

"He said to tell you that he preferred to think of it as payment toward a debt he owes."

Gwendolyn wanted nothing more than to tear the MacCullough's note into a thousand pieces, march up the hill to the castle, and hurl them into his arrogant face. But she knew what such a grand wedding would mean to Kitty. There would be tables laden with every manner of meat and pie, freshly tapped casks of whisky, piping and singing that would go on until dawn. And all of this feasting, revelry, and dancing would be presided over by the prodigal prince of the clan. It would be a night her sister would remember for the rest of her life. And one Gwendolyn wouldn't be able to forget, no matter how hard she tried.

She sighed. She had been willing to sacrifice so that Kitty could have a fine wedding. She just hadn't realized the cost would be so high.

"You may inform the MacCullough that I will accept his offer," she told Tupper, "but that he should know better than anyone that some debts can never be repaid."

# Chapter Twenty

THE PIPES NO LONGER mourned for Ballybliss's lost prince. Castle Weyrcraig blazed with light, its ghosts finally laid to rest. The villagers swarmed up the hill, their colorful tartans and plumed bonnets in open defiance of the Crown's Act of Proscription, which had banned all manner of Highland dress after Bonnie Prince Charlie's defeat at Culloden.

As they spilled through the newly restored wrought iron gates into the torchlit courtyard, their laughter ringing in the crisp night air, a solitary figure watched from a window high above, searching their joyful ranks for the one face he feared he would not find.

Although some of the finest workmen from Scotland and England had spent every waking moment of the last two months patching cracks and rebuilding walls, the castle seemed more of a ruin to Bernard than it had before. He missed the solitude. He missed the dark.

He missed her.

Leaning against the window frame, he briefly closed

his eyes. He missed Gwendolyn's courage, her defiance, her softness in his arms. Her absence had left gaping holes and jagged cracks that no amount of mortar could fill. There were so many words left unspoken between them, so many questions she hadn't given him the chance to answer.

For over two months, he had fought to stay away from her, telling himself that nothing had changed since that stormy night he'd first found her in his courtyard. He might dress like a gentleman and live like a prince, but he was still a beast at heart—a creature with no conscience or remorse.

He was haunted by the fear he'd glimpsed in her eyes that night on the beach. It was almost as if she were more afraid of Bernard MacCullough than she'd been of the Dragon. Not that he could blame her.

He watched the villagers stream through the gates that had been thrown wide to welcome them. They had no idea that they were marching into a trap. Before this night was done, they would be begging to hand over the traitor who had destroyed his family. Perhaps it would be best if Gwendolyn stayed away. It wasn't as if he could ask her blessing on what he was about to do.

Bernard straightened, giving the ruffled cuffs of his shirt a practiced flick. The time for indulging his regrets was done. His adoring clansmen were waiting to toast the health of their host, and he was only too willing to oblige them.

✦ ✦ ✦

Gwendolyn sat at her father's bedside, determined to linger there for as long as she dared. She wished she could spend the entire evening with her nose buried in the latest pamphlet from the Royal Society for Improving Natural Knowledge by Experiment, but she hadn't the heart to abandon Kitty on her wedding day. She sighed, already missing her sister. After tonight, she would never again have to worry about waking up with Kitty's elbow in her ear.

The merry sound of piping drifted through the closed shutters. The ancient wood did little to muffle the music and laughter ringing through the glen. Thanks to the laird's gracious generosity, no doubt the revelry would grow more raucous as the night wore on and the freely flowing whisky loosened tongues and inhibitions held in check for years.

Her papa twitched in his sleep. He'd been fretful all day—jumping at shadows, tugging at her hand, and muttering about the wrath of dragons until Gwendolyn had wanted to climb into the bed and bury her own head beneath the pillow. It was such a pity, she thought, that he would never know that his youngest daughter was about to become the wife of a future viscount.

The door creaked open and Izzy came bustling in, looking taken aback to find her there. "Why are ye dallyin', lass? Yer sisters left for the castle nearly an hour ago."

Gwendolyn rose and busied herself with tucking the blanket beneath her father's chin. "Papa's been very restless today. I was thinking that perhaps I should stay with him while you go and make merry with the rest of the villagers."

"And what business does an auld woman like me have with makin' merry? Makin' merry is for those still young eno' to get a rise out o' the sap in their veins." Izzy jerked her head toward the door. "Go on with ye, lass. I'll look after yer father. Yer sister would never forgive ye if ye missed her weddin'."

Still avoiding Izzy's eyes, Gwendolyn plumped up the pillows. "If you reminded her of what a bad day Papa has had, I'm sure she would understand."

Izzy planted her hands on her hips. "Kitty might understand, but I'll be damned if I do."

Gwendolyn bowed her head, ceasing her aimless motions. "I don't know if I can go back to that place. I'm not ready to face him."

Izzy shook her head. "In all the years I've known ye, lass, I've never known ye to back down from a battle. I don't know what that young rogue did to ye up there in that castle, but it shames me to think ye'd let anyone, man or beast, keep ye from yer sister's side on the most important day of her life."

Gwendolyn slowly lifted her head, considering Izzy's words. The maidservant was right. It was selfish of her to let her own apprehension cast a shadow over Kitty's happiness. She stole a look at the bed. Her papa slept without stirring, at peace for the first time in that endless day.

"Very well, Izzy, I'll go." Gwendolyn's pulse quickened as she took her shawl from the back of the chair.

"Not dressed like that, ye won't," Izzy retorted, eyeing Gwendolyn's brown woolen gown. "I'll not have ye bein' mistaken for one o' the kitchen maids at yer own sister's weddin'."

She hurried out of the room, returning a few minutes later with several yards of shimmering taffeta draped over one arm. Gwendolyn gasped.

It was the sky blue sacque gown she had worn that last night at the castle. Dawn had just begun to streak the sky when she had ripped it off and hurled it into the corner of the loft, hoping never to see it again. She had assumed it had been disposed of, but Izzy must have rescued it and painstakingly repaired the tears in the fragile fabric.

"Yer mother had such fine things before she married yer father," Izzy said, stroking one rawboned hand over the sleek taffeta. "But she never truly had need o' them. Lady Leah's beauty was on the inside and would have shone through even the ugliest of rags." She held her offering out to Gwendolyn, her sharp eyes dulled by a fine mist. "Much like yer own."

Tears stung Gwendolyn's eyes as she gently folded the gown into her arms. The brusque old maidservant had given her a much greater gift than she realized. Wanting to give her something in return, Gwendolyn stood on tiptoe and kissed Izzy's cheek.

Turning a full shade redder than her usual color, Izzy shooed Gwendolyn toward the door. "Go on with ye, lass. Ye haven't the time for such nonsense, and I haven't the patience. That randy young Englishman's likely to have yer sister's petticoats up and her drawers down before you can trot yer arse up the hill."

Gwendolyn hurried up the cliff path, no longer able to resist the song of the pipes. Their pagan wail stirred her blood, made her ache to cast off her own inhibitions and dance with abandon by the icy glow of the moon hanging in the northern sky. The night seemed to whisper her name just as it had at Castle Weyrcraig, coaxing her to embrace the seductive dangers of the dark.

The sleek taffeta of her skirts rustled around her slippers. She touched a hand to her hair. After changing gowns, she had traded her woolen snood for a pair of tortoise-shell combs that allowed soft ringlets to escape from the French knot at her nape.

A carriage waited outside the courtyard gates, its patient horses draped with a profusion of flowers and ribbons. After the wedding, Tupper and Kitty would be departing for Edinburgh for a brief honeymoon. A heady journey indeed, Gwendolyn thought wistfully, for a lass who would have been content to spend her entire life within the sheltering walls of the glen.

Although the castle windows blazed with light, most of the merriment seemed to be confined to the courtyard. Standing torches ringed the walls, banishing the shadows with their luminous glow. Aphrodite presided over the revelry, both her head and her mocking smile restored to their former beauty. Servants worked their way through the crowd, bearing trays laden with food and drink. Their scarlet livery and powdered wigs earned more than a few sniggers from the Highlanders.

Auld Tavis was wheezing out a jaunty melody on the pipes, his bony chest heaving as if every note would be his last. Lachlan strummed along on the strings of his clarsach, accompanied by drums, fife, and fiddle. Even though Reverend Throckmorton looked like a drab crow amongst a flock of preening robins in the severe black of his breeches and coat, it appeared he had decided to turn a blind eye to the clan's petty rebellion. A smile lit his puckish face as he clapped along in time to the music, missing more beats than he hit.

It didn't take Gwendolyn long to locate her radiant sister. Tupper clasped Kitty's hands in his as they led two lines of dancers through a galloping reel. A halo woven from wild roses and dried sprigs of heather crowned Kitty's dusky curls, making her look even more angelic than usual.

Kitty's dimples deepened as she spotted Gwendolyn. She broke from the line of dancers, dragging a winded Tupper along behind her. "I was beginning to think you weren't coming!" She relinquished her grip on her husband-to-be just long enough to give Gwendolyn a fierce squeeze.

Gwendolyn squeezed her back. "I wouldn't have missed it for the world, kitten. Or perhaps I should call you 'cat,' since you'll soon be a grown-up married lady."

Tupper beamed down at his betrothed, his broad

face flushed with exertion and pride. "In a very short while, you can call her Mrs. Tuppingham."

"I thought perhaps she'd prefer 'Mrs. Dragon,'" Gwendolyn replied, giving him an arch glance.

Kitty scowled and punched him on the arm. "You shouldn't tease so. I still haven't quite forgiven him for that wicked little charade."

"After tonight, you'll have the rest of your life to make me pay," Tupper reminded her, bringing her fist to his lips.

"And don't think I won't," Kitty purred.

Before their flirting could disintegrate into open cooing, a line of dancers galloped past, grabbing them both back into the reel.

"Don't go away! I'll be back!" Kitty shouted over the music and laughter, throwing Gwendolyn an apologetic glance.

Gwendolyn sighed as she watched them whirl away from her. She was supposed to be the sensible sister. Why couldn't she have fallen in love with someone as sweet-natured and uncomplicated as Tupper?

The thought made her look furtively across the courtyard. There was no sign of the MacCullough.

In a shadowy corner, a lass and lad were sharing a lingering kiss. Gwendolyn didn't realize she was staring until the girl lifted her head and looked straight at her.

Cheeks burning, Gwendolyn headed for the nearest buffet table. The music was climbing to a feverish pitch that made her blood feel too hot for her veins. Nine months from now, there would doubtlessly be a rash of babes born in the village, some begotten willingly and others forced upon women drunk or foolish enough to wander away from the protection of the light. Wishing she had remained at her father's bedside where she belonged, Gwendolyn helped herself to a fluffy scone. Perhaps if she ate enough of them, she would grow too fat to ever again squeeze out the door of her home.

The pastry was halfway to her mouth when she heard a familiar high-pitched titter. She turned to find Nessa and Glynnis bearing down upon her.

Nessa wrinkled her pert nose. "For heaven's sake, Gwennie, must you make such a pig of yourself?"

"As much as she's eaten in the past two months," Glynnis said, "you'd think the MacCullough refused to feed her the last time she was his guest."

Gwendolyn's fingers tightened on the scone, crumbling it into bits. She was growing weary of her sisters' baiting. "Oh, he fed me. He fed me sumptuous banquets of nectar and ambrosia while I reclined on cushions of pure silk."

Nessa and Glynnis leaned forward as one, mesmerized by the uncharacteristic huskiness of Gwendolyn's voice. Although she didn't realize it, several of the nearby villagers also paused to listen.

"He would pop plump, succulent grapes into my mouth one by one, then kiss away each sparkling drop of dew that fell upon my quivering breast."

Nessa gasped and Glynnis clapped a hand over her

mouth, but Gwendolyn was too busy savoring their reaction to realize that their attention was no longer on her, but on something just over her right shoulder.

"After I was all done licking the nectar from his fingertips," she continued, allowing a lascivious smile to curve her lips, "he would lay me back among those very cushions, tear off all my clothes, and make mad, passionate love to me all night long."

"There's no need to flatter me, Miss Wilder," said someone standing just behind her. "I expect your sisters, as kindhearted as they appear to be, would not be disappointed to learn that even a man of my stamina might require a brief nap between such vigorous . . . shall we say . . . exertions?"

The smoky baritone with the lilting hint of heather washed over Gwendolyn, followed by an icy flush of horror. After waiting just long enough to make sure God wasn't going to answer her prayer and allow the ground to open up and swallow her, she slowly turned to find herself glaring up into the smirking face of Bernard MacCullough.

"Don't you ever grow weary of sneaking up on people?" she demanded.

Had she believed he possessed even an ounce of shame, the downward sweep of his thick, dark lashes might have been quite convincing. "I realize my rudeness is unforgivable, but if I announced my presence everywhere I went, how would I be able to eavesdrop on such *delicious* conversations?" He arched one dark eyebrow, bringing to mind the torrid scene Gwendolyn had just described to her sisters.

As far as she was concerned, he had picked a wretched time to embrace his heritage. In defiance of the Crown's edict, he wore a short kilt and a matching scarlet and black plaid draped over the dazzling whiteness of his shirt. The froth of lace at his wrists and throat only emphasized the masculine strength of his imposing chest and long limbs. His knees were bare, his lower legs encased in tartan stockings and leather shoes. His thick, dark hair brushed his shoulders.

It might have been a trick of the torchlight, but he seemed to be both the boy Gwendolyn had loved for more than half her life and the man she had always dreamed he would become. She felt as if she were nine years old again, yearning for something she could never have.

"Good evening, m'laird," Nessa chirped as she and Glynnis took turns curtsying, bobbing up and down like the windup birds in a mechanical clock.

"Good evening, ladies," he replied, his gaze never straying from Gwendolyn's face.

At that moment someone wrested the pipes away from Auld Tavis while someone else began to weave a beguiling melody on fife and clarsach. It was a ballad they all knew, one that bemoaned the fate of a young girl foolish enough to give her heart to the first lad who looked her way.

Bernard held out his hand, his eyes darkened by an

emotion Gwendolyn couldn't begin to fathom. "Shall we dance, Miss Wilder?"

The crowd fell into a sudden hush, leaving the strains of the song to swirl around them—sweet, seductive, and dangerous.

Gwendolyn gazed down at his hand. Once she had trusted not only her hand to him, but her heart. Once she had been a fool.

She lifted her gaze to his face. "Is that an invitation or a command, m'laird?"

"Which would you prefer?"

"From you? Neither." Gwendolyn turned on her heel, fully intending to leave him to the mercy of her twittering sisters.

"Then consider it a command. Like it or not, I'm still your laird and master."

Gwendolyn whirled around with a snap of her skirts. "That's where you're wrong, Bernard MacCullough. No man will ever be my laird and master."

The villagers were openly gawking now, such outright defiance of their laird's will unthinkable.

A smile slowly curved his lips. "I wouldn't be so sure of that, lass, if I were you."

He seized her hand, but instead of drawing her into the dance, he began to march toward the castle. Gwendolyn had no choice but to stumble along behind him, once again the Dragon's captive.

# Chapter Twenty-one

"OF ALL THE SMUG, high-handed . . ." Gwendolyn sputtered as she marched along behind Bernard. "You can hide behind the MacCullough tartan all you like, but man or beast, you're still a bully!"

"And you're still a brat," he retorted without slowing his long strides.

"Just what do you intend to do about it? Lock me in the tower?"

He snorted. "If I did, none of your clansmen would come to your rescue. I'm sure they believe it my divine right to claim any one of the village lasses for my pleasure."

As if to prove his point, the servants and stray merrymakers they passed in the entranceway took one look at his face and went bolting for the door.

To Gwendolyn's keen relief, he bypassed the stairs, hauling her instead toward the great hall. As they passed beneath its graceful archway, she gasped.

The Dragon's bogies had been at it again.

The moon was no longer free to spy on the hall's occupants. The roof had been repaired, the shattered beams replaced, the ceiling plastered and painted. A bronze chandelier strung with tiers of wax tapers dangled from the center beam, casting a soft glow over the freshly polished table. The faded pastel linen that had once draped the walls had been replaced with rich burgundy damask. A pair of crossed claymores hung over the mahogany mantel, which had been refinished and buffed to a warm sheen.

Velvet drapes of a verdant forest green shrouded the windows overlooking the courtyard. As Bernard led her past the table, she tried desperately not to remember the night she had been so foolish as to try and tame a dragon with her kiss.

A pair of leather wing chairs nestled before the fire. Bernard gave her a gentle shove toward one of them, and she sat. She wasn't surprised to find Toby draped across the warm hearthstones like a plush catskin rug. He roused himself from his stupor just long enough to give her a somnolent blink. He was obviously under the impression that she'd stepped out of the room for two minutes, not two months.

While she perched stiffly on the edge of the chair, her host moved to the sideboard and poured two glasses of port.

He held out a glass to her. "It will have to do, I'm afraid. I'm fresh out of kitten's blood."

Toby, apparently offended, bounded off the hearth

and went trotting from the room, his fluffy tail twitching.

"No thank you. I'm not thirsty," Gwendolyn said. "But I am famished. Haven't you any refreshments?"

"No nectar and ambrosia, I fear," he replied silkily, "although there might be a grape or two around here somewhere."

Hoping to steady her frazzled nerves, Gwendolyn took the glass from his hand and tossed back its contents in one swallow. A heady warmth spilled through her, loosening her tongue.

"So is it customary to drag a woman off by her hair if she refuses your invitation to dance? Is that how it's done in the drawing rooms of London?" She toyed with the empty glass. "Of course, I've been told that it wasn't the drawing rooms you preferred to frequent."

He took a leisurely sip of the port. "When you have to make your own way in the world, you soon discover that it's more sensible to pay for your pleasure in advance. There are far fewer regrets come morning."

Gwendolyn rose to set her glass on the mantel. She toyed with the braided gold tassels adorning the hilt of one of the claymores, trying to avoid his eyes.

"If you'd like," he said, reaching around her to rest his glass on the mantel next to hers, "I can extinguish the candles so as to spare you the unpleasant task of looking at me."

"No!" Her reply came out with more passion than she intended.

He stood next to her, so close she could feel the heat of his breath stirring her hair. Gwendolyn knew it was a mistake to close her eyes, but the familiar aroma of sandalwood and spice was more intoxicating than aged Scotch whisky.

"Look at me, Gwendolyn."

"I can't," she whispered, her voice choked.

"Why not? Because I'm not your precious Dragon?" His voice softened. "You're wrong, Gwendolyn. I'm the same man who kissed you." He brushed his lips against the corner of her mouth, but she turned her face away. "The same man who held you in his arms. The same man you . . ."

*Loved.*

He wasn't cruel enough to say it.

"No you're not," she said, squeezing her eyes shut. "You're Bernard MacCullough, laird of Castle Weyrcraig and chieftain of Clan MacCullough."

"That boy is dead," he said flatly. "You were right about him all along. He died in this very hall nearly fifteen years ago, the victim of his own misplaced faith in his fellow man. He died, but I lived." He caught her chin in his hand, tilting her face toward his. "Look at me, Gwendolyn. See me!"

If he had been rough with her, Gwendolyn might have been able to resist him. But his grip was as gentle and compelling as she remembered. She slowly lifted her lashes.

His face was no longer masked by shadows, but open

and vulnerable. Her helpless gaze searched his features, finding the same brow she had traced with her fingertips, the same lips that had so tenderly kissed her. Despite its beguiling familiarity, it was still the face of a stranger.

"You're right," she said softly, backing out of his embrace. "You couldn't be Bernard MacCullough, because the boy I knew could never have fought for the English. He would never have sold his sword or his soul to his father's enemies."

Bernard gazed at her for a long moment, bitterness darkening his eyes. "Slipped your dirk right between my ribs, didn't you, my dear?" He reached out to smooth his fingers across her cheek. "The English may shoot you through the heart, but at least you'll see it coming."

He retrieved his glass from the mantel and crossed to the sideboard to pour himself another glass of port. "The redcoats killed my father, but it was his own faithless clansmen who betrayed him into their hands."

Gwendolyn's heart sank. "You haven't forgiven them, have you? You're just biding your time until you can make them pay for what they did to your family."

Bernard finished off the port. "Oh, I'm all done biding my time."

"I don't know what you mean to do," she said, giving the window an apprehensive glance, "but I implore you not to ruin this night for my sister."

"Do you really think I'd spoil Tupper's wedding?" He gave her a reproachful look. "I'm not that much of a monster. I have every intention of waiting until Kitty and Tupper are safely away on their journey to Edinburgh before I make my little announcement."

"Your announcement?"

Bernard poured himself another glass of port and lifted it in a toast. "If my loyal clansmen don't bring me the thousand pounds that was paid for my father's life by dawn tomorrow, I'm going to evict them."

For a long moment, Gwendolyn couldn't speak. She'd heard of ruthless English landlords driving native Scotsmen from the land they'd shared for centuries, but she couldn't fathom one of their own doing it. "You wouldn't . . . you can't . . ."

Bernard slammed the glass down on the sideboard. "The hell I can't! It's my land and I can do whatever the bloody hell I please with it!" His burr deepened as his temper blazed, betraying a glimpse of that stubborn boy who had been determined to climb a tree simply because Gwendolyn had told him not to.

As the full implication of his words sank in, her horror deepened. "But they've lived in Ballybliss all their lives. Their parents have lived here . . . their grandparents. . . . They don't know anything else. Where will they go? What will they do?"

"They won't have to worry about it, will they, if they bring me the gold?"

"You don't want the gold, do you?" Gwendolyn said softly, chilled by the ruthless cast of his features. "You never did. You want the man who's been hoarding it all these years. You don't want justice. You want revenge."

"I stopped believing in justice the night I watched my mother die, choking on her own blood. I started believing in revenge when Cumberland's men came and dragged me away from everything I had ever known, everything I loved—including my father, who was fighting for his every breath as he watched them bind his only son and carry him away like so much live-stock."

Gwendolyn bowed her head. "There's obviously nothing I can say to change your mind. So if you'll excuse me, m'laird, I will go pack my things."

Bernard stepped in front of her. "You don't have to go."

She recoiled, flinging out one hand to keep him at a distance. "You must be mad if you expect me to just sit here by your cozy little fire and toast your brilliant plot to evict an entire village of people who are dependent upon your goodwill for their very survival!"

"I meant that you don't have to leave Ballybliss." He took a step toward her. "Or me."

Gwendolyn slowly lifted her gaze to his face. "Just what are you asking of me, sir?"

"I'm asking you to stay. Here. At Castle Weyrcraig. With me."

Gwendolyn had to struggle to catch her breath. "The villagers may believe me to be your mistress, sir, but I would think that neither you nor I should be under any such delusions."

"I'm not asking you to be my mistress. I'm asking you to be my wife."

At first Gwendolyn thought he must be making some sort of heartless jest, but there wasn't a hint of humor in his eyes. It was his very grimness that made him look so vulnerable. He looked less like a man who had just asked a woman to marry him than a man prepared to drink poison.

She sank into one of the chairs, remembering all the times she had dreamed of hearing him utter those very words. When Gwendolyn was only seven, Nessa had discovered her accepting a proposal from the kitchen hound, whom Gwendolyn had attired in a handsome cloak sewn from a scrap of scarlet and black tartan she had filched from the castle. Her sisters had teased her mercilessly and insisted upon addressing her as "M'lady Pup" for months afterward.

But now the joke was on them. She could be the wife of the MacCullough. She could sleep in his bed each night and wake up in his arms every morning. He could give her dark-haired babies with eyes the color of emeralds and not a single inclination toward plumpness. Together, the two of them and their children could reign over the glen—the abandoned glen that had once rung with the laughter and music of Clan MacCullough.

Gwendolyn slowly came to her feet and faced him. "Very well, m'laird. If you wish, I shall marry you." Before triumph could spark in his eyes, she added, "But only if you'll forsake your vengeful scheme and allow the villagers to remain in Ballybliss."

Bernard gazed at her for a long moment, frustration and admiration warring in his eyes. "Am I to understand that you're offering me your body in exchange for their absolution?"

Ignoring the flush she could feel creeping up her throat, Gwendolyn boldly held his gaze. "I'm offering you the opportunity to pay for your pleasure in advance. So you'll have fewer regrets come morning."

"You've piqued my curiosity, Miss Wilder. Suppose my part of the bargain didn't include a proposal of marriage? Would you still be willing to make such a noble sacrifice on their behalf?"

Gwendolyn hesitated only long enough to catch her breath. "Aye, I would."

As he closed the distance between them, she believed he'd come to claim his prize. But instead of taking her into his arms, he cupped her cheek in his hand. "I'd be lying if I said I wouldn't do almost anything to make you mine. But as tempting as your offer might be, I'm afraid I shall have to decline. I've waited fifteen years for this moment, and no one is going to take it away from me." As his fingers sifted through the softness of her hair, she caught a glimpse of the raw regret that lay beneath his determination. "Not even you."

Withdrawing his hand, he turned and started for the archway.

"Not even if I can tell you who betrayed your father to the English?"

Her words weren't much more than a whisper, but

they stopped Bernard in his tracks. He slowly turned back to her.

"Who?" The single word tolled like a death knell in the taut silence.

Gwendolyn lifted her gaze to his face, no longer able to stop the tears from spilling down her cheeks. "I did."

# Chapter Twenty-two

As BERNARD DRIFTED BACK into the room, his expression disbelieving, Gwendolyn sank into a chair, staring straight ahead.

She folded her hands in her lap, her voice dispassionate despite the tears that were coursing down her cheeks. "Do you remember when I fell out of the oak tree and nearly killed you?"

"Of course I remember. You were such a funny little thing—all prickly and proud. I couldn't decide whether you needed to be spanked or kissed." His frown deepened. "I still can't."

"I stumbled onto the redcoats' camp almost as soon as I left you that afternoon. I was so angry that I wasn't paying any mind to where I was going. The next thing I knew, one of them was holding me by the braids while his companion poked me in the belly and said, 'I do believe we've captured ourselves a plump little Highland partridge. Shall we let it go or roast it on the spit?' " A shaky little hiccup of a laugh escaped her. "I must confess that I truly thought they meant to eat me. You see, Ross had told me that Cumberland and his men frequently dined on Scottish children." She slanted Bernard a rueful look. "But I suppose that wasn't nearly so foolish as believing that you might come charging to my rescue again."

Bernard groped blindly behind him for a chair, sinking down as if his legs no longer possessed the strength to support him.

"One of the men said, 'She has the look of a spy, don't you think?'" Gwendolyn mirrored the soldier's scowl without realizing it. "'Perhaps we should torture her to see if she has any secrets.' I doubt that they meant to do much more than tickle me, but at the time it seemed a most dire threat. And I only had one secret." She looked Bernard dead in the eye. "Yours."

When his face betrayed no change in expression, she rose from the chair and began to pace in front of the hearth. "Don't you dare think that I told them just because I was afraid! I was still furious at you for calling me a child, a 'mere slip of a girl.' I wanted to punish you for not trusting me. For not—"

She bowed her head, unable to go on. "So I told them that our laird's son would be escorting a most esteemed guest to the castle that night. A true hero . . ."

"A prince among men," Bernard whispered, running a hand over his face.

"The redcoats gave each other a most peculiar look then, and I managed to wriggle away and run for home. I never even realized the significance of what I'd told them. Until it was too late. So you see," she said fiercely, "there was no bargain with Cumberland and there was no thousand pounds. If you're seeking the traitor who destroyed your family, you need look no further."

Her passion spent, Gwendolyn sank back into the chair. The shame she'd kept buried for all those years was so overwhelming that she wouldn't have been able to summon up more than a token protest if Bernard had pulled one of the claymores from the wall and proceeded to whack off her head.

He continued to sit with his head bowed and his eyes covered by one hand. When his condemning silence stretched beyond the tolerable, Gwendolyn stole a furtive peek at him from beneath her lashes.

His shoulders were heaving, his cheeks wet with tears. She almost rose to go to him, but when he lowered his hand, she realized that it wasn't sobs wracking his frame, but helpless snorts of laughter.

Gwendolyn gaped at him, wondering if her terrible confession had caused him to take leave of his senses. She'd never seen him laugh with such abandon before. It brought about a most remarkable transformation, wiping away the strain and bitterness that usually edged his features. He looked like a boy on the brink of manhood again, with all of his hopes and dreams shining brightly before him.

He shook his head, grinning at her as if she were some sort of delightful creature fashioned solely for his amusement. "For a lass blessed with both beauty and brains, you've some daft notions, Gwendolyn Wilder. I never could understand why you kept defending the villagers, even after they tried to feed you to a bloody dragon and burn you at the stake. But you blame yourself for their predicament, don't you? Why, you were even willing to bargain away your precious virtue to a devil like me! And no wonder you were so angry when you found out who I really was. You must have believed that because of your 'betrayal' we had no hope of a future together." He swiped tears of mirth from his cheeks, surveying her dumbfounded expression with disarming affection. "I suppose it's not very funny to you, is it, sweeting?"

Still grinning like a fool, he moved to kneel in front of her, covering her icy hands with his big, warm ones. He spoke slowly and deliberately, as if he were speaking not to the woman she was, but to the little girl she had been. "Cumberland's attack on Castle Weyrcraig was a major military undertaking. There was no possible way he could have planned it all in one afternoon."

"But those soldiers . . . the redcoats—"

"—were already on MacCullough lands when you stumbled across their camp. As were the cannons they would later use to destroy the castle." He caressed her knuckles with his thumbs. "They were just a pair of cruel men toying with a frightened child. Don't you see, Gwendolyn? You couldn't have told them anything that they didn't already know."

She frowned, struggling to absorb the enormity of what he was telling her. "Do you mean to suggest that they already knew your father had offered sanctuary to Bonnie Prince Charlie?"

"That's exactly what I'm suggesting." Bernard cupped her face between his hands, both his touch and his expression brimming with tenderness. "There was a traitor in the village that day, my darling, but it wasn't you."

With those words, he leaned forward and kissed the softness of her mouth, absolving her of a sin she had never committed.

"Oh, Bernard!" She touched her trembling fingertips to his cheek. "All these years I've been so ashamed because I thought I'd killed you!" Thinking only to hold on to the wonder of it all, she threw her arms around his neck. "I wouldn't have deliberately harmed a hair on your head, I swear I wouldn't, no matter how arrogant and insufferable you were."

He chuckled into her hair. "Don't you mean 'no matter how arrogant and insufferable I *am*?' "

Still clutching fistfuls of his plaid, Gwendolyn leaned back in his arms as another astonishing realization struck her. "And Papa . . . oh, Papa . . ."

Bernard smoothed a stray lock of hair from her cheek, leaving his fingertips to linger against her skin. "What about your father?"

Gwendolyn felt her heart contract with a familiar mixture of pride and pain. "Papa tried to make it to the castle that night. He was the only one who had the courage to try and warn your father that Cumberland's men were coming. But somewhere along the way, the redcoats attacked him. He was beaten so badly. . . ." She shook her head, biting her lower lip. "I always believed I was to blame. . . ."

Gwendolyn was so caught up in spilling out all of her misguided guilt that she didn't see Bernard's smile fade, didn't feel the warmth seep out of his touch. "Exactly when did your father leave the manor that night?"

She frowned. "It was just after dark. Shortly before we heard the first cannon blast."

Bernard sat in absolute silence for almost a minute, then without a word of explanation gently detached himself from her arms and moved to take one of the swords down from the wall over the mantel, his movements as cold and methodical as she had ever seen them.

Bewildered by his abrupt desertion, Gwendolyn came to her feet. "What are you doing?"

He swung around, gripping the hilt of the claymore in one white-knuckled fist. "Your father suffered an attack all right, my dear. An attack of conscience."

His face grim, he strode past her and out of the hall.

Gwendolyn remained riveted in place, her mind struggling frantically to reach a conclusion that was as impossible as it was undeniable.

"Papa," she finally breathed, the word both oath and prayer.

Realizing that she had already wasted several precious minutes, she hiked up her skirts and went sprinting after Bernard.

✦ ✦ ✦

It wasn't the laird of Castle Weyrcraig who came striding through the courtyard that night, but the dangerous creature who had been born out of its fiery ruins.

As he passed through the wrought iron gates and started down the cliff path, his face more beautiful and terrible than any beast's, the villagers fell into step behind him, unable to resist his unspoken authority. Some retained enough of their wits to grab a torch from one of the iron sconces that ringed the walls, while others simply trotted along at his heels like befuddled sheep.

None of them had any idea where he was going, but it had been so long since they'd had anyone to lead them that they didn't care. Where he went, they would follow.

Gwendolyn stumbled down the castle steps and raced through the gates, but found her path blocked by a shuffling wall of villagers.

"Bernard!" she shouted, fighting to be heard over the confused din of the crowd. She jumped up and down in a vain attempt to catch a glimpse of him over the sea of bobbing heads.

Spurred forward by a tantalizing hint of scarlet and black, she shoved and clawed her way past the stragglers in the back, only to be caught up in the mob's midst and swept toward the village on a relentless tide. As she was driven along, she caught fragmented glimpses of a curious Nessa, a bewildered Kitty, a pale and worried-looking Tupper. But there was no time to stop. No time to explain or plead for help. Not if she hoped to save one man's life and another man's soul.

Bernard strode through the streets of Ballybliss, not ceasing until he came to a dead halt in front of the manor.

As the villagers hung back, their excited murmurs dying to silence, Gwendolyn fought to break through their ranks. She trod soundly on Ross's foot, ignoring his bellow of pain.

Just as she broke free and reached Bernard's side, he threw back his head and roared, "Alastair Wilder!"

Gwendolyn snatched at his sword arm, but he jerked away from her. "Leave me be, lass! This is between your father and me. It has naught to do with you."

"You don't understand! My father isn't the man you remember him to be. The beating he took from Cumberland's men changed him. He's never been the same since that night."

"Neither have I," Bernard replied, his jaw set in stone. "Alastair Wilder!" he shouted again as if she hadn't even spoken.

A curtain twitched in one of the front windows of the manor. *Izzy*, Gwendolyn prayed, *let it be Izzy*.

She grabbed Bernard's arm again, refusing to let him shake her off this time. Despite the barely suppressed violence coiled in his muscles, she knew he would never strike her. "He's mad, Bernard. Completely and utterly mad. He hasn't had possession of his senses since you left Ballybliss." She softened her grip, convinced that if she could just get him to look at her, she might be able to reach him. "No matter what he may or may not have done in the past, he's nothing now but a defenseless old man."

Bernard slowly shifted his wary gaze to her face. But Gwendolyn had no time to savor her triumph, for at that moment the door of the manor came creaking open and Alastair Wilder appeared in the entrance, garbed in a faded nightshirt and armed with a claymore even more ancient than the one in Bernard's hand.

"I've been waitin' for ye, Ian MacCullough," he snarled, his voice more vibrant than it had been in years. "I knew the devil himself couldn't keep the likes of ye in hell forever!"

# Chapter Twenty-three

ALASTAIR WILDER STAGGERED into the street, dragging the sword alongside him. "Aye, I knew ye'd come," he said, squinting up at Bernard. "It may have taken ye fifteen long years, ye stubborn auld bastard, but I never once stopped lookin' over my shoulder."

"Papa?" Gwendolyn whispered, struggling to reconcile this sharp-tongued vulture with the sweet-tempered old man she had left napping in her father's bed.

"Papa?" Glynnis and Nessa echoed, drifting to the front of the crowd while Kitty clung to Tupper, her face as white as her gown. Izzy hung back in the shadows of the doorway, her broad face grim.

If Bernard was surprised to find himself face-to-face with the unknown enemy who had haunted him for all those years, he hid it behind a rigid mask. Nor did he betray so much as a flinch to find himself addressed by his father's name.

Gwendolyn's limp hand fell away from his arm as he took a step toward Alastair. "How could you? You were his steward. His friend. He trusted you above all other men."

Alastair wagged a bony finger at him. "If ye'd have truly trusted me, Ian, ye'd have heeded my advice. I couldn't let ye destroy us all with yer noble ideas, yer romantic notions about restorin' Scotland's rightful king to her throne. I tried to warn ye! I begged ye not to offer shelter to that traitor, but ye wouldn't listen. If I hadn't given Ailbert a hundred pounds to stop the clan from comin' to yer defense, ye'd have gotten us all butchered, just like those poor fools at Culloden."

Ailbert went paler than Kitty, but Bernard didn't spare the blacksmith so much as a contemptuous glance. "At least you'd have died like men."

"Wrong or right, a MacCullough always stands to fight, eh?" Alastair shook his head sadly. "There wasn't much left standin' once Cumberland finished with you, was there?"

Bernard's fingers flexed around the hilt of the claymore, and for one chilling moment Gwendolyn thought he was going to strike her father down where he stood. Instead he said, "I'm heartened to learn that it was concern for your fellow clansmen that drove you to betray your laird, not greed."

Her papa shrugged his bony shoulders. "Cumberland already had all the evidence he needed. He was goin' to make an example of you whether I took the gold or not."

"But you took it anyway, didn't you?"

Confusion clouded Alastair's eyes for the first time

since he had emerged from the manor, making him look like the papa Gwendolyn knew, the papa she loved.

"I wouldn't have taken the gold if it hadn't been for my Leah," he said plaintively. "She deserved finer things than I could give her. She never once complained about not havin' enough, but I wanted her to have so much more." He passed a hand over his eyes as if to blot out a memory he could not bear. "She was always so generous. She died tryin' to give me a son."

Izzy stepped into the torchlight, her massive arms folded over her chest. "It wasn't the babe that killed her, ye auld fool. Aye, losin' the babe sapped her strength, but it was shame that killed my lady. Shame that her own husband would've sold the chieftain of his clan. When ye told her what turrible thing ye'd done, she sent ye out into the night to warn the MacCullough. But it was too late, and when ye returned to her, ye were naught but a gibberin' madman."

The sword slid from Alastair's hand, landing in the dirt with a muffled thud. Tears began to slip silently down Gwendolyn's cheeks as he sank to his knees, his bravado melting away to reveal what he really was—a tired old man with a broken mind and a broken heart.

Pushing past Bernard, Gwendolyn went to her father's side and knelt next to him in the dirt. "It's all right, Papa. I'm here."

"Gwennie? Is that you, Gwennie?" He fumbled for her hands, clinging to them like a frightened child. "I had a turrible dream. I dreamt the Dragon came back for me. You won't let him take me, will you, lass?"

"No, Papa, I won't let him take you." She glanced over her shoulder, but it was impossible to read the expression in Bernard's eyes as he watched them together. Turning back to her father, she said, "I need you to think very hard, Papa. I need you to tell me where you hid the gold."

"I did it for her," he whispered, the familiar fog descending over his eyes. "All for her. I wanted her to have it. So she could buy fine things."

It took Gwendolyn no more than a shuddering breath to realize what he was trying to tell her. "Oh, Papa," she said, stroking his paper-soft cheek. "Mama never wanted fine things. She only wanted your love."

As he began to rock back and forth in the dirt, Gwendolyn swiped fiercely at her cheeks, trying to scrub away the last traces of her tears before lifting her eyes to Bernard's face. "I hope you're satisfied now, m'laird. I believe you'll find your precious gold buried in the side yard. In my mother's grave."

Bernard shook his head, an emotion that looked dangerously like regret shimmering in his eyes. "You know I didn't come for the gold, Gwendolyn. I came for him."

"Well, you can't have him!" she cried. "Can't you see that he's been punished enough?"

"I'm his laird," Bernard said quietly. "That's for me to decide."

"Do you honestly believe that cutting down a pathetic old man will make everything better? Will it right the wrongs of the past? Will it somehow turn back time and make you the boy you once were? Will it bring back your parents?"

Something flickered across his face, telling her she had struck a raw nerve. She pressed on, knowing she had no choice.

"Look at your clansmen, Bernard. Aye, they made a mistake just as my father did—a terrible mistake. And they've been paying for it ever since. Not because of your father's curse, but because of their own shame." The villagers shuffled their feet nervously, as if unsure whether to stay or bolt. "By returning to Ballybliss, you've given them pride in their name and a hope for the future. And you have it within your power to give them something even more precious than pride or hope. You can give them mercy!"

"Damn it to hell, woman!" Bernard roared, his mask slipping to reveal a face twisted in a spasm of grief. "I don't have any mercy left to give!"

Gwendolyn rose and moved to stand between the two men she loved. "Very well, then. If it's blood you want, then it's blood you'll have. Mine."

Bernard's eyes narrowed. "Just what are you offering me?"

Gwendolyn shrugged. "What else? Revenge? One life for another."

As he began to move toward her, claymore in hand, Glynnis made a choked sound and Kitty buried her face in Tupper's coat. Izzy unfolded her arms, but Gwendolyn stayed the glowering maidservant with a warning shake of her head. As if unable to watch what was going to happen next, Izzy abruptly turned and ducked back into the manor.

Only Gwendolyn watched unflinchingly as Bernard approached, because she knew something the rest of them did not.

She knew the Dragon's heart.

Despite her faith in that heart, she had to set her chin a little higher to keep it from quivering. It was as if she were once again bound to that stake in the castle courtyard, watching her destiny melt out of the shadows.

Then Bernard tossed the claymore to a startled Lachlan.

He stretched out his hand. Gwendolyn was a breath away from taking it when that hand closed like a vise around her wrist.

"What do you think you're doing?" she asked, staring stupidly at her captive arm.

"Taking you up on your offer." He drew her hard against him, then leaned down until his lips were less than a breath away from her own. "If I can't have your father, Miss Wilder, then by God, I'll have you."

# Chapter Twenty-four

As Bernard started toward the cliff, giving a dazed Gwendolyn no choice but to follow, Nessa thrust herself into their path.

"Forgive me for interfering, m'laird," she said with a flutter of her silky lashes, "but if it's revenge you want, then I'm the lass for you. Our dear, sweet Gwennie has already suffered enough at your hands."

"How very kind of you to notice," Bernard replied.

Glynnis appeared out of nowhere. "Don't be ridiculous, Nessa. As the eldest, I should be the one allowed to atone for Papa's sins." She flattened one hand against Bernard's chest. "I can assure you, m'laird, that I'm fully prepared to slake your hunger for vengeance."

Bernard gently returned her hand to her. "While I find your concern for your sister's welfare quite . . . um, touching, I'm afraid such a sacrifice won't be necessary."

Offering each of the crestfallen sisters a curt nod, he

continued toward the cliff, his fingers laced through Gwendolyn's. He'd barely taken three steps when another obstacle appeared in their path. Although the top of the man's graying head barely came to Bernard's breastbone, he was armed with an expression of dogged self-righteousness and an enormous black Bible.

"Should I choose a second and send for my pistols, sir?" Bernard asked, coming to a halt. "It won't be dawn for a few more hours, but perhaps we could pass the time with a reading from one of the Psalms."

Reverend Throckmorton's hand trembled as he reached to adjust his spectacles, but his reedy voice was as sharp as a whip. "The pistols won't be necessary, lad, unless you persist in this madness. As the spiritual authority appointed to this village by both the Crown and our almighty God, I cannot in good conscience allow you to drag this poor child back to that castle for your own nefarious purposes. She's already spent a fortnight in your company without benefit of a chaperone or the church's blessing. Her reputation may have been soiled beyond repair, but her soul might still be salvageable."

"I can assure you," Bernard said, his voice just silky enough to make several of the nearby villagers exchange apprehensive glances, "that you won't find another soul in this village that could compare to Miss Wilder's."

The reverend had enough decency to look abashed. "Which is exactly why I cannot allow you to take her unless your union is sanctioned before God."

The two men regarded each other in stony silence. Beads of sweat popped out on the reverend's brow, but it was Bernard who finally sighed his defeat.

He drew Gwendolyn in front of him. "It seems the good reverend here is determined to give us his blessing whether we want it or not. So what say you, sweeting? Would you care to marry me?"

Bernard's words brought Gwendolyn back to reality. She turned her wrath on the hapless minister. "How could you ask such a thing of me? He's a coldhearted, unforgiving ogre without an ounce of mercy or compassion in his arrogant soul!"

"You heard the lady. The matter's settled. Now if you'll excuse us . . ." Bernard smoothly sidestepped the reverend, leaving him hugging his Bible to his chest.

Bernard and Gwendolyn had nearly reached the outskirts of the village when a shadow fell across their path. As Bernard looked the towering behemoth before them up and down, a speculative gleam lit his eye. If his years with the Royal Navy had taught him one thing, it was just how rare it was to find a worthy adversary.

Izzy hefted the ax in her hand to her shoulder, her curls bobbing like a nest of adders. "If ye care to keep that bonny head o' yers, lad, ye'll do right by my lass just as the reverend says. I might not have looked after her as well as I should've, but I'll be damned if I'm goin' to just stand by while some randy scoundrel makes off with her without so much as a by-yer-leave."

Bernard looked over his shoulder to find the reverend's face wreathed in an angelic smile.

Bernard swept Izzy a gallant bow. "Never let it be said that I could refuse a lady with an ax. Come, Gwendolyn." He tucked her icy hand in the crook of his arm. "It seems you're to become my bride."

Gwendolyn and Bernard were married at the manor less than an hour later. Unwilling to miss a moment of the spectacle, the villagers crowded into the smoky kitchen, taking turns gawking at their chieftain and his sullen bride. Never before had there been so many heartfelt tears shed at a Highland wedding.

"It was supposed to be *my* wedding!" Kitty wailed, staining the silk of Tupper's frock coat with her tears.

"He was supposed to be *my* husband!" Glynnis whined, honking into her lace handkerchief.

"It's not fair! Why does Gwennie have all the luck?" Nessa sobbed, sniffing frantically to keep her own nose from turning an unsightly red. Suddenly her eyes brightened. "He may have a wife, but he'll still have need of a mistress, won't he?"

Tears of paternal pride kept fogging up Reverend Throckmorton's spectacles while Marsali's sallow baby sent up a howl that drowned out most of the vows. Even the stoic Izzy, who had planted herself firmly behind the groom just in case he decided to bolt, was seen lowering her ax long enough to dab a sentimental tear from her cheek.

Only the bride remained dry-eyed as she repeated the words that would bind her to Bernard MacCullough for as long as they both should live. Someone had plucked the halo of roses from Kitty's curls and placed it on Gwendolyn's head, from where it kept sliding down over one glowering eye.

The ceremony had to be interrupted twice—once when Lachlan caught Auld Tavis sneaking out to the side yard to try and dig up the gold, and again when Gwendolyn's father climbed out of his bed for the second time that night and wandered into the room wearing nothing but a plumed bonnet and a vacant smile.

Someone had had enough foresight to send for the carriage that was supposed to take Kitty and Tupper to Edinburgh, and it was into that carriage that Gwendolyn was bundled after Bernard had brushed her lips with a chaste kiss and promised to worship her with his body. He sank into the velvet-upholstered seat opposite her, giving the door a sharp rap to signal the driver.

As the carriage rolled into motion, the villagers sent up a rousing cheer. The joy on their faces made it plain that they believed their debt to their laird had finally been paid in full, leaving them free to get on with the business of living.

As the carriage creaked its way up the cliff path, Gwendolyn's anger slowly gave way to apprehension. She stole a look at Bernard, finding it hard to believe that he was now her husband. Before, he could only steal what he wanted from her, but now she belonged to him body and soul.

Yet this man seemed more of a stranger to her than

the faceless creature who had once slipped into her bedchamber. Fighting shyness, she gazed out the opposite window. But the moonlight sifting through the shadows only reminded her how many hours of darkness were left before the dawn.

Bernard must have noticed her faint shiver. Tugging the pin from the MacCullough badge, he drew off his plaid and wrapped it around her shoulders. He had clung tightly to her hand while they exchanged their vows, but now that they were alone, he seemed almost reluctant to touch her.

As he settled back in the seat, Gwendolyn said, "Congratulations, M'lord Dragon. It appears you'll have your virgin sacrifice after all."

He returned to gazing out the window, his profile as stony as the landscape. "You should never offer a man anything you don't want him to take. Especially—"

"—a man like you?" Gwendolyn finished softly.

Before he could agree with her, Castle Weyrcraig loomed out of the darkness.

The carriage drew up before the gates, and a footman came running out to throw open the door. As Bernard escorted her to the castle, Gwendolyn remembered that stormy night when he had carried her through this very courtyard in his arms. And now she was returning to this place not as his captive, but as his bride.

A man garbed all in black greeted them at the door. "Good evening, sir. Shall I have Cook prepare a late supper for you and your . . ."—he peered down his long patrician nose at Gwendolyn, his hesitation betraying volumes—*"lady?"*

Bernard shook his head. "That won't be necessary, Jenkins. I want you and the rest of the servants gone. Take the longboats and spend the night on the ship."

"But, sir," the man protested, plainly scandalized by the suggestion that he abandon his duty, "what if you should require something during the night?"

Bernard rested a possessive hand against the small of Gwendolyn's back. "I can assure you that I'm more than capable of providing my *lady* with whatever she needs."

His words sent a dark shiver down Gwendolyn's spine. At least before there had been Tupper. Now she would be utterly at the mercy of a man who had already confessed that he had none. Before the servant could hasten to obey his instructions, Bernard was gently, but firmly, guiding her toward the stairs.

The main staircase was no longer littered with fallen stones and draped in shadows, but swept clean and lit by two rows of flickering candles set in iron sconces. The splintered railing of the gallery had been replaced by sturdy mahogany carved with fanciful scrollwork. Gwendolyn expected to find such cozy touches everywhere they went, but as they started up the winding stairs that led to the tower, a blast of chill wind whipped right through Bernard's plaid. The scattered rubble made it plain that no workman's hand had been allowed to alter the desolate chaos of the stairwell.

They rounded the first turn, bringing Gwendolyn

face-to-face with the jagged hole in the north wall. Civilization might be slowly reclaiming the rest of the castle, but here the night still reigned in all of its wild and tempestuous beauty.

The stars were strewn across the brooding sky like glittering shards of ice. The waves crashed against the rocks at the foot of the cliff, churning the sea into a bubbling cauldron.

Bernard's hand tensed, and for one dizzying moment Gwendolyn actually believed he might hurl her over that precipice to punish her for her father's betrayal. Then his arm stole around her waist, drawing her back from the brink. Closing her eyes, she sank against him.

"Watch your step," he murmured, urging her past the chasm.

The panel door at the top of the stairs creaked open at his touch. Moonlight streamed through the bars of the grate, casting a hazy glow over the half-melted tapers and rumpled bedclothes.

The trunk in the corner sat open, spilling out an array of lace and ribbons. Manderly's *The Triumph of Rational Thinking* was still sprawled on the floor. Everything was exactly as Gwendolyn had left it.

"So did you save all of this for me," she asked, "or were you hoping the villagers would leave another virgin on your doorstep?"

Bernard leaned against the panel, folding his arms over his chest. "I was rather hoping for a strumpet this time. Virgins are too damn much trouble."

"Speaking of strumpets," she said, drifting over to

the trunk to finger a length of ribbon, "I would have thought you'd have returned these gowns to whichever one of your light-o'-loves they once belonged to."

"I'm afraid that won't be possible." He paused, his mouth tightening. "They belonged to my mother."

The ribbon slipped through Gwendolyn's fingers. She smoothed the pleated taffeta skirt of her gown.

"My mother was a practical soul without a vain bone in her body, but my father delighted in surprising her with the most beautiful bolts of fabric Paris and London had to offer." Bernard picked up the book and leafed through its gilt-edged pages. "The books were his. He always hoped I'd take more of an interest in them, but I was too busy hunting and hawking. I fancied myself a warrior, not a scholar."

"He was very proud of you, you know."

Bernard tossed the book on the table. "I didn't prove myself to be much of a warrior the night Cumberland took the castle."

"You stayed alive, didn't you?"

"Only because one of Cumberland's officers was a cunning bastard with a hatred for all things Scots and an unnatural appetite for pretty young boys."

For a moment, Gwendolyn couldn't even draw breath. "He didn't . . . ?"

"He wanted to. Oh, it was subtle at first—a ribald jest here, a threat there, a casual touch. Until the day he cornered me in the woods on the march to Edinburgh." Bernard inclined his head, his face shadowed by an old shame. "He held me down. Tried to put his fat, filthy hands on me."

"What did you do?"

He lifted his head, meeting her fierce gaze with one of his own. "I killed him. I gutted him with his own knife. When it was done, I stood over him, my hands dripping with his blood, and I felt nothing—no shame, no remorse, no regret."

If he had thought to disgust her, he had failed. Gwendolyn felt nothing but a savage gladness that the man was dead.

"They would have executed me, but they decided it would be more fitting to let the Royal Navy break my spirit. When they took me aboard the ship in Edinburgh, the captain had me locked in the hold, in one of the compartments that had once been used to transport slaves. It was no bigger than a grave, and they gave me just enough bread and water to keep me alive long after I began praying to die."

Gwendolyn closed her eyes, trying not to imagine that proud, bright-eyed boy, who had spent his entire childhood roaming the mountains and moors, locked away in the darkness, choking on the stench of his own filth.

"How did you keep from going mad?"

He shrugged. "Maybe I didn't. By the time we reached England, I was little more than an animal, un-recognizable even to myself. When we docked, they dragged me out of the hold and threw me at the feet of a Royal Navy admiral. At first I thought he was like the other one. So I lunged at him. If I hadn't been so weak, I might have succeeded in tearing out his throat with my teeth. He could have had me hanged for that, but instead he ordered that every man on that ship be stripped to the waist and given twenty lashes for so sorely abusing a child." He shook his head. "All I could think was '*How* dare *the bastard call me a child*?' "

Gwendolyn bit back a tremulous smile.

"Admiral Grayson was a decent sort for an Englishman, rather stern, but not unkind. His wife had died before she could bear him a son, so he took an interest in me. When I was old enough he purchased a commission for me, and when I left the navy he prevailed upon his well-heeled friends to invest in my shipping business. I had always planned to return to Ballybliss someday, but I felt it only fair to wait until after his death."

For the first time, Gwendolyn could understand Bernard's loyalty to a people who were supposed to have been his sworn enemies. She could understand why he had learned to talk like them, to dress like them, and to fight at their side.

As she drifted toward him, the plaid slipped from her shoulders to the floor. He watched her approach through wary eyes, but made no move to stop her, not even when she reached up to touch her fingertips to his cheek. She had once searched his features for some terrible disfigurement, but now she realized the scars she had been seeking weren't on his face, but his soul.

"My poor Dragon," she murmured, stroking the

curve of his jaw. "They treated you like a beast, so you had no choice but to become one."

He caught her wrist in his unyielding grip. "Damn it, Gwendolyn, I don't want your pity!"

"Then what do you want from me?" she implored, tilting her face to his.

"This," he whispered hoarsely, shifting his hungry gaze from her eyes to her lips. "I want this."

# Chapter Twenty-five

BERNARD BROUGHT HIS MOUTH down on hers. His tongue was hard and hungry as it pressed into her, licking to life a searing flame of desire. Gwendolyn twined her fingers through his hair, the sweet, hot flicker of her tongue inviting him to work his dark magic, even if there be nothing left of her when he was done but a smoldering heap of ashes. She should have been afraid, but this place, this night, this man had cast a spell upon her, banishing all of her fears and inhibitions.

She sighed as his lips abandoned hers, but that sigh deepened into a moan of pleasure when they blazed a scorching trail from the corner of her mouth to the softness of her cheek.

"God, I love your dimples," he muttered. "And I intend to taste every one of them before this night is done."

He pressed his lips to the vulnerable hollow at the base of her throat. Nuzzling his way past her pounding pulse, he captured her earlobe between his teeth, then sent his tongue swirling through the wildly sensitive shell of her ear.

Gwendolyn gasped, unprepared for the sharp explosion of longing in her womb. Bernard caught the helpless sound in his mouth, muffling it with a groan of his own. She had believed he meant to feast on her, but she was the one being sated, by every hungry stroke of his tongue, every greedy brush of his fingertips against her skin. She was so lost in his kiss that she wasn't even aware that his deft hands had unfastened her bodice and bared her to the waist until she felt the cool night air caress her naked breasts.

Before she could shield the generous globes with her hands, Bernard had covered them with his own. He filled his palms with her, then caught her throbbing nipples between forefinger and thumb, gently teasing and tugging until a mewling sob of pleasure escaped her.

"I can't believe you don't know how beautiful you are," he whispered in her ear. "You're so soft, so sweet, so round in all the places a man most wants to touch."

As if to prove his point, he slid his hands from her breasts to her bottom, urging her hips against him. He lavished her mouth with kisses as he rocked against her, the rigid length straining against the front of his kilt seeking an even deeper softness.

Gwendolyn gasped as that exquisite friction ignited a fresh spark, one so wild and so hot it threatened to incinerate her where she stood. Sliding her hands beneath his shirt, she feathered her fingers against the taut plane of his abdomen. His heated skin quivered at her touch.

"If your fingers stray so much as an inch lower," he said through clenched teeth, "this wedding night will be over before it's begun."

Gwendolyn slid her hand upward, stroking the lightly furred muscles of his chest. "I've waited over half my life for this night. I want it to last forever."

"Then I'll do all I can to stop the dawn from coming."

As Bernard gathered the voluminous sacque gown and slipped it over her head, she closed her eyes, thankful that there were no corsets or petticoats to hinder him. He gently urged her drawers down her legs until there was nothing left for her to do but step out of them and stand before him, as naked as a newborn babe.

He gazed down at her, the glint of appreciation in his eye so keen that she thought he might lift his kilt and take her right there against the door.

Instead, he swept her up in his arms and carried her to the bed. After spending most of her life with her feet planted firmly on the ground, Gwendolyn found it a heady thrill to be lifted like that.

Bernard followed her down to the feather mattress. His weight should have crushed her, yet she welcomed the possessive thrust of his tongue, the hot and heavy fullness of his manhood pressing against her belly.

When he leaned away from her to drag off his shirt and unwrap his kilt, she quivered in anticipation of his return. Bars of moonlight fell across the bed, making her his captive once more. They bathed her in a lambent glow, but left him in darkness.

She could only imagine how she must appear to him—sprawled naked across the satin sheets like one of those wanton, voluptuous demigoddesses who gazed down upon them from the mural above. Although his eyes were in shadow, she could feel his gaze upon her, making her flesh tingle.

When he spoke, every trace of his years in England had been banished from his lilting burr. "This was my room when I was a lad, you know. I spent many a sleepless hour lying on my back, gazing up at that accursed mural. I used to dream that one of those goddesses would come tumbling out of the heavens and into my arms." His breathing was audible in the darkness. "And now she has."

A flush crept up Gwendolyn's throat and her breasts began to tighten and ache, as if begging for some small morsel of attention. It was sweet torture, knowing he would touch her, but not knowing when or where.

A shiver of yearning rocked her as he lowered his head and touched the very tip of his tongue to one of her throbbing nipples. She arched against him, her fingernails scoring the sheets as the gentle tug of his teeth and lips coaxed a surge of molten nectar from between her thighs.

Before she could catch her breath, he was pressing a reverent kiss to the dimple at the inner curve of one knee. His beard-roughened cheek tickled her calf, but his lips were moist and warm. As his mouth began to drift higher, urging her thighs apart, she began to tremble.

He ran his hands over the virgin cream of her belly. "There's no need to be afraid, my bonny angel. I'm not a beast tonight. I'm simply a man who wants nothing more in this world than to make love to his bride."

*His bride.*

Gwendolyn had almost forgotten that such sinfully delicious delights could actually be sanctioned by God. Which was why she wasn't prepared for the shock of Bernard's big, warm hands curling around her bottom, lifting and spreading her to accept the sweetest and most unholy of kisses.

She clutched at the rough silk of his hair as unspeakable pleasure curled through her. Gazing up at the goddesses in the mural through dazed eyes, she wondered if they'd ever known such forbidden ecstasy. Persephone gazed back at her with knowing eyes. Psyche's flushed cheeks and parted lips were a mirror of her own.

Then Bernard shattered both her and the heavens with nothing more than the artful flick of his tongue. She was still shuddering with tremors of raw bliss when his mouth closed over hers, feeding her the ambrosia of her own desire.

"Had I known being fed to a dragon would be so sweet," she murmured into his mouth, "I might have gone willingly to that stake."

"Ah, but the taste of you only whets my appetite," he growled, grazing her throat with his teeth.

The hungry stroke of his fingers left no doubt as to what would satisfy him. He pressed two of them deep inside of her, using the dew his mouth had coaxed from those lush petals to prepare her for what was to come. As his shadow covered her, blocking out the moonlight, Gwendolyn began to tremble again.

He cupped her face in his hands. "You were brave enough to defy a dragon in his own lair. Don't tell me you're afraid now."

"I'm not," she whispered, tenderly stroking his hair from his brow. "I'm terrified."

Bernard gazed deep into her eyes. "So am I."

His hoarse confession gave Gwendolyn the courage to open her legs to him. As he buried himself deep within her, a ragged groan tore from his throat. Gwendolyn might have cried out herself had his pleasure not seemed to be so much more powerful than her pain. The ache of accommodating him was quickly eclipsed by the primal thrill of being filled to the brink by his throbbing length. There would be no escaping this stake, and as Bernard began to glide in and out of her, each thrust driving him deeper, Gwendolyn realized she no longer wanted to escape.

She wrapped her arms around him and clung for dear life. He could no longer hold himself apart from her—not the boy she had adored, nor the man she had loved.

She arched against him, eager to embrace all that he was and all that he ever would be—angel and demon, boy and man, beast and prince, husband and stranger.

She no longer rebelled against his tender mastery, but rejoiced at being a captive to the pleasure he would lavish upon her.

Bracing his palms on each side of her head, he rocked into her, all the while gazing into her eyes with an urgency as fierce and driving as the ancient rhythm building to a crescendo between her thighs. "You told me you were once half in love with me," he reminded her. "Well, I'm a greedy bastard and I'm not willing to settle for half. I want it all."

At that moment, he shifted his body, angling his strokes so that each plunge of his hips abraded the tender bud nestled at the peak of her damp curls.

The words he sought broke from her on a wail, driven forth by a relentless tide of pleasure. His body went rigid, seized by the same convulsions of ecstasy that wracked her womb. In the glen below, several of the villagers lifted their eyes to the castle and signed crosses on their breasts, swearing that they had once again heard the Dragon's roar.

Gwendolyn stood in Bernard's arms on the table below the grate, watching the moon drift toward the sea. The ship that had first brought him to her was still anchored in the inlet, its masts silhouetted against the falling moon. Despite his most valiant efforts, they both knew the night couldn't last forever.

As the last traces of the moon's silvery wake disappeared beneath the swells, his arm tightened around her waist. She leaned the back of her head against his shoulder, sighing wistfully.

Although there seemed to be no shame in their nakedness, Gwendolyn was further emboldened by the dark. Turning in Bernard's arms, she slipped to her knees before him.

As the softness of her lips flowered against his abdomen, he gently twined his hands through her hair. "What are you doing, woman? Trying to drive me mad?"

Since there were no words to speak what was in her heart, Gwendolyn gave him the only answer she could. His hands fisted in her hair and his head fell back, the muscles in his throat cording as he uttered a groan of raw rapture. Gwendolyn had been seeking to atone for her father's sins, but instead she found herself exalted by this potent combination of power and vulnerability, both Bernard's and hers. She was no longer his captive, but a willing supplicant on the altar of his pleasure. Her absolution was sweeter than anything she had anticipated, but not nearly as sweet as the moment when Bernard dropped to his knees and pressed her cheek to his thundering heart.

Although the rosy glow of dawn was already beginning to warm the chamber, Bernard sat in the shadows beside the bed, watching Gwendolyn sleep. With her golden hair and pale skin, she was a creature of the light, defying the darkness with her very existence.

He leaned back in the chair, the kilt draped over his lap. Any other time he would have wished for a glass of port and a cheroot, but he wasn't yet ready to vanquish the taste of her from his mouth.

She was curled on top of the sheets, her cheek lying on her folded hands, her lips still swollen from his kisses. His groin tightened. Shortly before dawn he had learned just how generous those lips could be.

He reached to stroke a tendril of gold from her brow. For the first time in fifteen years, his urge to protect was stronger than his urge to destroy. Even if the danger he most needed to protect her from was himself.

He could no longer ignore the dried stains on the sheets, the rusty flecks marring Gwendolyn's pale thighs.

*May vengeance be upon yer heads*
*'Til innocent blood be shed.*

As his father's curse echoed through his mind, Bernard dropped his head into his hands. He had shed the blood of an innocent, only to discover that nothing had changed. He had warned Gwendolyn that the boy she had once loved was dead, but until this moment, Bernard had never truly grieved for him.

That boy would have never sought to punish her for her father's transgressions. He never would have forced such a ridiculous travesty of a marriage upon her. He would have given her the wedding she deserved. And the wedding night.

She would have had clean sheets and fresh flowers

and a fire to warm her while her lady's maid helped her out of her gown and into a virginal white nightdress. She would have sat on a stool before the mirror while the maid drew a brush through her hair and perhaps answered a few questions to allay her fears about the night to come.

He wouldn't have come to her in darkness, but by candlelight, offering her a glass of wine to soothe her nerves before stealing a few chaste kisses. Then he would have carried her to the bed, gently laid her back among the pillows, and made love to her with all the consideration she deserved. He certainly wouldn't have subjected her to one feverish coupling after another without giving her tender young body any time to recover from his brutish attentions.

Bernard lifted his head, tracing the graceful curve of Gwendolyn's back with his despairing gaze. That boy could have given her so much—a home, his children, his heart.

Bernard wanted to believe he could still give her those things. But every time he looked at her he would remember the bargain her father had struck with the devil and just what that bargain had cost him.

Memories he'd denied himself for over fifteen years came flooding back—the warm, briny scent of his pony after a hard rain; the deep rumble of his father's exasperated chuckle; the tenderness in his mother's touch as she brushed a lock of hair from his brow. Alastair Wilder's treachery had robbed him of his past, and now it seemed it would rob him of his future as well.

His enemy finally had a face. And it was the face of a man he had once admired and respected. A man his father had trusted with his life and the life of his family. By betraying that trust, Wilder had earned Bernard's undying hatred.

Surely it would be only a matter of time before that hatred poisoned everything he touched—even Gwendolyn.

It was just as he had feared. Her kiss, willingly surrendered, had doomed him to walk in darkness for the rest of his days. Only now he was cursed with the knowledge that darkness wasn't the absence of light, but the absence of her.

The Dragon came to Gwendolyn in her dreams. She was curled up on a bed of sandalwood and spice when his shadow fell over her.

Reluctant to wake up, she kept her eyes closed even as she opened her arms to him, murmuring his name. At first she thought he meant to slip between her thighs again—to ease the hollow ache that was satisfied only by his presence. But, instead, he gathered her into his arms, then gently touched his lips to her brow, her dimpled cheek, the corner of her mouth.

"Is it morning?" she murmured, nuzzling her lips against his throat.

"Not for me," he whispered, his arms tightening around her.

She snuggled deeper into their warmth. "Then do I have to wake up?"

"No, angel, you can sleep as long as you like." Planting a kiss on the softness of her lips, he eased her back to the mattress. He tucked the soft folds of his plaid around her, his hands lingering everywhere they touched.

His shadow drifted away from her. Gwendolyn burrowed into the tartan cocoon, secure in the knowledge that her Dragon would be watching over her while she slept.

When Gwendolyn opened her eyes again, there was a beast sitting on her chest. Once she might have shrieked to make such a discovery, but now she simply thought how astonishing it was that she could breathe while encumbered with so much dead weight. Toby returned her drowsy blink with one of his own.

"How do you stay so fat?" she inquired of him. "I know it's not from eating mice." His whiskers twitched, his expression so contrary that she had to laugh. "I suppose you'd like to ask the same thing of me."

In reply, he extended his claws and began to knead the plaid. Gently heaving him aside before he could puncture one of her lungs, Gwendolyn sat up.

This time, she didn't have to wonder how the cat had gotten into the tower. The panel door was half-ajar and Bernard was nowhere in sight.

"I hope he's gone to fetch us both some breakfast," she told the cat, stretching her stiff muscles. Noting the steep slant of the sun through the grate, she added, "Or lunch."

A naughty little smile curved her lips. Not even that dour English manservant of Bernard's could blame her for languishing in bed half the day, since it had been his master who had kept her up for half the night.

The villagers had been right about one thing. The Dragon's appetites *were* insatiable.

Gwendolyn collapsed on the pillows, giggling like a schoolgirl. The sheets no longer smelled only of sandalwood and spice, but of an earthy musk redolent of their loving. She breathed deep, savoring the memories it evoked.

She smiled up at the mural, musing over the parallels between Psyche's story and her own. Like the Dragon, Cupid had come to Psyche only at night, making her promise never to try and see his face. Gwendolyn struggled to remember more of the story her mother had once told her. Prompted by her jealous sisters, Psyche had broken her vow, stealing a glimpse of Cupid's face while he slept. But when a drop of hot oil from her lamp spilled upon his arm, he had awakened. Angered by his bride's betrayal, he had flown away, vowing never to see her again.

Gwendolyn's smile faded. She sat up, becoming aware of how very quiet the castle was. Since Toby was still sulking at being evicted from her chest, she didn't have even his purr to break the silence.

She rose and slipped into her rumpled gown, then

wrapped the plaid around her shoulders. Some childish whisper of hope made her close her eyes just as she had done in the ruins of the chapel on the night she had gone in search of the Dragon.

This time, there was no bone-deep certainty of Bernard's presence. There was only a vast emptiness, underscored by the unsettling hush that had fallen over the castle.

Opening her eyes, Gwendolyn dashed across the tower and scrambled up onto the table.

Bernard's ship was already drifting out of the inlet, its sails unfurled to catch the southerly breeze.


By the time Gwendolyn reached the peak of the castle, she was gasping for breath. The wind whipped at her hair, momentarily blinding her as she ran to the battlement.

She leaned over the wall, her nails digging into the stone as she spotted the ship approaching the horizon. Before a rush of hot tears blurred her vision, she saw a lone figure standing at the stern of the ship, his black cloak billowing about his broad shoulders.

She wondered if he could see her. He might have been able to see the sun glinting off her golden hair, but he couldn't have seen the sobs that wracked her shoulders or the tears coursing down her cheeks. She stood there, refusing to crumple as long as there was the smallest chance that she might be visible to his eyes.

As the ship melted into the misty horizon, Gwendolyn sank to her knees on the cold stone, burying her face in her hands. She couldn't have said how long she remained like that. It could have been only moments, or an eternity. But when she heard a footfall behind her, she jerked her head around, hope flaring in her breast.

Tupper stood there, compassion shining in his soft, brown eyes. "This was delivered to the manor a short while ago," he said gently, holding out his hand. "I suppose he didn't want you to be alone when you read it."

Gwendolyn smoothed the creamy paper beneath her hand, then slid her fingernail beneath the familiar dab of crimson wax that had been used to seal it.

Bernard's elegant scrawl lacked its usual flair. The forceful slashes and graceful loops were marred by ink blots and smears.

"My lady," Gwendolyn read softly. "The curse has been broken. Both you and Ballybliss are free. I tried to warn you that I was no longer the boy you once loved. After what transpired between us last night, you must surely believe me."

Tupper blushed, but Gwendolyn refused to feel even a flicker of shame.

"From this day forward," she continued, "no man will ever be your laird and master, because you will be the MacCullough, the chieftain of Clan MacCullough and lady of Castle Weyrcraig. I've arranged for the thousand pounds your father accepted from Cumberland to be delivered to you so that you might do what is best for the clan and the castle. A thousand pounds will follow each year until my death."

Gwendolyn faltered. "You once asked me for the truth and I refused you. Last night you asked me for mercy and I refused you that as well. All I have left to offer you now is the one thing that was never truly mine to take—your freedom." Gwendolyn was forced to read the last through the tears streaming from her eyes. "I leave you with both my name and my heart. Ever yours, Bernard MacCullough."

She bowed her head, crumpling the paper in her fist. Looking nearly as miserable as she felt, Tupper fumbled in his waistcoat pocket for a handkerchief and waved it at her.

Gwendolyn climbed to her feet, batting it aside. "Damn him, Tupper! Damn his arrogant soul to hell!" Hugging the plaid around her shoulders, she turned back to the sea, letting the wind sear the tears from her eyes. "Does he think everything can just go back to the way it was before he came to this place? Does he think I can just go back to pretending that dragons don't exist?"

Tupper shook his head helplessly. "I'm sure he believed he was only doing what was best."

Gwendolyn whirled around. "Yet he has the sheer gall to try and convince me that he's no longer the boy I remembered? He is *precisely* that boy! Smug. Bullheaded. Arrogant. Always trying to decide what's best for others without bothering to consult them. Why, he hasn't changed one whit!"

"He can be very stubborn once he gets a notion into his head. Perhaps in time . . ."

"I've already waited fifteen years. How long am I supposed to wait for him this time? Twenty years? Thirty? A lifetime?" She shook her head. "Oh, no! I've no intention of wasting another second of my life waiting for Bernard MacCullough to come to his senses."

Tupper stuffed the handkerchief back in his pocket. "So what do you mean to do?"

Gwendolyn straightened to her full height. Dashing the last of her tears from her cheeks, she drew the plaid around her shoulders as if it were the mantle of some ancient Celtic queen. "You heard his words, Tupper. I'm the MacCullough now. And wrong or right, a MacCullough always stands to fight."

# Chapter Twenty-six

HE'S QUITE THE BEAST, isn't he?"

"That depends on whether you're referring to his temper or his wit. I've heard that a single lash from that tongue of his can flay the hide from even the most clever of conversationalists."

"I wouldn't be adverse to receiving a tongue-lashing from him. Provided it took place while my Reginald was in the country, at one of his interminable hunting parties."

That husky quip earned a round of scandalized titters from the speaker's companions.

The object of their speculation brought his champagne glass to his lips, pretending not to overhear the conversation taking place just over his left shoulder. Fortunately, his hostess had an overbearing fondness for the Greek Revival style of interior decoration, giving him a wide variety of columns to lurk behind.

"My husband heard a rumor that he isn't even English," offered another woman. "Apparently, he's been masquerading as one of us for years simply to disguise the fact that he's actually"—she paused for dramatic effect—"a Scot!"

From the shocked gasps that greeted her revelation, she might as well have pronounced him an escaped Bedlamite.

"That explains his temper, doesn't it? Scots are a savage lot, given to ravishing virgins and speaking whatever is on their minds." The woman spoke as if these traits were equally abhorrent.

"Did you hear what he told Lady Jane after she cornered him in the drawing room and spent three quarters of an hour extolling her niece's matrimonial virtues?"

The rustling of fans indicated a new flurry of excitement. "Oh, no. Do tell!"

The speaker deepened her shrill voice three octaves in a crude impression of Bernard's baritone. " 'If I were seeking a wife, my lady, which I most certainly am not, she wouldn't be a simpering chit with more bosom than brains.' "

As the women dissolved into gales of laughter, Bernard lifted his glass in a bleak toast to a lass who had been blessed with both.

"Perhaps it's not his own wife he needs to satisfy his appetites," suggested the husky-voiced siren, "but someone else's."

As she and her tittering companions drifted away in search of fresh blood, Bernard brought the glass to his lips again. He was surprised to find it empty. If he kept swilling the foul-tasting froth at this rate, he would end up propping himself up with the column instead of hiding behind it.

He'd been back in London for less than a month, but he'd spent most of that time sleeping too little and drinking too much. It was no wonder he was getting a reputation for beastly behavior. He'd never been one to suffer fools gladly, but now it took little more than a sidelong look to earn a snappish retort or a growled set-down. Had Lord Drummond not been a loyal investor in his shipping firm and one of Admiral Grayson's oldest friends, he would have declined the duchess's invitation and remained at his sparsely furnished town house, his only company a stack of neglected ledgers and a bottle of port.

Waylaying a passing footman, Bernard traded his empty glass for a full one. He had taken a deep swallow before he realized he was no longer alone. One of the women who had just spent the last ten minutes dissecting his charms, or the lack of them, had emerged from the greenery of the potted fern at his elbow.

"My lady," Bernard said, offering her a curt nod.

"Oh, pardon me, sir." Her ingenuous blink was at odds with the throaty purr of her voice. "I mistook you for my husband."

"I believe that would be Reginald, wouldn't it? Tell me, does your devoted Reginald suspect that you go out prowling for fresh game whenever he's off hunting it?"

The woman's rouged mouth widened into a shocked little *o* before curving into a feline smile. "My, you do have the keen ears and sharp teeth of a beast, don't you? If you're trying to frighten me off, I should warn you that I've always been one to appreciate frankness in a man." Her hungry gaze licked from the polished toes of his boots to the gleaming crown of his hair. "Among other things."

Bernard almost wished he could return her appreciation. There was no denying that she was a beauty. Her dark hair had been whipped into a towering confection and dusted with a shimmering layer of powder that perfectly matched the alabaster of her face. Her lips were full and red, her cheekbones chiseled. She wore a black velvet ribbon around her slender throat and a mischievous patch of silk on her cheek where a dimple should be. Beneath the sleek satin of her bodice, a whalebone corset cinched her waist into a span he could have probably encompassed with his hands, while a frilled stomacher forced her creamy breasts upward until they threatened to spill from their constraints.

Yet, despite the broad panniers that gave her slender hips the illusion of softness, there was no disguising the hardness in her eyes. She looked brittle, prone to being shattered with a touch. There was nothing warm or solid about her. Nothing a man could hold on to . . . or sink himself into. . . .

Bernard pushed away from the column, fearing for a moment that he might actually stagger. "I'm glad that you appreciate frankness in a man because, quite frankly, I must beg you to excuse me."

"But you can't go yet, sir. Supper hasn't even been served!"

Bernard lingered just long enough to sweep her a polite bow. "I fear I wouldn't do it justice, my lady. I seem to have lost my appetite."

The fog muffled the click of Bernard's bootheels against the damp pavement as he strode toward his town house. His cloak swirled around his ankles with each step, but did little to warm him. This wasn't the crisp cold of a Highland evening, but a dank chill that seemed to sink deep into his bones. A murky blanket of soot hung over the ragged roofs and brick chimneys, dulling the shine of the distant stars to a wan flicker. The stilted hush made him realize just how keenly he missed Tupper's cheerful blathering.

He belonged to this fog- and soot-shrouded city now. He was no longer Gwendolyn's Dragon or chieftain of Clan MacCullough. He was just another faceless stranger among many.

He drew a cheroot from his pocket and lit it. Once, the restlessness that edged his soul would have sent him out to prowl the night. But his old haunts and the women who inhabited them had lost their allure, the victim of those few sweet hours in Gwendolyn's arms.

He heard a muffled footfall behind him. He turned, but found the street deserted and draped in shadows. The lamps did little more than make hazy dents in the fog. He cocked his head, but the only sound he heard was the faint sizzle of the burning cheroot in his hand.

Tucking the cheroot in the corner of his mouth, he

resumed his trek. He hadn't been back in London long enough to make any new enemies. Unless perhaps he'd insulted the wrong man's wife with one of his scathing set-downs.

But an outraged husband was more likely to call him out than follow him home. And Bernard wouldn't even begrudge him the privilege. At least being dispatched by a pistol ball in a duel would be quicker and more honorable than drinking himself to death.

As he turned down the street where he lived, his steps slowed. Who would have thought a London town house nestled within the tidy confines of Berkeley Square could manage to look more lonely and forbidding than a Highland ruin perched on the edge of a cliff? Lamps burned a cheery welcome in the windows of the neighboring houses. Somewhere a door opened and closed, briefly freeing the merry tinkle of a pianoforte and a child's burst of laughter. Bernard's house waited for him at the end of the street, dark and silent.

He was just starting up the front steps when a glint of light in one of the second-story windows caught his eye.

He paused, his hand on the wrought iron railing. He would have sworn he'd given Jenkins the night off. He waited for several minutes, gazing up at the darkened windowpanes, but that ghostly flicker did not come again. Shaking his head, Bernard unlocked the door, promising himself that he'd never again forsake port for champagne.

He dined on a cold supper of beef and bread, then remained closeted in his study until the tidy rows of figures in his ledgers began to blur before his eyes. Exhaustion weighted his steps as he climbed the stairs leading to his bedroom, but it was well after midnight before he finally drifted into a fitful sleep.

An unearthly wailing jolted him awake. He sat straight up in the bed, recognizing the melancholy music of the pipes. Their song abruptly ceased, leaving him to wonder if he was dreaming.

Phantom footsteps. Ghostly flickers of light in a deserted house. The eerie wail of bagpipes in the heart of London.

If he wasn't dreaming, he thought, then he must be going mad. He fumbled for the candlestick and tinderbox he'd left on the nightstand. At the exact moment he realized they were gone, he realized something else as well.

He was no longer alone.

Someone was in the room with him, someone whose breathing was a whispered counterpoint to the thundering of his heart. Reaching beneath his pillow, Bernard silently withdrew the loaded pistol he always kept there.

He leveled the mouth of the weapon at the shadows. "Who the hell are you? And what are you doing in my house?"

A match was struck. A candle's wick flared to life.

"There are some who call me the chieftain of Clan MacCullough and others who call me the lady of Castle Weyrcraig, but you, sir, may call me M'lady Dragon."

# Chapter Twenty-seven

Watching Gwendolyn Melt out of the shadows was like watching the sun emerge from a bank of storm clouds. The unexpected radiance made Bernard's eyes sting. She was a vision in lavender silk. The flowing lines of her sacque gown complemented the voluptuous curves of the body beneath. Her hair cascaded around her face in soft golden curls, while her blue eyes shimmered with warmth.

"Now I know I'm dreaming," he muttered. He closed his eyes, but when he opened them again, she was still there, regarding him with bemused tolerance.

"You'd best lower that thing before it goes off."

It took Bernard a dazed moment to realize that Gwendolyn was referring to the pistol. He slowly complied. "That wasn't very smart of you, stealing my candlestick but not my gun. I could have shot you, you know."

"No you couldn't." Her dimples deepened. "It's not loaded."

Disgusted more with himself than with her, Bernard tossed the gun to the table. "So where have you stashed Tupper and his pipes? The attic?"

"The cellar. But don't worry about him. I left Kitty there to keep him company. They're on their honeymoon, you know. I convinced them that coming to London with me would be even more of an adventure than Edinburgh."

"A new wardrobe. Honeymoons for your family. I'm glad to know you're putting that thousand pounds I left you to good use."

"And why shouldn't I?" She lifted one eyebrow. "I earned it, did I not?"

Bernard was speechless for a moment. "Is that why you think I left you the gold? As payment for your services?"

She shrugged. "What else was I to think? When I awoke that morning, you were gone and the gold was there."

Bernard was on the verge of throwing back the sheet so he could get up and pace the room when he remembered that he had always scorned nightshirts. His breeches were draped over the chair next to the door. Unless Gwendolyn had stolen them as well.

Folding his arms across his chest, he scowled at her. "Some treasures, my lady, are beyond price."

She might have blushed, but the flickering candlelight made it impossible to tell. "Or perhaps they're only worth what one is willing to pay for them."

Bernard eyed her warily. "So why are you here,

*M'lady Dragon*? Have you come to seek a virgin sacrifice?"

"If so, I've come to the wrong place, haven't I?" Gwendolyn sat down on the end of the bed, just out of his reach. "Actually, I'm not seeking a virgin, but a trustworthy solicitor."

"I can't imagine why you'd have need of one of those. Unless, of course, you plan to make a habit of breaking into houses to the accompaniment of bagpipes."

She gave his foot an affectionate pat. "Don't be silly. I wish to discuss the possibility of obtaining an annulment, or even a divorce if necessary."

Bernard sank back against the headboard, unprepared for the icy chill that shot down his spine. "You would divorce me?"

"And why not? You offered me my freedom, didn't you? Surely you didn't think I'd be content to molder away in that damp pile of stones for the rest of my life. You might not wish to marry again, but I have no intention of spending the remainder of my days"—she slanted him a provocative glance—"or my nights . . . alone."

"I've only been gone for a few weeks. Have you already chosen my successor?"

She shrugged. "I've found there to be no lack of suitors in Ballybliss. There's Ross, for instance."

Bernard almost came out of the bed, breeches be damned. "Ross? Are you out of your bloody mind? He tried to feed you to a dragon *and* burn you at the stake."

Gwendolyn fluffed out her skirts as if oblivious to his

consternation. "That may be true, but I've seen a much gentler side of him since I became the MacCullough. He's been ever so attentive." A prim little smile played around her mouth. "Not a day passes by that he doesn't bring me a bouquet of heather or some other small token of his affection. Of course, if Ross and I don't suit, there's always Lachlan. The lad's been quite heartbroken since Nessa cast him aside for the tinker's nephew."

"For God's sake, woman, you can't marry Lachlan! He has hair sprouting from his ears."

Gwendolyn blinked at him. "Isn't that supposed to be a sign of virility?"

Bernard would have sworn he was done with being a beast, but he came within a heartbeat of growling at her. "Only if you're a gorilla."

Frowning, Gwendolyn rose and paced beside the bed. "Perhaps you're right, sir. I fear I was on the verge of making a terrible mistake. You've given me much to think about."

"Thank God for that," he muttered.

After another minute of such pacing, she turned to face him. "Perhaps it would be best if I seek a suitor right here in London. Once I might have lacked the confidence to do so, but you were the one who convinced me I had much to offer a man. And you're not the only one who thinks so." She clasped her hands in front of her as if reciting out of a child's primer. "Current fashion may dictate that a woman be as slight as a sylph, but a discerning fellow will always appreciate a healthy breeder."

Bernard leaned forward, fully prepared to call out the scoundrel guilty of filling his wife's head with this shocking notion. "Who told you such a thing?"

"Why, Tupper's great-aunt Taffy, of course. She was kind enough to take us all in when Tupper's father disowned him for marrying a penniless Scottish lass. She was so furious with the viscount that she's decided to disinherit him. Upon her death, her entire fortune will go to Tupper."

"Should he outlive her," Bernard said grimly, thinking the prospect highly unlikely given his friend's part in this ambush. Growing weary of Gwendolyn's dancing just out of his reach, he yanked the sheet off the bed and wrapped it around his waist. "Just how do you propose to meet these prospective suitors of yours? Shall I introduce you?" He stood, sweeping the bedpost a courtly bow. " 'Hullo, David, old chap. This is my wife. Would you care to marry her?' "

Gwendolyn laughed. "You'd frighten them all off with that terrible glower of yours."

He took a step toward her. "I haven't done a very good job of frightening *you* off, have I?"

"On the contrary, it was you who fled from me. And just why was that?" She tapped her lips, pretending to search her memory. "Oh, yes, it was 'because you were no longer the boy I once loved.' But you forgot to take one thing into account. I'm not a little girl anymore." She flattened her palms against his chest, sending a shiver rippling through the taut muscles of his abdomen. "I don't need a boy. I need a man."

Her boldness was irresistible. Capturing one of her wrists, Bernard slid her open hand downward over the sheet until it was molded to the fire blazing at the cradle of his thighs. "Then you've come to the right place."

Her fingers tensed. She gazed up at him through her lashes, her breath coming as short and fast as his own. Drawing her into his arms, he lowered his lips to hers. Her mouth was plump and sweet and ripe for the taking, like sun-warmed strawberries drizzled with fresh cream. Bernard groaned as her tongue sought his, making him wild with urgency.

As he fell back on the bed, drawing Gwendolyn down to straddle him, all of his noble resolutions to go slow, to be gentle were replaced by one all-consuming desire.

To be inside his wife.

It took him less than three long, hot, open-mouthed kisses to work his hands beneath her petticoats. Instead of tugging her drawers down around her hips, he simply used his fingers to widen the narrow slit in the silk at the apex of her thighs. Two more kisses and he had those same fingers gliding in and out of her in a rhythm his body was aching to duplicate. She followed the pace he set, instinctively arching toward the pleasure he would give her.

Bernard shoved the sheet aside. The next time Gwendolyn sank down on top of him, it wasn't his fingers that slid deep inside of her.

She shuddered, her tender young body squeezing

him in a vise of raw delight. She had wanted a man and he had given her every inch of one.

He reached up to stroke her flushed cheek. "We can slow down now, angel. I want you to enjoy this ride every bit as much as I intend to."

Determined to do everything in his power to make sure she would, Bernard filled his hands with her hips and guided her into a rhythm that was just slow and sinuous enough to madden them both. The effort made a feverish sweat break out all over his body, but he knew it was worth it when flickers of rapture began to dance across her beautiful face.

He waited until her head fell back and a deep-throated moan escaped her parted lips before slipping one hand beneath her skirt. All it took to turn her moan into a wail was the teasing caress of one fingertip across her quivering flesh.

Bernard's own control snapped. He seized her hips, no longer willing or able to contain the driving rhythm of his strokes. His desire to be inside of her had been supplanted by a need that was even more powerful and primal. He clenched his teeth against a savage roar as his seed came spilling from his loins in a blinding rush of ecstasy.

As Gwendolyn collapsed against him, he wrapped his arms around her, holding her as if he would never let her go.

# Chapter Twenty-eight

WHERE IS SHE?" Bernard demanded as he strode into the dining room of Taffy Tuppingham's Mayfair mansion.

Tupper froze, a scone smeared with butter and jam halfway to his mouth. Kitty dabbed at her lips with her linen napkin, her striped poplin morning gown and lace cap making her look remarkably elegant and mature for a Highland lass who had just turned eighteen. Rather than dining at opposite ends of the table as was customary, the newlyweds sat side by side, near enough for Kitty to twine her stockinged foot around Tupper's calf.

A nervous footman trotted into the room at Bernard's heels. "Forgive me, sir. I tried to tell him that your aunt never rises before noon and absolutely refuses to receive callers until after two o'clock, but the gentleman would have none of it."

Tupper nodded at the frazzled man. "That's all right, Dobbins. He's no gentleman."

As the footman slunk out of the room, Bernard slammed his palms down on the polished table, feeling every inch the beast with his hair uncombed and his cravat hanging loose around his neck. "Where is she? What have you done with my wife?"

Tupper took a sip of chocolate from a delicate Wedgwood cup. "Have you misplaced her?"

"When I awoke this morning, she was gone from my bed."

Tupper frowned. "That's most odd. You've never had any trouble keeping women in your bed before."

"I've never married one before either, have I?" Bernard snapped.

Tupper shook his head. "I simply can't have you spoiling my wife's delicate digestion with all of this growling and baring of teeth. If you must know, Gwendolyn left for Ballybliss shortly before dawn."

"Ballybliss?" Bernard straightened. "*Ballybliss?* I can't believe you were fool enough to let her go!"

"And I can't believe *you* were fool enough to abandon her in the first place," Tupper retorted.

Bernard sank down in the chair opposite him, rubbing the back of his neck. "To be honest, neither can I. Although at least I had the common decency to leave her a note."

Exchanging a look with her husband, Kitty drew a folded piece of vellum from the pocket of her skirt. "Before she departed, my sister asked me to give this to you."

Bernard took the missive, recognizing his own stationery. Gwendolyn must have filched it from his study before he arrived home the previous night. He wasn't surprised to discover that her handwriting was as graceful and precise as she was.

"If you ever wish to spend another night in my company," he read, "it will cost you more than a thousand pounds." Bernard waved the piece of paper at Tupper. "Just what am I supposed to make of this?"

"Whatever you choose, I would imagine," his friend replied, helping himself to a forkful of kipper.

Bernard was still gazing down at the note when Kitty gave his sleeve a tug. "Forgive my impertinence, m'laird, but I simply have to ask. Why *did* you leave my sister?"

It was hard to hold on to his anger beneath the wide-eyed sincerity of Kitty's gaze. It was even harder to remember that she was also the daughter of the man who had destroyed his life. He couldn't very well confess that he was afraid he would spend the rest of his life punishing Gwendolyn for their father's sin.

He opened his mouth to lie but instead found himself uttering a truth he'd kept even from himself. "I suppose I didn't believe I could ever be worthy of her."

Tupper chuckled and caressed his wife's cheek, earning an adoring glance for his trouble. "Then you're a bigger fool than I thought. Since when has any man ever been worthy of the woman he loved? It's only by God's grace that they love us in spite of ourselves."

Bernard gently folded Gwendolyn's note and slipped it into the pocket of his waistcoat. "What if it's too late,

Tupper? What if God doesn't have any grace left for the likes of me?"

"There's only one way to find out, my friend."

Bernard sat in silence for several minutes before rising and starting for the door.

"Where are you going?" Tupper asked, coming to his feet.

Bernard turned in the doorway. "Home, Tupper. I'm going home."

The pipes were calling him home.

As Bernard flew through the mountain passes and lonely glens, he could hear their music over the rhythmic thunder of his horse's hooves. They no longer wailed a lament to mourn all he had lost but soared in a jubilant song to celebrate all he hoped to win.

He was finally able to put a name to the hopeless yearning that had plagued him for fifteen years—homesickness. He was homesick for the salty sting of the wind that blew off the sea, the rippling music of the burns gurgling over their rock-strewn beds, the melody of English being spoken with a lilting burr. He was even homesick for the drafty old castle that had come to symbolize the ruin of all his dreams.

The towers of Castle Weyrcraig appeared in the distance, silhouetted against the night sky. Bernard reined his horse to a halt, remembering all the times his parents had been waiting there to welcome him home. Times when his mother would scold him for lingering too long in the damp while his father ruffled his hair and challenged him to a game of chess or a reading of some epic Gaelic poem. He'd never had the chance to bid farewell to either of them, but as he gazed over that moonlit glen to the castle beyond, it was as if he was finally free to let them go.

During all the years he'd spent plotting his return to Ballybliss, he had never once thought of it as going home because he'd believed there would be no one waiting for him once he got there.

But he'd been wrong.

A girl had been waiting for him. A girl who'd grown into a woman with a kind, brave, and constant heart. Instead of pity, she had offered him compassion. She had trembled beneath his hands yet given herself willingly into his arms. She'd taken mercy upon him when he'd had none to offer her and tempered his fury with tenderness.

He could only pray she hadn't given up on him yet.


The village of Ballybliss slumbered peacefully in the castle's shadow. As Bernard walked his horse through the deserted streets, he saw a single light burning in the window of the manor.

He tugged on the reins, bringing his mount to a halt. That cozy square of light seemed to mock all his noble intentions. Before he even realized what he was going to do, he was standing on the front stoop of the manor, his hand poised to knock.

Izzy swung open the door before his knuckles could touch the wood. His first instinct was to duck, but as far as he could tell, she was unarmed.

"What is it ye want, lad? If ye wait a few weeks, there'll be no need to finish what ye started. The good Lord'll do it for ye."

"I just want to see him," Bernard said.

Izzy gave him one long, hard look before stepping aside to let him pass. Taking up her basket of mending, she sank back into her rocking chair, her joints creaking. While she seemed content to darn stockings by the light of the kitchen fire, a lamp burned brightly at the bedside of the man in the next room.

Alastair Wilder was curled up on his side like a child. He had kicked off his blanket, exposing a body stripped of all but sinew and bone.

His eyes fluttered open as Bernard's shadow fell across the bed. It took them several seconds to focus, but when they did, anger glinted in their red-rimmed depths. "That must have been some bargain ye made with the devil, Ian MacCullough. To keep yer youth and vigor while I wither away like an auld man's cock."

Bernard couldn't think of a single reason to dispossess the old man of the notion that he was conversing with his long-dead friend. In truth, he felt almost as if his father were speaking through him.

"It was you, not I, Alastair Wilder, who made the bargain with the devil. You sold your soul and mine for a thousand pounds in gold."

"And I've been payin' for it every minute o' every day since," Wilder spat out.

"As have I," Bernard countered.

Wilder cocked his head to the side, eyeing him with more than a trace of cunning. "So why have ye come here? To take yer revenge on a daft auld fool?"

Before Bernard had time to ponder that question himself, Wilder's gnarled hands closed around his wrists with surprising strength. He tugged, guiding Bernard's hands toward his throat.

"Wouldn't ye just love to fasten yer hands round my scrawny throat? Don't it give ye pleasure to imagine me gaspin' my last while ye squeeze the life out o' me?"

Hypnotized by the old man's singsong coaxing, Bernard gazed down at his hands as if they were the hands of a stranger. He wouldn't even have to use his hands. He could simply press the heather-stuffed pillow over the old rogue's smug face and hold it there until—

It was almost as if Wilder could read his thoughts. "Go on, lad," he whispered. "Izzy won't tell anyone. She's eager eno' to be free o' me. She might even help ye convince my daughters I perished in my sleep."

*His daughters.*

Gwendolyn.

Bernard shifted his gaze to Wilder's eyes. They weren't glittering with fear, but hope.

Shaking his head, Bernard pried himself free of the old man's grip. "I'm not going to help the devil do his work. I'm afraid you'll just have to wait until he comes to collect."

As Bernard turned away from the bed, Wilder pounded on the tick, his eyes filling with tears of impotent rage. "I know ye still want me dead! I can see it in yer eyes! I can feel yer hatred boilin' through yer veins like acid!"

Bernard turned at the door. "You're not worthy of my hatred, Alastair Wilder. All I feel for you is pity."

He strode from the room, missing the bitter twist of Wilder's lips as the old man muttered, "Then ye're as great a fool as ye always were, Ian MacCullough."

He wasn't coming.

Gwendolyn huddled between two stone merlons at the pinnacle of Castle Weyrcraig, her feet tucked beneath her, and Bernard's plaid wrapped around her shoulders.

Every day for the past week, she'd made the arduous climb to the parapets of the castle and spent endless hours gazing out to sea. But on this, the seventh night of her vigil, there was still no sign of a ship on the horizon.

The frigid bite of the rising wind made her shiver.

Bernard might not be coming, but winter was, and she feared it was going to be the longest, coldest one of her life. In the past few days she had even dared to hope that she might spend it huddled in that decadent bed in the tower, warmed by a roaring fire and the heat in her husband's eyes. Hugging the plaid around her, she tilted her head back to gaze up at the stars. They glittered like shards of ice, near enough to touch yet forever out of her reach.

She had stood on this very spot and told Tupper that wrong or right, a MacCullough always stands to fight.

Well, she had fought, but she had lost, and her sense of defeat was more bitter than she had anticipated. She felt much as she had all those times when Bernard had ridden his pony beneath the oak tree without ever glancing up to see the little girl huddled in its branches. A little girl who would have given him her heart for nothing more than a smile or a kind word.

Unfolding her stiff limbs, Gwendolyn stood, stealing one last look at the sea. There wasn't so much as a hint of light to break the inky blackness of the waves. Bowing her head, she turned toward the stairs.

Her breath caught in her throat. A man stood there, veiled in shadows. If it hadn't been for the wind rippling his cloak, she might not have seen him at all. She had no way of knowing how long he had been watching her.

"What sort of coward would spy on a woman from the shadows?" she called out, biting her trembling lip.

"Only the worst sort, I'm afraid," he replied, stepping into the moonlight. "The sort who's spent half his life running from ghosts. The ghost of his past. The ghost of his parents. Even the ghost of the boy he used to be."

"Are you certain you weren't running from me?"

Bernard shook his head helplessly, his dark hair

whipping in the wind. "I could never hope to escape you, because you're here"—he touched a hand to his chest—"in my heart."

Gwendolyn felt tears well up in her eyes. She was on the verge of running into his arms, when a ghostly white shape appeared on the stairwell.

"Papa!" she cried. "How did you get here? Where's Izzy?"

Her father clung to the stone wall, barefoot and wearing nothing but a faded nightshirt. "I might not walk so good," he wheezed out between gasps for air, "but I'm still man enough to sneak past a dozin' auld woman and steal a horse."

"He must have followed me," Bernard said. "I stopped at the manor on my way here."

"Why?" Gwendolyn asked, wary of the guarded expression in his eyes. "It's a bit late to ask for his blessing on our marriage, don't you think?"

All her questions were forgotten as her father staggered forward and she saw the claymore in his hand.

# Chapter Twenty-nine

FOR ONCE HER FATHER'S HAND did not waver. It held steady and true as he glided forward, leveling the deadly blade at Bernard's heart.

Bernard began to back toward her, spreading his cloak to make himself a larger target. "Put down the sword, old man. Your battles are long over."

"They could've been over when ye came to my bedside and stood starin' down at me with those devil's eyes o' yers. All ye had to do was finish it. But, no—ye chose to spit in my face instead."

As Bernard moved within her reach, Gwendolyn clutched at the back of his cloak. "I don't understand, Papa. What did he do to you?"

"He offered me his pity, lass, that's what he did. As if he had the right!" A sneer twisted Alastair's lips as he shifted his contemptuous gaze to Bernard. "I've no need o' yer stinkin' mercy, Ian. Ye may be laird o' Clan MacCullough, but ye're not God!"

He lunged forward, closing half the distance between them.

Bernard flung out an arm to hold Gwendolyn back, but she ducked beneath it, taking her rightful place at her husband's side. "He's not Ian. He's Bernard, Ian's son. And you mustn't hurt him. I won't stand for it."

Her papa searched Bernard's face, his rage slowly giving way to bewilderment. "Bernard? It can't be. The lad is dead."

"No, Papa, he survived Cumberland's attack. And he's grown into a fine man—strong and true and kind." She stole a look at Bernard to find him gazing down at her, his green eyes burning with emotion. "He's everything I always hoped he would be."

Her father's face crumpled. The sword slipped from his hand to land on the stones with a dull clank. "I suppose I'll have to take yer word for it, lass." A sad little smile touched his lips as he shook his head at her, his eyes gleaming in one of their rare moments of lucidity. "Ye're a good girl, Gwennie. Ye always have been."

His eyes remained clear when he turned them on Bernard. "I may be a daft auld man, lad, but I was right about one thing. Only God can offer me mercy."

He turned, but instead of limping toward the stairs as they expected him to do, he went lurching for the parapet. Gwendolyn froze, rooted to the stones. For a fraction of an eternity Bernard didn't move a muscle, but after taking one look at her stricken face, he bit off an oath and went barreling toward her father.

He caught her father's calves just as the old man sought to fling himself between two of the merlons. The struggle should have been an easy one, but her father's desperation to end the life that had brought him so much misery seemed to imbue his wiry limbs with inhuman strength. As the two men grappled at the edge of the wall, Bernard's cloak billowed around them, caught in the relentless grip of the wind.

They teetered there, balanced between the past and the future.

Her spell of terror broken, Gwendolyn lunged for them, terrified that they were both going over. She grabbed for Bernard's cloak, tugging with all her might. But the wind tugged back, seeking to rip the heavy fabric from her hands.

Her father slipped over the edge. The muscles in Bernard's throat corded with the effort as he sought to keep the elderly man from plummeting into the churning sea.

Bernard began to slide after Alastair, no longer able to battle both the wind and the dead weight. Gwendolyn clawed for his back, but she was afraid to loosen her grip on the cloak.

Blinding panic assailed her. All Bernard had to do to save himself was let go of her father. If he didn't, she was going to lose them both.

Her strength was nearly spent when a massive arm banded with muscle from a lifetime of wrestling with iron pots and heavy washtubs shot past her, wrapping itself around Bernard's shoulders. Before Gwendolyn could catch her breath, Izzy had hauled them all to safety.

She and Bernard collapsed against the parapet. Her papa continued his fitful struggles until Izzy drew back her massive fist and slammed it into his jaw, sending him crumpling into a boneless heap.

"You should have let me do that," Bernard said grimly, massaging his shoulder. "Although I might have enjoyed it more than was strictly necessary."

Izzy shook her head, her hair rags bobbing like a nest of Medusa's snakes. "Don't think I didn't. The daft auld rascal should've known better than to try to escape me."

Still shaking her head, she heaved Alastair over her shoulder as if he weighed no more than a sack of potatoes and went marching for the stairwell.

Tears coursed down Gwendolyn's cheeks as she struggled to absorb all that had just taken place.

Bernard had risked his own life to save her father's.

He had chosen the future over the past.

He had chosen her.

Laughing through her tears, she gave him a fierce shake. "Damn you, Bernard MacCullough. I'm tired of you almost dying on me. If you do it again, I'm going to kill you!"

He grinned, looking exactly like the boy she had fallen in love with all those years ago. "I wasn't afraid for a minute. Don't you know that dragons can fly?"

"So you're back to being M'lord Dragon, are you?" she asked, stroking his cheek.

Bernard sobered as he gazed down into her eyes. "For the first time in my life, I know exactly who I am. I'm the man who loves you. The man who wants to spend the rest of his days making you happy."

Instead of melting into his arms as he'd expected, Gwendolyn scowled up at him.

"Why on earth are you looking at me that way?"

"I'm trying to decide if you'd have married me if Izzy hadn't been standing over you with that ax."

"There's only one way to find out." He tenderly folded her hand into his. "Gwendolyn Wilder . . . um, MacCullough, would you marry me?"

She inclined her head, giving him a demure glance from beneath her lashes. "If you mean to make me your bride again, there's something I must confess. I'm afraid I let some wicked scoundrel steal my virtue. I'm no maiden."

"Wonderful," he pronounced, sweeping her up in his arms. "Then I won't feel like such a beast for carrying you back to my lair and ravishing you."

"My beast," she murmured, cupping his face in her hands.

As their lips met in the most enchanted of kisses, Gwendolyn would have almost sworn she heard the song of the pipes soaring above the castle on wings of joy. In the village below, several of the townsfolk sat bolt upright in their beds, listening in awe as the jubilant melody thundered through the glen.

For years after that, the sons and daughters of all who had heard that unearthly music would tell their sons and daughters of the thrilling time when a fearsome Dragon had surrendered his heart to a brave and beautiful maiden, winning a happy ending for them all.

## About the Author

✦ ✦ ✦

*USA Today* and *Publishers Weekly* bestselling author TERESA MEDEIROS was recently chosen one of the Top Ten Favorite Romance Authors by *Affaire de Coeur* magazine and won the *Romantic Times* Reviewer's Choice Award for Best Historical Love and Laughter. A former Army brat and a registered nurse, she wrote her first novel at the age of twenty-one and has since gone on to win the hearts of critics and readers alike. The author of twelve novels, Teresa makes her home in Kentucky with her husband and two cats. Readers can visit her website at www.teresamedeiros.com.

*Be sure to look for*
*Teresa Medeiros's splendid new romance*

# A Kiss to Remember

A Bantam hardcover on sale in July 2001

# Bestselling Historical Women's Fiction

## ❑IRIS JOHANSEN❑

___28855-5 THE WIND DANCER ........$6.99/$9.99

___29968-9 THE TIGER PRINCE .........$6.99/$8.99

___29944-1 THE MAGNIFICENT ROGUE ...$6.99/$8.99

___29945-X BELOVED SCOUNDREL ......$6.99/$8.99

___29946-8 MIDNIGHT WARRIOR .......$6.99/$8.99

___29947-6 DARK RIDER ..............$6.99/$8.99

___56990-2 LION'S BRIDE .............$6.99/$8.99

___56991-0 THE UGLY DUCKLING .......$6.99/$8.99

___57181-8 LONG AFTER MIDNIGHT ......$6.99/$8.99

___57998-3 AND THEN YOU DIE ........$6.99/$8.99

___57802-2 THE FACE OF DECEPTION ........$6.99/$9.99

## ❑TERESA MEDEIROS❑

___29407-5 HEATHER AND VELVET .......$5.99/$7.50

___29409-1 ONCE AN ANGEL ..........$5.99/$7.99

___29408-3 A WHISPER OF ROSES ........$5.99/$7.99

___56332-7 THIEF OF HEARTS .........$5.99/$7.99

___56333-5 FAIREST OF THEM ALL ......$5.99/$7.50

___56334-3 BREATH OF MAGIC .........$5.99/$7.99

___57623-2 SHADOWS AND LACE ........$5.99/$7.99

___57500-7 TOUCH OF ENCHANTMENT. . $5.99/$7.99

___57501-5 NOBODY'S DARLING ........$5.99/$7.99

___57502-3 CHARMING THE PRINCE ........$5.99/$8.99